Damien's gol
her in as if he wanted to devour her.

Suddenly uncomfortable for an entirely different reason, Caro crossed her legs and folded her arms, something she rarely felt the need to do. She hated it even more when she realized she was responding to that intensely male look. Ordinarily she reacted negatively to such looks from men, but this time it was as if someone had poured heat through her veins and it was pooling between her thighs.

She looked away, then glanced at Damien again. His expression had changed, appearing merely interested. Had she imagined that lustful look?

Maybe the department was right. Maybe she was losing her mind.

Books by Rachel Lee

HARLEQUIN NOCTURNE
***Claim the Night* #127
***Claimed by a Vampire* #129
***Forever Claimed* #131
***Claimed by the Immortal* #166

HARLEQUIN ROMANTIC SUSPENSE
**The Final Mission* #1655
**Just a Cowboy* #1663
**The Rescue Pilot* #1671
**Guardian in Disguise* #1701
**The Widow's Protector* #1707
**Rancher's Deadly Risk* #1727
**What She Saw* #1743
**Rocky Mountain Lawman* #1756

SILHOUETTE ROMANTIC SUSPENSE
Exile's End #449
Cherokee Thunder #463
Miss Emmaline and the Archangel #482
Ironheart #494
Lost Warriors #535
Point of No Return #566
A Question of Justice #613
Nighthawk #781
Cowboy Comes Home #865
Involuntary Daddy #955
Holiday Heroes #1487
        "A Soldier for All Seasons"
**A Soldier's Homecoming* #1519
**Protector of One* #1555
**The Unexpected Hero* #1567
**The Man from Nowhere* #1595
**Her Hero in Hiding* #1611
**A Soldier's Redemption* #1635
**No Ordinary Hero* #1643

HARLEQUIN SPECIAL EDITION
The Widow of Conard County #2270

*Conard County
**Conard County: The Next Generation
***The Claiming

Other titles by this author available in ebook format.

RACHEL LEE

was hooked on writing by the age of twelve and practiced her craft as she moved from place to place all over the United States. This *New York Times* bestselling author now resides in Florida and has the joy of writing full-time.

CLAIMED
BY THE
IMMORTAL

—

RACHEL LEE

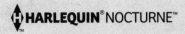

Recycling programs
for this product may
not exist in your area.

ISBN-13: 978-0-373-88576-3

CLAIMED BY THE IMMORTAL

Copyright © 2013 by Susan Civil Brown

Printed in U.S.A.

Dear Reader,

Writing The Claiming series has been a lot of fun. I've been able to break out a bit, and I have to admit that dealing with alpha heroes who are prisoners of their own desires has been an interesting contrast to the books I normally write. Immortals whose very lives can be threatened by love has been a different sort of challenge for me.

Researching the background details has also been a lot of fun. I've explored esoteric avenues that have been illuminating and sometimes surprising.

But mostly I've enjoyed the characters. They have minds of their own and often lead me down surprising paths as they tell their stories. In this book an assertive female cop takes on an arrogant vampire and proves herself a good match for him. I so very much enjoyed it.

I hope you enjoy it every bit as much.

Hugs,

Rachel

Chapter 1

Police sergeant Carolyn Hamilton stared at her captain with utter disbelief. He was a large man with one of those Irish mugs that seemed to perpetually smile, even when it was totally inappropriate to. Like now. "I'm suspended?"

"Not suspended. Indefinite medical leave, Caro."

"I'm fine! There's nothing wrong with me."

"Except for seeing things that are impossible."

She glared at him, grinding her teeth. Captain Malloy was usually a good boss. Until today she had even liked him. "I saw what I saw."

"That's the problem, isn't it," he said kindly. "Men don't get lifted into the air and impaled on the horns of a stuffed elk head by invisible forces. Just doesn't happen."

"I saw it happen. *You* explain how he got there."

Malloy shook his head. "I'm sure we'll figure it out. In the meantime, you were involved in a shoot-out last week and that can have unpredictable effects. Delayed shock, that sort of thing."

"Captain…"

But he shook his head sternly. "Take the time, Caro. I don't want anything to keep you from getting promoted to detective next month."

That effectively silenced her, although it didn't prevent her from grinding her teeth some more. She'd worked hard for that promotion. If he was going to hold that over her head, she'd better do as told.

But she didn't have to like it.

At least he didn't ask for her badge and her service pistol. She grabbed a few things from her desk, then headed over to Robbery-Homicide to talk to her friend and mentor, Detective Pat Matthews.

"I'm out of here," she told Pat, a striking woman in her forties with short, steely hair and equally steely eyes.

"Not suspension?"

"Medical leave. Indefinite."

Pat waved a hand as if to reassure her. "After that shooting last week…"

"Pat, I never even had to draw my gun."

"That's not the point. You go running around here talking about that guy being impaled, your credibility will be shot. Understand? So you're going to take this leave with all the grace you can muster, and you can probably come back in a week or so if you just don't talk about this anymore."

"I know what I saw."

Pat's eyes softened a shade. "I believe you. I believe that you saw it. I believe you didn't imagine it. But we're cops, Caro. We don't handle that kind of stuff, not as part of our jobs and not as part of our worldview. You need to stop talking about it."

"Great. I see a guy murdered and have to shut up about how it happened."

"Only around here," Pat said. She pulled open a desk drawer and hunted around a bit, then handed a business card to Caro.

"Messenger Investigations?" Caro asked.

"Jude Messenger handles the kinds of things we don't. The kinds of things we can't. He's on the weird side, evidently suffers from some medical problem that makes it impossible for him to tolerate daylight, but he's never let me down yet. You talk to him about this, Caro. He won't think you're crazy."

At that moment, Caro honestly didn't know if that was good or bad. She had to admit her story sounded nuts, but she had actually seen it happen. What would it mean about a guy who would believe it without seeing it?

"I'm serious," Pat said quietly. "This isn't cop stuff. This is Jude Messenger stuff. He's good, he's honest and you can trust him."

Caro wandered the streets for two hours after leaving the station. She was back in civvies, her pistol at her waist under her navy blue jacket in a belt case. Its weight seemed to be all she had left to remind her of who she was.

Worse, she continued to feel watched. It had started right at the moment she had witnessed that man's killing, and the feeling hadn't left her since. She was a little psychic but had always kept that to herself, knowing her grandmother's insistence that she was descended from a long line of witches wasn't any kind of proof that would hold water with her fellow policemen.

And she should have had the sense not to mention what she had seen in that house. What in the world had made her think it was her duty to relay a story no one would believe? Simple, stupid honesty, that's what. Because it was her job to help solve such crimes, not impede investigations by withholding information.

Hah!

Now here she was, wandering the darkening streets alone, with neck-prickling certainty that whatever had killed that man was now keeping its eye on her. Who the hell would believe that?

But she couldn't ignore it any more than she could ignore what she had seen. Finally, not knowing what else to do, she caught a bus to go see Jude Messenger.

She found Messenger Investigations in one of the seedier parts of town. Not unusual for a P.I. who probably made less than the average cop. The office was just below street level, but there was a light on over the door, making it possible for her to see the steps.

At the bottom, facing the closed door, she hesitated. He wasn't going to believe her. She didn't know how much more of that she could take. Yet Pat had recommended him.

She scanned the signs beside the door, saw the agency kept night hours only, but Pat had warned her that Messenger was ill. She also saw a security camera and a button to push for entry.

It seemed like a lot of security for a small-time P.I. She pressed the button, though, and heard a voice say, "Can I help you?"

A young woman's voice that sounded just a little suspicious. Cataloging impressions was second nature for Caro after eight years as a cop. Why would the woman be suspicious?

She shrugged the thought away. "I'd like to see Mr. Messenger. Detective Pat Matthews sent me."

The magic words worked, because she heard a buzzer and was able to open the door.

She stepped into a dark hallway that put her immediately on high alert. Light spilled from an open doorway. She headed for it and stepped into an ordinary-looking office furnished with a desk, two computers, three chairs and a sofa.

What wasn't ordinary was the young woman who greeted her. Enough black eye makeup to keep a cosmetic company in business. Spiky dyed-black hair, scarlet lipstick, and a combination of black leather and lace clothing that straddled the border somewhere between punk and stripper. Not your typical receptionist. Who was this Messenger guy?

"Have a seat," the woman said, indicating a chair near her desk. "I'm Chloe Crandall, Jude's assistant."

This day was just getting better and better, Caro thought as she sat in the metal chair with a padded leather seat. Who had a receptionist who dressed like this? A lunatic?

"So Pat Matthews sent you," Chloe continued cheerfully. "You work with her?"

"I'm a cop, yes."

"Cool. Pat's a great lady. What can we do for you?"

Caro's mouth locked closed. Absolutely nothing about Chloe inspired her to tell her story. "I need to talk with Mr. Messenger."

"Most people do," Chloe answered perkily enough. "That's why they come here." At least she didn't seem offended by Caro's reluctance to talk to her. Instead she leaned over and pressed a button on the desk phone. "Boss? Pat sent someone over to see you."

Less than a minute later, a door to Caro's left swung open. A dapper man, all in black, stood there smiling at her. For an instant, though, she didn't notice anything except how strange his aura was.

Seeing auras was part of life for Caro. Most everybody walked around surrounded by glowing rainbow colors that could give her clues to their moods or their states of health if she chose to pay attention.

But never had she seen an aura like this: all one color, a deep wine-red that hugged his body more closely than usual. She blinked, tamping down her awareness, telling herself it must be his illness. Yes, it had to be.

She rose. "Mr. Messenger, I'm Caro Hamilton. Sergeant Caro Hamilton. Pat Matthews tells me you might be able to help me."

He nodded slowly, still smiling. "Please, come in. My colleague is in my office, as well. That won't be a problem, will it? You may need his help, too."

Caro shook her head, although the idea of telling her story to two strangers was enough to make her reluctance grow to near dread. Then she reminded herself the worst had already happened: she was considered nuts and had been put on medical leave. The worst these people could do to her was laugh her out of this office.

Inside Jude Messenger's windowless office she noted nothing unusual except what appeared to be an old cavalry saber on the wall. The room was heavily paneled, lit only by a couple of desk lamps. Two leather wingback chairs faced a large walnut desk, the kinds of chairs she was used to seeing in a lawyer's office. Upscale for this part of town, certainly.

Rising from one of them was a man who nearly took her breath away. He was only a few inches taller than average, like Jude, but he literally resembled one of the effigies of Teutonic knights she had seen in Templar churches in Europe years ago. She hadn't realized a face like that could be real, but she was looking at one, with the prominent jaw, the blade of a nose and pronounced cheekbones. She had thought carving a face into stone had simply been difficult, but here she was looking at just such a rigid and sharp face. He smiled faintly, softening his harsh features, and tossed his head a bit to throw raven-black locks back from his face.

"Damien Keller," Jude introduced him. "He hails from northern Germany. Damien, this is Sergeant Hamilton."

Damien stuck out his hand and Caro automatically shook it, but as her surprise at his appearance faded, she noticed something else: he had the same odd aura as Jude. What was going on here? Did he have the same illness? His skin did feel just a bit cool.

Unfortunately, she couldn't ask. So she settled in one of the offered chairs and tried to focus instead on what she needed to say. Amazing how difficult this felt when she'd managed to get in trouble at work by refusing *not* to talk about it.

"What can we do for you?" Jude asked.

She met his oddly golden eyes and felt as if concern poured out of them. A glance at Damien gave her the same feeling.

Then her heart skittered. They *both* had golden eyes? She shook her head a little. Maybe they were related. They *had* to be related, given their auras and their eyes.

"Sergeant?" Jude prompted.

She dragged her gaze back to him. "Just call me Caro. I don't know where to begin."

"At the beginning is usually a good place," Jude said. His voice was pitched soothingly, filled with calm and patience. Damn, he was good.

"You're going to think I'm crazy," she said, "but here goes. Three nights ago we received an emergency dispatch.

A man, Andrew Pritchett, had called saying his family was being murdered."

Jude's nod encouraged her.

"Anyway, six of us responded. We had to break in the front door, and we split up. One went to the back of the house, four went upstairs. And I...I went into a closed room off the main foyer. I opened the door with my gun drawn, and there was a guy standing there, looking for all the world as if he were going out of his mind with terror. My first thought was that someone was in that room with him. I keyed my radio, calling for backup, but before anyone could get there..."

She stopped, looking down, swallowing hard. The memory was etched vividly in her mind, rising up now as if it were happening this very moment. No one pressed her.

At last she drew a deep breath. "This is where it gets crazy. I saw that man—I *saw* him—lift up straight off the floor. He levitated at least six feet right in front of my eyes. I tried to move, but I couldn't figure out what was going on, and then before I could do a thing he flew hard across the room. The next thing I knew he was impaled on the horns of a stuffed elk's head about eight feet above the floor."

"Good God," Messenger said. Damien uttered something that sounded about the same in German.

"Yeah." She drew another breath, this time a shaky one. "My backup came piling in then, but it was too late. In less than a minute the guy was dead. He was later identified as the caller, Andrew Pritchett. But there was no one else in that room. No one."

She fell silent, awaiting judgment.

"I believe you," Jude said.

"As do I," Damien added. "I've seen many strange things over the years. Such a thing is possible."

She jerked her head up then, looking at them both. "You have?"

"Most definitely," Jude said. "Which is why Pat sent you to us. But what do you want us to do about it?"

"I'd like to catch the killer," Caro said hotly. "Of course. But..." Again she hesitated, because this was probably the hardest thing of all to believe.

"Yes?" The prompt was quiet.

In for a penny, in for a pound, she told herself. *Just spit it all out.* "There was no one in that room. No one. No mechanical means were used to kill that man either. But I... felt something. Something I can't describe. Something that saw me. Something that's been watching me ever since."

The expected dismissal didn't come. Jude's expression turned grave. She looked at Damien Keller, and then wished she hadn't, because his golden eyes were drinking her in as if he wanted to devour her.

Suddenly uncomfortable for an entirely different reason, she crossed her legs and folded her arms, something she rarely felt the need to do. She hated it even more when she realized she was responding to that intensely male look. Ordinarily she reacted negatively to such looks from men, but this time it was as if someone had poured heat through her veins and it was pooling between her thighs.

She looked away, then glanced at him again. His expression had changed, appearing merely interested. Had she imagined that lustful look?

Cripes, maybe the department was right. Maybe she *was* losing her mind.

"All right," Jude said. "We need background on this. Can you give me the incident address?"

She reeled it off. "There's not much in the newspaper about it yet, except for a family of five having been killed.

They'd been thrown around like rag dolls and died from trauma, according to the medical examiner."

"I won't be looking in newspapers." Jude punched the intercom button on his phone. "Chloe, get me Garner. And then find me everything you can on the murders over on Duchesne Street and the victims."

Chloe's voice responded sarcastically. "Sure, boss. Will next week do?"

Jude punched off the intercom without responding. Apparently he was used to attitude from his assistant. He returned his attention to Caro.

"This thing you feel. Is it threatening? Is it getting stronger?"

"It's certainly not fading," she said finally. "I've been trying to ignore it, but I'm not succeeding."

"And you first noticed it when you saw the man killed?"

She nodded. "It was almost as if some invisible eyes suddenly settled on me. Like a shift in the atmosphere. And once it fixed on me, it hasn't gone away." She sighed. "This is so hard to explain!"

"You're doing just fine," Jude said. "But you're not sure it's getting stronger?"

"It's strong enough," she retorted tartly. "Maybe it *is* intensifying. *Thickening* would be a good word. But I'm not really certain. Maybe it's just eating away at me, this feeling of being watched all the time."

"All right. I'd like you to stay here for a while if you can. I have someone coming who can…sense this thing, for lack of a better word. He might be able to tell us something."

Considering her own psychic abilities, she had no trouble swallowing that line. But she *was* beginning to feel a bit amazed to have fallen in with people who seemed to accept these things.

How rare was that?

"I can stay for a while."

"Good. Chloe can make you coffee or tea, and if you're hungry, she can order you something to eat. In the meantime, just like you cops, we're going to gather every bit of information we can."

She hesitated, biting her lip. "I'm not sure I can afford you," she admitted. Maybe she should have thought of that before coming here, but now there was no escaping it. Before they went any further, she had to know how much of a hole this was going to place in her budget.

"Don't let it concern you," Jude said pleasantly. "I owe Pat a few favors. Let's just call this one of them. She *did* send you here, after all."

She couldn't argue with that, because Pat must have had those favors on her mind. She knew what Caro made and wouldn't have made a recommendation Caro couldn't afford. "Thank you."

Jude waved her thanks away. "I'm glad to help."

For the first time, Damien entered the conversation. His voice utterly lacked an accent, which surprised her in someone who came from Germany. Only reluctantly did she look at him again, but there was nothing hungry in the way he looked at her now. So she must have imagined it, right?

"Will you feel safe going home alone later?" he asked.

Good question. "I've been going home alone since it started." And that was not much of an answer, even to her own ears. As a cop, she knew evasion when she heard it, even if it was her own.

"We'll talk more about that later," Jude said. Rising, he ushered her to his outer office. "Chloe? Beverage, food, whatever Sergeant Hamilton would like."

"Sure," Chloe said. "I'll just add it to the heap you just dumped on my desk."

Jude just shook his head, sighed and disappeared back into his inner office, closing the door behind him.

"I can look after myself," Caro said, trying not to sound irritable.

Chloe laughed. "That was for his benefit. I live to give him a hard time. I'm hungry, too, anyway. So let me pull out the delivery menus."

Damien Keller was relieved when the door at last closed behind Caro Hamilton. He noticed all the things about her that an ordinary man would notice: her lithe but generous figure, her rich dark hair that might have been spun from the finest dark chocolate, her bright gray eyes. He even noticed the mantle of authority she wore despite her uncertainty. He liked strong, self-confident women.

But he was also a vampire and he noticed a great deal more: the scent of her blood, the beat of her pulse, the aromas that perfumed the air as her moods changed. Whether she knew it or not, would admit it or not, Caro was frightened.

That fear called to him as strongly as the richness of her blood or the throb of her heart. It added to the Hunger that had been born in him the instant he had been changed. That Hunger was an almost irresistible pull, calling to him the way water called to a man after days in a desert. Compulsion. Need. Thirst.

With Caro, the compulsion was stronger than anytime in recent memory. It clouded his thoughts, preventing him from wondering why he Hungered so strongly for her.

He had long since learned to control it, but he didn't like having to do so. Restless now with needs he could not assuage, he paced Jude's inner office while Jude worked on his computer.

The winter nights were shortening. He had come here

intending to stay only a short while, intending to return to Cologne the instant the rogue vampires had been eliminated. They had been eliminated several months ago, and now his window of opportunity was shrinking.

He needed to get back home to where there were women who would gladly slake his Hunger and count themselves lucky. Caro had reminded him of the power of that need, and he yearned for those easy delights, delights which he had been denying himself ever since he had come to aid Jude.

Because Jude did not approve. Because Jude felt as if he must protect weakling humans.

Damien didn't despise humans. He found them quite enjoyable in so many ways. They had gifts to offer he could find nowhere else. But he'd been here too long if one single woman could cause a reaction like this in him.

He wanted her. He wanted her entirely too much, yet she had barely crossed his path. Already his mind was imagining ways he could take her to that paradise known only to vampires and their human lovers. But Jude would be furious, and as a guest in Jude's city, he didn't want to misbehave. Certain courtesies overruled need, or they would all become the monsters they were entirely capable of being.

"Damien?"

He turned toward Jude and saw wisdom looking back at him from golden eyes so like his own. "She got to you."

"It's been a while," he said frankly.

Jude laughed shortly. "I remember what it's like."

But of course, Jude had wed a human. Worse, he'd claimed her, making the human his mate in a way that no vampire could escape except through his own death. Damien had always counted himself fortunate never to have tasted that particular obsession, and Jude's current happiness gave him no cause to change his mind. Claiming had always struck him as insane.

"I'm thinking it's time to return to Cologne."

Jude cocked his head. "Missing your harem?"

Damien snorted. "They are not that at all. Just a handful with whom I share delightful moments of passion."

"Food," Jude said bluntly.

"They are that, too," Damien agreed. "Contented food." Unlike some others of his kind, he had absolutely no qualms about what he was: a predator who hunted with sex as his lure. It wasn't as if he killed his lovely little humans.

"Well, if you must, go." Jude shrugged. "I've enjoyed your company. So has Terri. She likes your stories. I'll get Creed to help me with this case. Or Luc."

Damien hesitated. There was still that delightful morsel in the next room, and she had awakened him as he had not felt awakened in a very long time. A mystery, one which he thought he might enjoy solving. And perhaps, as was always possible, she might come to him freely enough that Jude would not object.

"I'll stay awhile longer," he decided. "She woke my curiosity."

"*Just* your curiosity?" Jude asked drily. But he didn't press the issue. Instead he glanced at his computer and said, "Chloe's coming through. I can see she's downloading things. Let's go."

Damien followed Jude into the next room with a mixture of reluctance and excitement. There was challenge in the air, he realized. The challenge of solving a problem, the challenge of either wooing a woman or resisting himself.

But mostly, he decided, it was the challenge of a problem he hadn't seen in centuries. He was aware of unseen forces, and long ago, as a member of an esoteric Persian priesthood, he had had intimate knowledge of them.

With time those forces seemed to have largely weakened and he had wondered how much that had to do with lack of use. Perhaps they found it harder to draw energy in this modern world. Regardless he was looking forward to finding out what this one was and how it had been called.

It had been a while since he had felt seriously challenged. The idea quickened his step a bit.

Papers were stacking up on the out tray of the laser printer. Caro wondered where Chloe was getting all that information. The police were keeping the story close to their vests this early on, and reports to the press had so far been shocking only in that an entire family had been murdered. No other information, other than names and ages, had been released.

But the stack of paper was growing, and Chloe was gnawing her lip as she continued keying her way through computer screens.

What was going on here?

Jude and Damien emerged from the inner office and she looked up. Damien's gaze raked her, causing her to shiver pleasurably and unwillingly before he looked away from her.

What was wrong with her? She had far more important things to think about than sexual attraction to a man. Worse, attraction to a man with a very strange aura, and she had enough strange in her life as it was.

The door buzzer sounded, and Chloe jumped up. "I'll just get our food."

"How much have you got here?" Jude asked, picking up the pages from the printer.

"Police reports, M.E. reports and the crime scene investigation. You'll be glad to know they're done with the house."

Then she bounced out the door.

Caro hopped to her feet. "You don't have access to all that stuff. You don't have the authority." She was appalled that anyone could hack into information that should only be accessible to investigating officers. "That's not legal."

Jude, holding the sheaf of papers, tipped his head a little. "I have special permission for special cases."

She stood there, her mouth still open to complain. But Pat had recommended him, after all. Maybe they had some kind of agreement? She made a mental note to check with her.

Slowly she sank back onto the couch. "This shouldn't be possible," she muttered.

Damien answered. "There's a lot that shouldn't be possible, but as you've seen for yourself, it is."

She tossed him a glare. "One doesn't equal the other. Access to an ongoing investigation is severely limited."

"Unless," Jude drawled, "you're part of the investigation."

Now, what did he mean by that?

Still disturbed but realizing there might be good reasons for this, she settled down and accepted the lo mein that Chloe handed her.

She trusted Pat and Pat trusted Messenger Investigations. Pat was trying to help her. But she wondered if Pat had some kind of offbeat secret life.

Because there was no question that Messenger Investigations was entirely offbeat.

Chapter 2

Jude read through the papers he had in hand but passed only a few of them to Damien. Caro wondered why, and then decided some of the details of the investigation were probably useless to them.

Most of them, probably. Reams of highly technical details that weren't going to tell them much, if anything, about the invisible force she had encountered.

Hardly tasting the lo mein she was eating, she forced herself to stop watching the two strange men, and instead turned her attention to thinking through, yet again, exactly what had happened that night.

No police officer wanted to receive that kind of call—a man claiming his family was being murdered. Adrenaline went through the roof, of course, but an extraordinary dread built, the kind of dread you didn't feel when called to even the typical murder scene. A family. Somehow that changed all the parameters.

It was a very well-to-do part of town, a place where the usual crimes were burglary and robbery, with an occasional domestic thrown in. Not the kind of place where entire families were murdered. Hell, even the worst parts of this city couldn't lay claim to that.

Gang killings, drive-by shootings, they happened. And sometimes the innocent got caught up in them. But an entire family sleeping in their beds?

Extreme for any city, any neighborhood.

And then that *thing*. That unidentifiable something. And what truly troubled her about it was that it had had no feeling. No sense of evil had struck her. Simply a sense of power. Indifferent, directed power.

Somehow that was scarier than the stories her grandmother had told her. But it wasn't a story, she reminded herself. She had *seen* what it could do, felt it watching her and knew it was real. What had her grandmother said many times when a story scared her? Something about how she would have nothing to fear when she found her own power.

She had never believed in that power, or its ability to hold nightmares at bay. Now she was smack in the middle of a nightmare she couldn't claim was simply a dream.

Her stomach tightened and almost revolted at the lo mein as she began to wonder for the very first time how much her own stubbornness may have blinded her and limited her.

Then a golden-haired young man joined them. Apparently he had a key, as she had heard no buzzer. He appeared to be in his early twenties, and had adopted an appearance of elegant dishevelment. It suited him. He also had a winning smile.

But Caro viewed him from eyes aged by her job. Something about him struck her as naive, almost puppylike.

"This is Garner," Jude said. "Garner, this is our new

client. I want to know one thing and one thing only from you. Do you sense demon around her?"

Caro gasped. She couldn't help it. *Demon?* Jude had to be joking. But she had grown up with hints of such things. Her grandmother had been remarkably reluctant to speak that word *demon.* But there had been warnings of dark powers to be wary of, and constant lessons about things she must never do.

She hadn't believed most of it even as a child. For her those stories had been about as real as the volume of *Grimm's Fairy Tales* her grandmother had read to her from after her parents died.

The notion that she might have dismissed something real almost made her brain reel. She was a realist, living with some psychic senses that she couldn't entirely ignore, but she didn't accept the fantasy world of her grandmother. In fact, she had chosen to work against evil in the most realistic way possible—by becoming a police officer.

Now this?

Garner cast his blue eyes over her, then approached cautiously. "Not demon," he said with surety.

"Then what?"

"I don't know. There's something clinging to her, but it's not exactly a dark energy, and it's certainly not some discarnate entity. I've never seen anything like it."

"That's it, then," Jude said. "Go back to your life."

Caro was shocked by the dismissal, but Garner flashed a grin. "I'm curious," he said. "I want to pursue this."

"You're a demon hunter. This isn't a demon. All you do is give me headaches, Garner. You know that."

Garner shrugged. "You're lucky to have me."

"Sometimes."

The young man laughed and sauntered out.

A short while later, Jude tossed the papers onto Chloe's

desk. "These are no ordinary murders. I need to do some research. Damien, I want you and Caro to go to the house where the murders occurred. I want you to check for something unusual, something out of place, something that sets your hackles up."

"I can do that."

"No, we can't," Caro objected, rising as she put her food container to the side. "We can't enter a crime scene."

"The techs are done with it," Jude answered. He tapped the papers. "Finished. So we can. You've been in there before, and Damien won't leave any traces. But he might note something your crime techs didn't consider significant."

"Why should he?"

"Because he has different training. Just go and do it. And, Damien, see that she gets home safely, will you? I need to talk to Terri about some of the M.E. reports."

Caro felt utterly confused, but she wasn't given any time to ask more questions. Damien took her elbow in a way that brooked no argument and guided her toward the door.

"What's going on?" she demanded as they reached the street and Damien opened the door of a battered old car.

"We're going to take a very different look at the crime scene, Caro. Now get in, unless you want to walk home."

She didn't need to glance at her watch to know the buses had stopped running by now. She didn't need to look up and down the darkened streets to realize she didn't want to walk alone. She had a gun, she was a cop, but it wasn't ordinary criminals who frightened her now.

She glared at Damien. "You're very high-handed."

"Mainly because I don't have a lot of patience or time. Are you coming or not?"

Muttering inside her own head, she climbed into the car. This wasn't at all what she had expected.

But what had she expected? Some soothing private investigator who would listen to her, charge her a few hundred dollars and promise to look into it?

Instead, she had gotten a couple of guys who were determined to act right now. According to them, they weren't even going to charge her. But what did she know about these men, after all, except that Pat had told her to trust Messenger?

Crap.

For the first time she seriously wondered what Pat Matthews had gotten her into. But maybe Pat hadn't gotten her into anything. Maybe she'd gotten herself into this mess by refusing to shut her mouth.

They had to drive nearly all the way across the city to get to Duchesne, but traffic was light at this late hour on a weeknight and they made decent time.

Caro hardly noticed the speed of their travel. Something kept drawing her attention to Damien, as if he were a magnet and she couldn't look away. God, he was gorgeous in a medieval sort of way. And she needed him to talk, mainly to distract her from the crime one or both of them were about to commit.

Maybe Malloy had been right: maybe she was losing her mind, even though he hadn't quite said that. Unfortunately, however, that question was moving to front and center in her own mind. It was not a question she wanted to deal with right now, so she sought distraction.

"So you're from Germany?"

"Most recently, yes. From Köln, although you probably know it as Cologne. I've lived there a long time."

"How long have you been here?"

"A few months."

"You speak English incredibly well. No accent."

He glanced her way with a smile, his golden eyes almost

gleaming in the flash from some passing headlights. "I've had a long time to practice. A very long time."

"You said *recently*. Where did you live before that?"

"A lot of places."

"What was your most favorite?"

"Ah, that's a question. Every place has its charms. I certainly enjoyed Persia."

"Persia? You mean Iran?"

"Persia," he said firmly. "To me, it'll always be Persia."

He didn't look old enough to have called the country by any other name, she thought, then shrugged away the oddity. Probably something to do with politics.

She turned forward again, tensing as they drew closer to Duchesne. She dreaded going back into that house. And then she felt Damien look at her again, felt the lust as his eyes raked her.

The downside of being psychic. Or maybe the upside, because she now knew what she had to worry about with him. She could feel his attention as surely as she could feel that other thing that had attached to her. Maybe even more strongly.

Just feel flattered, Caro. He wouldn't try to pull anything. Besides, she knew she was capable of protecting herself against unwanted advances. If he got out of line, she could pin him to the ground in no time flat.

Then she heard him sniff a couple of times. She looked at him reluctantly, reacting again with a strong surge of hormones. She *had* to get that under control pronto. What the hell was the matter with her?

"You smell something?" she asked.

"You."

At once she felt her cheeks heat. She hadn't showered since before going to work that morning, and now she felt embarrassed. "That bad?"

"That good. You smell delightful."

Apart from a blossoming ball of heat at her center, her only response was to roll down the window and let in the icy night air.

He laughed.

At least he was a good sport, she thought. And quick to get the message.

Figuring that matter was resolved, she focused on the crime they were about to commit.

"You know," she said, "you could get arrested for this if the police still have the place sealed."

"No one will know except you."

That thought didn't make her any happier. It *had* been three days since the murders, and the techs were most likely finished, but sometimes they left a place sealed in case their investigation brought something to light that required them to come back. Regardless, she didn't have any *legal* right to enter the property now. Her part of the job was done. Oh, she might be able to argue for herself if they were caught, but what about Damien?

Lord, what was she getting herself into? But every time she remembered the way that man had levitated and then been *driven* right onto those horns, she remained convinced that the police were never going to solve this. Never. And what if this monstrosity killed someone else?

She'd never be able to forgive herself.

So breaking and entering was about to be added to her résumé. Lovely. Not.

Damien parked a few doors down from the house. Apparently he had some smarts to go with the good looks. The street was dark and deserted, and only an occasional house showed any light at all. Together they walked quietly beneath old trees, and Caro checked to be sure her badge was still in her pocket. It would be their only cover if cops questioned their reason for being out here at this hour. In neighborhoods like this, that was often a good question.

The yard was still ringed with police tape, and more of it was slashed across the front door, barring entry.

"If we're going to do this," Caro said, "we'd better enter from the back. Although I can't imagine what you think you're going to find."

"Neither can I. Trust me, I'll know it if I find it."

That was enigmatic enough to irritate her. But she swallowed her irritation and led the way through a neighbor's yard to the back of the house. Moonlight added a silvery glow to the night but washed out all color. Reluctantly, she followed Damien under the cordon to the back door. Someone had neglected to tape it. Or possibly someone had already entered. Her nerves tensed, given the possibility that right this moment there might be a burglary in progress. She unsnapped her holster and put her hand on her gun butt.

"There's no legitimate reason this door shouldn't be sealed."

"It seems odd they would have left it off."

"Someone could be in there now. But if there's no one, this is still breaking and entering."

"Then allow me to do the breaking part." He reached out, gripped the knob and with little effort turned it. The door swung open into yawning darkness.

They could have turned on the lights, but that could draw the attention of any neighbors who were awake. Damien instead reached into the pockets of his overcoat and brought out two small but powerful halogen flashlights. He passed her one.

"I don't smell anyone in here," he said. "The house smells empty."

She was supposed to rely on his sense of *smell?* Not

very likely. She drew her gun and thumbed off the safety. "We're not going to be able to see much," she remarked. "Let me go first. If there's a burglar in here, I'm at least armed."

He closed the door behind them. "I'm not counting on seeing. Stretch your senses, Caro. You felt that thing. You might feel its leavings. And if you close your eyes for a moment, what you'll smell is the detritus of the murders and an otherwise empty house."

That was almost something her grandmother would have said. Her initial response was to ignore his suggestion and assume someone might be in here. But then, tugged by some inner working she couldn't name, she closed her eyes and reached out with those senses she so rarely used.

Shock rippled through her as she realized with absolute certainty that the house was empty. How very odd.

Come to think of it, Damien's suggestion was odd, too.

He had no way to know she was psychic, but what he said made sense anyway. If she could feel the force, she might feel what had drawn it, or what it had left.

And she could definitely feel that thing that dogged her steps. As she stepped into the house, she felt it strengthen in some way.

She froze.

"What's wrong?"

She looked at Damien, who looked almost like a ghastly effigy in the indirect glow of the flashlight beams. "It's getting stronger, the feeling. The minute I stepped in here."

He turned, facing her. "Not good. Do you want to leave?"

"And be alone outside right now? With this thing flexing its muscles?" She shook her head. "Let's just get this done. And don't touch anything."

"I don't need to touch anything."

"What are you going to do? Smell it?"

"Perhaps."

She felt her jaw drop a little but snapped it shut and followed him. He was already working his way from the kitchen to the front of the house. Interestingly, he passed the ground-floor study and headed upstairs first.

"What I saw happen was downstairs," she argued as she followed him up the wide, curving staircase.

"But it started upstairs."

She couldn't exactly argue about that. The guy had called and said his family was being murdered, and they had all been found upstairs in bed like shattered rag dolls who had been dumped where they had slept.

She was grateful, however, for the thoroughness of the crime unit. Most of the grisly stuff was long gone, taken as evidence or to the morgue. What remained was some spray and splatter, and plenty of fingerprint dust, something she'd seen countless times.

It would still take a special cleaning crew to make this house habitable again, but that was not the concern of city officials.

In each room they stopped for a minute or two. The way Damien sniffed the air was a little unnerving, but Caro forced herself to ignore it and instead stretch her underused sixth sense to see if it could feel anything.

Unfortunately, she recoiled almost at once. Death was very much in the air. Death and pain. It hit her like a blow, and she staggered out of the room.

"Are you all right?" Damien was there, gripping her elbow. His golden eyes almost seemed to gleam.

"Death. Everywhere."

"I smell it. The pain, too. It's heavy in the air."

He could *smell* it? But why not? she thought miserably. Pheromones might linger as strongly as the stench of blood.

"Stay here," he said. "I'll finish looking."

But she followed him anyway, hovering on the threshold of each room, trying to pick out anything useful from the waves of terror, pain and death imprinted on the space.

She wondered if anyone could ever live comfortably in this house again. Or who would even want to.

At last they descended the stairs, side by side.

"Can you still feel the watcher?" Damien asked.

"Oh, yeah. It's right behind me."

He surprised her at the foot of the stairs, telling her to stop. "Just hold still. If Garner could sense it, maybe I can."

So she waited, curious, frightened and sickened, while he closed his eyes. This time he didn't sniff the air. He simply stood stock-still as if he was waiting for something.

Suddenly his eyes snapped open. "It's done here. It left its work behind but nothing else. Let's go."

"But you can feel it around me?"

He hesitated. "Yes. I can. I can't place what it is, but I think I encountered it once before. A very, very long time ago." He shook his head in frustration. "But still I can't place it. Now come."

He'd encountered this before? How was that possible? What exactly was he? Or Jude for that matter. They weren't like any private investigators she had ever met before.

Most P.I.'s operated to some extent like cops, gathering information for their clients. The difference was they mainly focused on things that were ugly in a different way, things that weren't crimes, like infidelity, concealed assets and sometimes missing persons.

Messenger Investigations seemed to operate in an entirely different ballpark. But that was why Pat had recommended them, she reminded herself. Because Messenger Investigations handled things the police couldn't. Like invisible murderers. An unnerved bubble of laughter tried to rise in her throat, but she swallowed it. Laughter would not soothe what had happened here anytime soon.

Outside she drew in lungfuls of fresh air, grateful to be out of that house. Only in returning to the outdoors did she realize how oppressive it had been in there. Suffocating, at least to someone with senses to detect it.

"Is the feeling of being watched lessening?" he asked.

"No." No, it wasn't. Not at all. Her neck prickled, and she couldn't help looking around the darkened backyard, and into the trees and blank windows of nearby houses. Nothing. But something was most definitely watching her.

"Let's get you home," Damien suggested. "I need to search my memory very hard. Something is familiar about this. I just wish I knew what."

So did she. Squaring her shoulders, she marched to the tape line, ducked under it and headed for the car. She didn't want to let a feeling terrify her, but she had felt, not seen, that thing that had killed a man right in front of her, and she had felt it turn toward her.

Just a feeling wasn't going to be a good enough reason to dismiss it. Not this time.

Damien grew increasingly irritable. At first it amused him, but not for long. What had he been thinking to accompany this woman? She was driving him insane with Hunger. Every whiff of her breath, every beat of her heart, every one of her scents from fear to moments of arousal when she responded to him.

But here he was, having volunteered for this tour in purgatory.

When they got back in the car, it was he who rolled down the windows this time. Too bad if she froze in the winter temperatures—he couldn't stand smelling her for another minute in the confined space. He'd lose it. Every bit of the self-control he'd so carefully practiced for centuries was about to desert him. Hunger, quieted for a while in the charnel house, had returned, hard and heavy, pulsing through every vein in his body and threatening to overwhelm him with its power.

And that could not be.

However, he was having a bit of trouble remembering why. After all, he knew without doubt that he could seduce this woman and leave her so content she'd never think of complaining.

What was so wrong with that? Jude kept talking about humans becoming "vampire addicted," but in Damien's experience that didn't always happen, and less so when a vampire was careful about both what he took and what he gave. It *was* possible to taste paradise in a way that left most humans simply thinking they'd had an extraordinary experience. Nothing wrong with that.

But the Hunger he felt for Caro exceeded anything he'd ever felt as a human, assuming he accurately remembered his human days. Instead of centering heavily in his groin, it filled his entire body with throbbing need that was impossible to ignore. If he didn't battle it down, eventually it would become so consuming that he wouldn't hear or feel anything else but the need raging in him.

He couldn't let it get that far.

"Can you roll up the windows?" Caro asked. "I'm cold."

"No." But then he relented, figuring that the wind coming in her side was probably blowing more of her scent toward him. So he hit the button and closed her side of the car, but left his own window open to beat the aroma back. It worked. Somewhat.

As she directed him toward her place, he fought internally with Jude and himself. Jude was a relatively young vampire. Perhaps his line in the sand came from lack of experience. Damien, thousands of years older, had learned ways to control his interactions with humans that didn't leave them "addicted." He hated that word, actually.

There were plenty of delights that could be shared by vampires and humans that left both able to walk away. He knew that for a fact.

So why shouldn't he indulge just a bit?

But even as the dark side of his nature tried to persuade him, the better side responded. Because she was Jude's client, because he was Jude's guest here. Rules of hospitality and all that.

Behave yourself, Damien. And while behaving himself hadn't been difficult in a long, long time, the fact was that having lived the past several months on the canned blood Jude purchased, he was Hungrier than ever for the taste of warm, fresh food.

That was one carefully managed indulgence that he was not entirely used to doing without.

He was grinding his teeth in frustration by the time they reached Caro's apartment building. He'd have loved to just dump her outside, but her admitted fear, and the sense he had of the thing around her, prevented him from doing so.

Whatever his personal problems, he had to do what he could to protect her…a protection that would be limited by dawn's arrival.

The thought frustrated him even more, mainly because he was sure, absolutely sure, that he had encountered this energy before. This thing that was tailing her. And if he didn't have entirely too many years of memories stacked up between him and it, he'd probably identify it quickly.

Sometimes he truly felt the weight of his years, and it never made him happy.

Caro couldn't figure out what she was supposed to do now. Her apartment was empty—she'd checked it out—and

Damien's contribution to the entire process was to stand in her living room and close his eyes. She was surprised he didn't follow the procedure she had, that any cop would.

But then she'd already figured out he wasn't anything like a cop. So how could he be a private investigator?

Regardless, she guessed he was testing the place with the sense he'd used at the victims' house: smell. Or something else. Watching him stand like a statue only gave her the opportunity to feel that wakening desire again. What was wrong with her? She couldn't remember if she had ever been so sexually drawn to a man. In fact, she was almost certain she'd never been.

In self-defense, she closed her eyes, too, reaching out with her sixth sense, and she felt that darkness watching her. An invisible force, an almost nonexistent thing that nonetheless had the power to frighten her.

Why had it fixed on her? And why wouldn't it go away? Using barely remembered skills, she tried to push it back, but it hardly withdrew at all.

For the first time in her life, she truly wished she had listened better to her grandmother.

Then she froze as she felt a whisper of movement in front of her. Snapping her eyes open, she found Damien standing in front of her, not six inches away.

What the hell?

He smiled, a very attractive smile, and despite herself she felt her heart accelerate with eager anticipation. Her mind started throwing up objections, but her body instantly reached the precipice of breathless anticipation and hope. It wanted his touches, and it wasn't listening to reason. Just like when she'd been young and stupid.

"You are so beautiful," he murmured.

Horse crap, her brain responded. She knew perfectly well she was no beauty. Passable, maybe, with even features, healthy skin and bright eyes. A little too plump for fashion, but that was the way she was built. When she put on her utility belt, she was convinced she looked dumpy.

But she'd heard the line before—the first line on the path to seduction. It had been a long time since she'd fallen for it.

She wanted to stiffen, to draw back to safety, but it was as if her feet were cemented to the floor.

"Lovely," he said softly, and reached out to touch a strand of her dark hair.

He was *touching* her? She hardly knew him. Her brain shrieked warnings as her body tried to purr.

Then his hand trailed down until it brushed over her breast. Silken waves of heat rolled through her and she realized she was in serious danger. Not from him but from herself.

Because it would be so easy to give in.

"Just let me…" He started to lean toward her. She felt her mouth lifting to welcome him as his hand closed over her breast.

With his other hand, he captured her wrists behind her back, arching her in a way that made her breasts more prominent. Looking into his darkening eyes, eyes that no longer appeared golden, she felt herself sinking into the miasma of longing and desire that wanted to melt her every muscle. All she wanted was to let this happen.

Then sanity hit her with a snap. His eyes were *black* now? He was making a pass that she wouldn't have tolerated from anyone, and she was *letting* him?

She stepped into him with all the training she had, all the strength she possessed, and yanked her wrists free. Then she grabbed his arm to twist it behind him, shoving upward with her other hand to his chin to give him a brain-rattling knock to reawaken his senses.

Who did he think he was?

But before her hand connected, before her grip on his arm tightened, he was gone.

Just like that.

Across the room from her, slightly crouched. And she had not seen him move. Suddenly unnerved, she yanked her pistol from the belt holster, thumbed the safety and aimed at him.

She stared at him, stared at his strange aura, tried to take in what had just happened.

The question burst from her. "Just what the hell *are* you?"

Chapter 3

He'd almost had her. He was sure of it. Very few could resist the Voice or the seduction when a vampire put his mind to it. But this one had. Somehow. And she'd gone at him in a way that had made him make the biggest mistake possible: he'd jumped away too fast.

God, where had his mind gone? Of course, he knew. It had gone to that sweetest and most demanding of places where the object of his Hunger had overruled him. He had been near the brink of madness with desire.

But after all these centuries it was embarrassing to have to question himself. Had Hunger truly pushed him into the stupidest thing he could have done?

Evidently so. And now he had to think fast because she was asking a question he should not truthfully answer, and because he'd embarrassed Jude. If this woman talked to her detective friend about this, Jude would be furious and have a lot of explaining to do.

It was not very courteous of him as a guest to have put Jude in this position. He had to fix this and fix it fast so that Jude wouldn't have to leave town to protect his identity, so that his wife, Terri, who was a medical examiner, wouldn't be forced to give up her job....

The import of what he had just done crashed through him like a tsunami, to be followed by waves of desperation nearly as strong. The Hunger and lust that had driven him now took a definite backseat to damage control.

He straightened, clearing his throat, and tried to evade the question as his mind raced over how to handle this. Unfortunately, after what had just happened, he didn't think he was going to be able to make her forget it.

But he tried anyway because there was no mistaking that, for at least a very brief time, she'd responded to his control. "Forget," he said in the Voice that most humans had to obey. "Forget this happened."

"I'm not about to forget this," she retorted hotly. "Just who do you think you are? You're supposed to be a private detective, you pervert!"

Pervert? That was entirely possible, and he didn't exactly object to the word either. Perversion was, after all, largely in the eye of the beholder. He wouldn't mind binding her with silken ropes and getting her to admit she wanted him, too. And she did. He had smelled her arousal around her as clearly as he could see her right now.

However, this was not solving the problem either. She was mad and needed to be soothed, the quicker the better.

"I was overcome by your charms," he said, which at least was true. She, however, astonished him by not believing it.

"Yeah. Really. As if you're a sixteen-year-old who thinks with your groin. You were out of line. Way out of line."

"I apologize."

But clearly that wasn't going to satisfy her either. Concern for Jude hung over him like a dark cloud.

He wasn't at all concerned for himself. Staring down the barrel of her gun might make her feel better, but for him it meant nothing. He was certain that, like most cops, she was trained to shoot at center mass. Any wound she could give him would not kill him unless she hit him in the head, the last place a cop was trained to aim for.

Regardless, he could move so fast the instant he saw her trigger finger tighten that she didn't have a hope of hitting him anywhere at all.

But of course he was not going to illuminate her. He'd already illuminated her far too much.

Amusement might have gripped him except for his concern about Jude. Never, not once in Damien's countless years, had a woman ever denied him. Now that one had, he realized he was in quicksand of his own making. How maddening. But for himself he didn't care. He could be gone faster than she would be able to see. No, other concerns pinned his feet to the floor, forcing him to battle his natural urges and ignore his own abilities.

He could almost see her thinking rapidly, and he suspected that was going to bode ill for his secrets, too. She had asked the one question that was most important, and he didn't think she'd forgotten it.

He wondered if Jude would see the humor in it when he explained that he couldn't tell a lie because of a vow he had made centuries ago. Not likely.

His only hope now, he supposed, was that Caro would disbelieve his answer and throw him out. Then he could let Jude tell him he was no longer welcome and could head back to Cologne. Surely that would appease all the parties who were going to be annoyed with him, from this woman to Jude to Pat Matthews. However, he had promised to hang around for a while just in case any more of those rogue vampires arrived to stir up things for Jude again by attacking innocents and trying to create a vampire-ruled world. Tell a lie or break a promise? The horns of a dilemma indeed.

His mouth lifted in half a grim smile as he contemplated the sword he was about to fall on.

But she didn't make him fall on it; she pierced him with it. All of a sudden her eyes widened, and she drew a sharp breath and said, "You don't exist!"

Unfortunately, he did. Of that much he was sure. Dead, undead, vampire or not, he most certainly existed. Now more than a little perplexed, he moved a little farther away, trying to give her space to feel safe and calm down.

He'd been an idiot and was willing to admit it. The question was how to get *her* not to make a big deal out of it.

Her eyes followed him, narrowing as they did so. "Your aura," she said.

"What about it?"

"It's not human."

That didn't exactly shock him. What shocked him was that she could see it. "Really?" He wondered if he should buy time by going on the attack. After all, not that many humans admitted to seeing auras. Maybe he could use that against her.

But as soon as he had the thought, he despised himself. While he might have slightly different rules of conduct because of his state of existence, that didn't excuse him from the important rules that governed the behavior of most intelligent beings, such as not attacking people based on who or what they were.

"Your aura," she said again. "It's not normal. It's all one color and too close to your body. Wine-red."

He looked down, but seeing auras was not among his gifts, sadly. While he could tell much from the ebb and flow of heat in a human body, that was not the same as an aura. "Really. I had no idea."

"But you still haven't answered my question, have you, *vampire?*"

In an instant the entire thing went from bad to worse. It was one thing for her to consider him a pervert but to know he was a vampire by his aura—a fact that would certainly give away Jude—was a disaster of epic proportions.

He cursed the urges and stupidity that had led him to dig this hole. Not since he was a newborn had he found self-control beyond his ability. Of course, he'd never met anyone who attracted him the way Caro did either, but that was no excuse for his biggest mistake: assuming his abilities would allow him to seduce her. He'd lived long enough to know that the Voice didn't work with everyone, long enough to know that getting his way was sometimes chancy.

Hell.

"You don't believe in vampires," Damien answered, which was certainly true but also an intentional misdirection on his part. He hoped it would work. It was certainly his last chance for a clean getaway that would harm no one.

But before he could be sure, she took a wholly confusing tack.

"I *wish,*" she groaned, "that I had listened to my grandmother." Then she lowered her pistol, sank onto a nearby chair and looked at him as if she wanted him to vanish.

Well, he could vanish, and quickly, too, he thought with bitter amusement, but that wouldn't make things better for Jude. "Your grandmother?"

"Yes, my grandmother. She used to tell me about things,

things from fairy tales. At least, I wanted to believe they were fairy tales."

"I'll gladly be a fairy tale for you."

Her head snapped up a bit. "Oh, no, you don't. You sit right over there," she said, pointing to another chair with her gun. "I want some answers."

He debated. He could slip out before she could stop him, race to warn Jude and then catch a wheel well on the next night flight to Europe, an utterly cowardly response that would have made bile rise in his throat, if he still had bile. Or he could sit out the inquisition and try to patch the damage. Which was clearly the only honorable choice left now.

He sighed. "You're troublesome, Caro."

"Me? I'm troublesome?" Her voice rose a bit with anger. "Who was it who just pawed me?"

"I didn't paw you. Please. I fondled you."

"Without my permission, which makes it pawing!"

"Actually, I could smell consent all around you."

"Oh. My. God." She put her face in her hand, but not before he saw her cheeks redden.

He decided that taking a seat might be the wise thing to do now, especially since he had just put her on the defensive. Just a little, but perhaps enough to settle this matter before it got worse.

Her head jerked up. "I don't care what you smell. Never do that again without my permission."

Well, he couldn't exactly promise that. Considering that her scents, including her anger, which was tinged with just a dash of fear, were calling to him almost irresistibly, he tried to find a response that would soothe her.

"Promise me," she demanded.

Truth again. Never in all his centuries had he so regretted taking that vow. "I can't lie to you," he said, "so I can't promise you that. I can promise to *try,* but nothing more."

"Why? Are you incapable of self-discipline?"

"I'm not incapable of it. Actually, I'm usually quite good at it."

"Then why not now?"

He sighed. "I gather you've never been deprived of something essential to life." While also true, this was yet another evasion. For some reason he wanted Caro even more than he wanted the usual mix of sex and blood, but he absolutely didn't want her to know that. She was on an edge right now and could teeter either way. Teetering the wrong way would cost Jude and his wife enormously.

"Sex isn't essential to life. Not even a vampire's."

How had they moved so quickly to her accepting that he was a vampire? But that wasn't the question before him right now, so he watched the puzzling emotions skitter across her face and tried to divine her reactions from her scents. Neither was really giving him a strong clue right now. Whatever she was feeling was scattered all over the place.

"Sex," he said finally, "is not essential to my survival. What goes with it is."

At that her face went utterly still. Then fury tightened her eyes. "You were going to take my blood without my permission?"

"Never." That he could say with absolute truth and certainty. "Never."

"Then…" She stopped. Drew a deep breath. Clenched her hands. "I can't believe this."

"Then don't." It would be excellent if she returned him to the pervert category and convinced herself that he wasn't a vampire at all.

But that was not to happen. "You really exist," she said quietly.

"So it seems."

She stared at him almost miserably, then slapped her hand on her thigh. "That does it."

"What does it?"

"I told you all about why I came to you. To Jude. Evidently you were part of the package and I need your help."

He regarded her warily. "I can remove myself from the package if you like."

"No, that won't change a damn thing. Because Jude has the same aura."

He'd blown it. He'd blown it to hell and gone. Now it was just a matter of how to deal with it, and right now he didn't have a single decent idea that could spare Jude and Terri.

"So," he said slowly, "are you going to expose Jude?"

At that she laughed. It wasn't a happy sound. In fact, it sounded edgy. "Sure. I just got put on medical leave because I refused to stop trying to tell my boss that I saw a guy levitate and get thrown across the room by an invisible force. If I go to anyone and tell them you and Jude are vampires, I can kiss my career goodbye."

"Oh." His instant sense of relief gave way to concern. "I didn't know your career was in danger."

"Because I didn't tell you. Do you think it makes me feel good to know my boss thinks I'm having some kind of breakdown? That if I don't shut up permanently I'll lose my promotion to detective? And now this! Oh, I really needed you on top of everything else."

She at last thumbed the safety on her pistol and shoved it back into her holster. Evidently she had remembered enough to realize how useless it would be against him. "I could put you in jail, you know. That was sexual battery. So keep your mitts to yourself."

He resisted the urge to remind her there was no way in hell she would get him jailed, but he decided to accept her warning as it was intended. For now, at least. Besides, as things began to settle, he began to feel urges. Urges to solve the mystery of Caro Hamilton and why she called to him so strongly. Urges to understand her quixotic mix of traits and beliefs. Urges to protect her. He halted himself there. *Protect her? Whoa,* as Chloe would say. Over the top, surely? But this woman was facing something that concerned him, and he was certain she couldn't deal with it alone.

Then she fell silent, staring gloomily into space, and he let her be. He had no idea how he could help her with any of her problems, except possibly the force that was hovering nearby even now. The cat was out of the proverbial bag, and he had to admit to a little shame that he had added to her problems when all he had been trying to do was share with her a few utterly satisfying moments of passion. He wondered if he would have been any wiser had he known the pressure she was under in addition to being stalked by some unseen and deadly power. Too late for an answer to that.

It was difficult to keep a rein on himself, though, sitting here in her small apartment, swamped in her scents, listening to the beat of her heart and smelling the fresh blood moving in her veins. The difficulty of it surprised him, and he blamed it on not having indulged in fresh food for so long. Certainly not since he was a newborn had his needs driven him to the point of utter folly. He prided himself on deciding who, what, where and when.

Tonight he'd lost control. That was enough to make him uneasy about himself.

Silken ropes wafted into his mind again. He knew how many women preferred to pretend they were helpless so they could indulge free of qualms of conscience. As long as they were bound, they could pretend it was all his doing. Strangely enough, they all came back for more.

But with Caro, those ropes probably wouldn't please her at all, unless they were on him. She seemed very much the type to want to be in charge. He could do that. In fact he wouldn't mind it at all. With this woman, he decided, he wanted her to be sure it was all her doing.

Right now, that didn't seem like even a remote possibility.

Thinking about it wasn't quieting his needs or his instincts either. The urge to pounce was building again. He was a predator and food, delightful food, sat only a few feet away. He must be mad to stay here. Sanity would dictate that he clear out of here fast and find some other food to satisfy the Hunger.

But there was that *thing,* that energy or force he could sense but not identify. Much as he wanted to escape temptation, he feared leaving Caro alone with whatever it was.

Maybe he could summon up one of the protective spells he'd learned so long ago. Make some kind of talisman for her protection. It would have been helpful, of course, if he weren't so out of practice. Few vampires needed the powers of a magus when they had so many inherent ones.

His skills and knowledge were now so rusty he feared to use them because he might *mis*use them. A lot of good he was.

Caro broke into his thoughts by speaking. Her tone was reluctant, her words slow.

"My grandmother," she said, "claimed to be a witch."

He spoke cautiously. "Really?"

"I don't mean the kind you see everywhere now. I mean an honest-to-goodness witch with real powers. She said I was descended from a long line of witches and that someday I'd discover my real powers and harness them. She tried to teach me, but I didn't listen very well. I didn't believe her."

"No?" She had captured his interest, only on a different level than the one already plaguing him. "But you see auras. And you sense…other things."

She looked glumly at him. "Believe me, I try to keep that to myself. Besides, plenty of people claim to see auras and be a bit psychic. They call themselves sensitives, not witches."

"No, but a witch is a very different thing. A true witch." Now he was on ground he knew well. "I'd hesitate to even use the term *witch* for what you're describing."

"What would you call it?"

He hesitated, seeking the term that would induce the least negative reaction in her. "That your grandmother was a mage."

She thought about that for a second. "Maybe. She was certainly right about your existence. But why not *witch?*"

"Only because it's become such a polluted word with so many different meanings attached to it by many. *Witch* is fine if you like. *Mage* is an older word, going all the way back to a Persian group of adepts. They were called *mogh,* and later Magi."

She looked thoughtfully at him. "You mentioned Persia. Were you a magi?"

"Magus. Singular. Yes."

She closed her eyes and drew a deep breath. "Wow. What just happened to reality?"

"Nothing. You've just seen a part you resisted before." He tried to take hope from the fact that she was talking to him, no longer waving her pistol at him, and that she no longer appeared furious.

Her eyes snapped open. They looked strangely hot and hollow. "I need time to think. You can go."

"I'd like to try to remember some protection spell or talisman first."

She shuddered a little. "I know. It's still here. What the hell is it?"

"I wish I could remember, because I'm sure I've encountered it before. But I'm concerned about leaving you with no protection."

"If I remember right, you're going to have to do that at dawn anyway."

"Yes, but the dark forces are weaker in the daylight. And this one seems reluctant to be observed."

"How can you know that?"

"Because," he said simply, "it hasn't attacked you yet. It may not have had enough strength right after the other murders. Perhaps you haven't been alone enough. But now I feel it's strong, possibly strong enough to attack."

"I feel it, too," she whispered. "It *has* been growing." She leaned forward, keeping her voice low. "Do you think the reason it attached to me was because I saw what it did?"

"Possibly."

She knotted her hands together. "My grandmother left me a bunch of old books. Maybe I need to start looking at them."

"I need to do the same. It's been a long, long time since I needed my skills."

"How old are you?"

He hesitated, then decided not to evade the question. "I was born in Persia when it was still Persia, in the days when Magi were respected."

Her eyes grew big. "That's a very long time ago."

"Yes."

Then she jumped up. "That does it. That's all I can take. Do whatever you want. I'm going to sprinkle some salt around my bed and go to sleep."

He hoped sleep would find her and the salt would work. But because he was sure of neither, he remained where he was, searching the endless corridors of his memory.

Caro couldn't sleep. She had locked her bedroom door and placed her pistol within reach, but those actions didn't reassure her one bit. Not when a creature of myth sat in her living room and some shadow seemed to cling to her.

After all that had happened, she felt as if her foundations had been shaken to the depths. Vampires. Some force that was strengthening and wouldn't leave her be. A guy who claimed to be a magus and to have lived probably a few thousand years. Her grandmother… God, she wished her grandmother were still alive. If for no other reason than that she could tell her, "Grandma, I believe you now."

Too late. The world she had refused to acknowledge had camped itself right in her living room and she wasn't prepared to deal with any of it because she had been stubborn and blind.

Just a few days ago, her world had been so orderly: she chased down bad guys and helped people who needed her. Now it was all chaos, and she didn't even know which strand to grab at for a lifeline.

But even as she tried to sort through all the changes to her world, her mind kept drifting back to Damien. A vampire. A magus, or so he claimed.

Her grandmother had spoken briefly of vampires. And while Caro couldn't remember the details—other than that they evidently lived forever and could be dangerous—she did recall that her grandmother hadn't entirely condemned them. But then, Grandma hadn't really condemned much, except outright evil.

Her memories were populated with creatures of myth. Faeries, shape-shifters, leprechauns and even trolls. They had seemed like fun stories, but now she had the proof she had lacked back then. At least she thought she did.

How did she know for sure that Damien was a vampire, except that he had moved too fast to be seen and had an odd aura? For all she knew, he was an alien from Sirius B.

The only certainty was that he was no ordinary human, and that the desire he had awakened in her was still thrumming in her body like an unanswered call.

She rolled restlessly beneath her covers, trying to ignore the desire. She didn't want or need involvement with a vampire, however temporary. Heck, right now she didn't want involvement with anyone, human, nonhuman, sexy or otherwise. Her career topped her priority list and she didn't want anything to get in the way of it.

However, the past few days had done a good enough job of that. Medical leave. Questions probably being whispered all over the precinct about whether she'd lost her marbles.

Somehow she had to deal with this situation, then get back to work and keep her mouth shut. Forever.

And getting laid by a vampire wasn't going to improve one damn thing. Not even if she craved it.

When she got to the part where she started wishing he would just come in and take her, she clambered out of bed and pulled one of her grandmother's books off the shelf in the bookcase beside her dresser.

Time to think about other things. Such as how to get rid of whatever was attached to her.

She'd worry later about how to fit vampires and all the rest of it into her worldview. Belief had become moot. Now all that mattered was dealing with this mess.

Damien knew the instant Caro left her bed. With his extremely acute hearing, he could detect her movements.

But something else shifted—that thing in the air—and it seemed to be redirecting itself toward her bedroom.

He had no idea if the salt she had sprinkled around her bed had helped protect her at all, although it was an old, familiar belief, but regardless, she'd done something to renew the thing's attention.

Which left him with only one choice: to become a witness. If his mere presence could hold the thing at bay because it didn't want to achieve notice, then he and Caro would have to work out something before dawn, even though these kinds of powers tended to weaken in the daylight hours.

Someday he intended to pursue that mystery of why so many things weakened in the daylight, but for now it was enough to be aware of it, and try to use it.

He rose in a swift, fluid movement and went down the short hall, opening Caro's door without knocking. As he did so, he felt her lock give and realized she would probably be angry about that, too. He sighed.

She was wearing pajamas covered with little rosebuds, reading a slim book by the glow of her bedside lamp. She lay on top of the covers with her ankles crossed and looked startled when he stepped in.

"What are you doing?" she demanded. "I locked my door for a reason."

"Witnessing. I hope."

At once she pushed up higher against the pillows. "What?"

"You did something. That thing focused on you again."

"Crap." She rubbed her eyes with one hand. "I broke the circle. I went to get a book, and I crossed it."

He walked around her bed, scanning the carpeted floor. "It's scuffed," he agreed. "Salt?"

She pointed to the box of kosher salt on top of her

dresser. He crossed the room to get it and sprinkled it all around her bed again.

Then he waited, his senses on high alert. The energy did not pull back.

"So much for salt," he said, and replaced the box. "Can you feel it?"

She closed her eyes briefly and nodded slowly. "What now?"

"We wait. With any luck, it doesn't want a witness."

He settled in a small chair in the far corner, aware that she was regarding him unhappily. But what could he do about it? He couldn't risk her life. Apart from his own feelings about such things, Jude had practically assigned him to protection detail. If that meant sitting here and stomping down on his own needs—as well as hers, to judge by some of the pheromones emanating from her direction—then he would do it. Duty was seldom an easy thing. If it were, it wouldn't be called "duty."

"What are you reading?" he asked, striving for distraction from the fact that he might be almost as much of a threat to her as that clinging force.

"My grandmother's diary. Well, it's not exactly a diary. It's all the things she wanted me to understand that I never wanted to listen to."

"Anything useful?"

"Not yet." She lifted a ribbon marker and placed it between the pages. "I may have heard her better than I thought, considering how much I resisted what she tried to tell me."

"How so?" He tried to look attentive, but the truth was that between her delicious aromas filling this room and the hovering threat, he was having a hard time paying attention to anything she said.

Instead, he noticed how her lips moved, how plump and

juicy they looked. He'd love to nibble on them. His eyes trailed over the beautiful pink of her cheeks, flush with life. He saw the pulse beating steadily in her throat, heard its rhythm and inevitably thought of how she would taste.

"Every woman is different," he heard himself say. As soon as the thought escaped him, he felt like an idiot. Had he lost every bit of his self-control? How did she do that to him?

But she shocked him. She didn't get angry. Instead, she looked curious. "How so?"

"You humans walk around missing some of the things that set you apart from each other. It's not that you each look different. You each *smell* different. You have your own unique scents. Even your blood is not the same, person to person."

"You'd know," she said a little sarcastically. But then her sarcasm melted away. "There is nothing," she said flatly, "that makes me any different. You just want me because I'm a human female."

He shook his head. "I wish it were so." Oh, how he wished it were that easy.

A faint frown knit her brows. "Why?"

"Because then I could walk out of here and get what I want. Unfortunately, because you're different, I could get what I need and not at all what I want."

She flushed faintly. Other eyes might have missed it in the dim golden light, but not his. He felt his pulse pound harder and had to force himself to remain in his seat.

"You want me, too," he said softly.

Anger flared from her eyes, so strong he almost felt the sparks. "So? What does that matter? It would only make a messy situation messier."

He couldn't really argue with that. Not with that energy hovering around. "That's possible," he agreed. "Or it might clear the air considerably."

"Sex never clears the air. It always adds complications."

"That's a sad thing to say."

"Well, it's true," she argued, sitting up higher and clearly still angry. "It's messy. Maybe men can just have sex and forget about it, but women are different. For us it's always an emotional experience."

"For me, too, but perhaps in a different way." He could, however, think of plenty of women who, over the centuries, had been happy to dally with him a time or two and then move on.

"I'm sure it's very different. Let's talk about something else. You're making me feel like I'm being stalked by a predator."

"I *am* a predator," he said, his voice turning hard. "That's what I am. The difference is that I never take anyone who is unwilling."

"Why should I believe that?"

"Because I haven't taken you."

He smelled it: the best aphrodisiac in the world. The room almost flooded with her response to his words, charging the air with sexuality and that delightful hint of fear. "You wanted to talk about something different," he reminded her as she tried to glare at him.

"Maybe you should just leave," she snapped.

"Not until I can't stay any longer. Not while that thing is still around."

Her frown deepened, but her scent didn't change. Ah, this one was going to be interesting. Supremely interesting after so many easy conquests. She was willing to fight herself as well as him. He liked it.

"How old *are* you?" she finally demanded once again, clearly determined to divert him because she couldn't get rid of him. She didn't want him to leave her alone with that dark energy, so she was going to tolerate him.

That amused him. No trouble accepting that he was a vampire but plenty of trouble accepting that he wanted her. "I don't know," he answered. "I stopped counting years a long time ago. What was the point? They just keep adding up."

"Do you really live forever?"

"We age. Slowly. Some faster than others. I seem to have aged very little."

Her lips puckered a bit, nearly driving him insane. "Could that be because you're a magus?"

At once he stilled and forgot all about his hungers and needs. An intriguing question. "I hadn't considered it. What made you think of that?"

"My grandmother. Until the day she died, no one thought she was much older than thirty-five or forty. She always said dealing with powers kept her young. But you said you were rusty? Or something like that."

"I've forgotten a lot because I haven't needed it. It's been a long time since I practiced my arts as a priest."

"Because you're a vampire?"

He shook his head, smiling slowly. "There was a time when that was considered an advantage for my work. That time passed."

"So everyone *knew?*"

"No, of course not. It was one of our temple secrets. Much better that way. Much more useful. We also severely limited our numbers."

Her brow knit momentarily. "Well, when you live forever, it would hardly make sense to have many of you."

"Exactly. Our numbers could make it very difficult to keep the secret, so we remained a small handful."

She gave a small shake of her head. "I can't imagine the things you must have seen."

"Someday, when we're past this, I'll tell you some of those things if you want."

It wasn't the time, he thought. Not now. Not when his neck was prickling with awareness of that energy, not when he could feel its heaviness in the very air. He changed tacks sharply.

"We've got to think of what to do with you come morning."

"I thought you said it weakened in daylight."

"Most of these things do. But that doesn't mean they're entirely gone. Read your grandmother's diary. Maybe it will jog something important in your memory. And I need to search mine. I'm sure there's something there. I *feel* it."

She nodded slowly and once again lowered her eyes to her book.

The tension in the room, though, was as thick as the sense of threat.

Forcing himself to sit as still as stone, he focused his attention on the preeminent problem of ridding the threat to Caro.

This thing was not an entity—it was an energy. Energies needed direction. That meant whatever it was had been summoned. The question was whether it was still being directed.

He looked over at Caro and saw that she had finally fallen to sleep. He let time tick by until about a half hour before dawn. The back of his neck had begun to burn with awareness of the coming day. He couldn't wait much longer.

Pulling out the phone Jude had given him, he called his friend. "We've got to find a way to protect Caro during the day. And I've got to find out everything possible about the victims."

"Bring her over here," Jude said. "Chloe can keep an eye on her today, if keeping an eye on her will be enough."

"It may be. I'm getting the sense that this energy doesn't want to be witnessed in action. At least not yet."

"Then bring her here. For our edification, I have a background search running on the victim and his family. Anything else you want?"

"A bookstore. The kind of place that caters to would-be mystics and mages."

"I know of several. I'll pull the list together."

He closed the phone and found Caro watching him from sleepy eyes. "What now?" she asked.

"We go back to the office. Quickly. You must not be alone."

Chapter 4

The embrace of night once again wrapped the city in its heart. The vampires awoke and reclaimed their world.

Damien entered the office not ten minutes after Jude emerged from his inner sanctum. Terri appeared a few minutes later, dressed in casual clothes and heading for the coffeepot.

Caro watched the movement around her and spent a few minutes getting to know Terri, Jude's wife. She could tell by Terri's aura that the woman was still human, and the idea made her a wee bit uncomfortable, although she couldn't exactly say why. Some atavistic response to vampires not being normal?

But according to her grandmother, they were part of the natural world, no different from anything else under the sun—or moon in this case. Evil, her grandmother had always maintained, was a choice not a fate.

She'd been struggling all day to deal with the wild

changes in her belief system, and she was slowly coming to realize that while she had rejected her grandmother's beliefs, she hadn't entirely escaped them.

She wasn't as shocked by the existence of vampires as she was by her own stubborn refusal to accept it for all these years. And here she had thought she was open-minded.

"You've figured it out, haven't you?" Terri asked as they stood leaning against the counter in the tiny kitchenette, drinking coffee from mugs.

"That they're vampires? Yes."

Terri nodded. She was a small, pretty woman with raven-black hair and bright blue eyes. "What are you going to do about it?"

"Not a thing." Caro gave a sharp, mirthless laugh. "I'm already up to my neck in hot water because I saw a man levitate and get thrown through the air by something invisible. How much will it help my case to say I know two vampires?"

Terri's smile was wry. "I heard about it."

Caro's heart sank. "I was afraid everyone was gossiping about it. Damn, it's going to be hard to go back to work."

Terri shook her head. "I didn't hear gossip, so I wouldn't worry about it. I'm working the case as M.E. and that was part of the information reported to me."

Caro's heart lifted a bit. "They at least told you what I saw?"

"It was passed on to me verbally. Trust me, it's not in the written reports."

"So who told you?"

"A man you're probably pretty angry with right now. Captain Malloy. I know he put you on leave, and why he had to do it, but he included the information anyway. As he said, 'You never know.'"

Caro almost heaved a huge sigh of relief. "I thought he believed I was losing my mind."

"I don't know about that. But he kept it out of the written reports, which protects you, and he passed it on to me privately, which says something."

Caro nodded as a burden seemed to lift from her shoulders. "So what's your impression?"

"That it would have been physically impossible for that man to get impaled that way by normal means, unless he'd been dropped from the ceiling on those horns, not thrown across the room. However, it's indisputable that my office had to take the guy down from the wall."

Caro nodded, savoring the vindication, however small it was. "So what are you going to put in *your* report?"

"Death from impalement by means unknown. What else could I put? Nobody but you saw what happened and the guy was found hanging on a wall on the horns of an elk. Someone else can wrestle with how it happened. I only need to report the facts."

Caro smiled crookedly. "I tried to report the facts."

"Eyewitnesses mess things up from shock. I'm not suggesting that you did, but it's a great cover for you. Just let it go at that, Caro. Some people are happier labeling things *unknown* than they are dealing with the truth. And speaking of shock…how are you handling the vampire thing?"

"Maybe I'm still in shock, but right now it doesn't seem like a terribly big deal. My grandmother used to talk about them. What about you?"

Terri laughed and turned to dump her coffee in the sink. "I threatened Jude with his own sword. I'll tell you about it sometime, but right now I have to run or I'll be late."

Caro lingered a few minutes longer in the kitchen, trying to imagine Terri, who was tiny, threatening Jude with a sword. That actually seemed like a rational response to her, and she wondered at her own lack of upset. Maybe Terri was right. Maybe she'd suffered too many shocks in a short space of time.

Maybe she was just numb.

Well, except for that ever-present desire to jump in the sack with Damien, which was even more nuts than seeing that guy impaled, when she came right down to it. What the heck did she really know about Damien? Not enough to trust him with her body and her most vulnerable emotions.

Certainly not.

She refreshed her mug and returned to the office to find Damien and Jude in deep discussion.

"The victim," Jude said, looking up as she joined them, "appears to be clean in all his dealings. No hint of anything unsavory. Same for his family."

Caro couldn't keep quiet. One thing she had learned on her way to making detective was how dangerous it could be to assume the obvious. "We're presuming the guy was the intentional victim here. Maybe he was collateral damage. Anyone in that family could have done something wrong."

Jude looked at Damien and they appeared to agree.

"You're right," Damien said. "For all we know, the mother may have been dabbling with dark powers. Or one of the teens. There may be no purpose behind these killings at all."

"Which only makes them harder to solve," Caro admitted grimly. "But it remains that we narrow our focus too much if we assume the father was the intended victim."

"He just seemed the likeliest," Damien said. "He was a real-estate developer. The mother didn't have a career. The kids were in school. Although these days, just going to school seems to be enough to set off the worst in some people."

Caro couldn't deny that. "It's sad but I see it too often.

Some kids gang up on some other kid. Just to gang up. We need to look more closely at that. Who knows what one of the victim's children might have done if they were being picked on badly? Or if they were picking on someone else?"

"I'll get on it," Jude said.

Chloe, sitting at her desk, sighed. "You mean I'll get on it."

"No, you're going to get some rest so you can keep an eye on Caro tomorrow."

Chloe rolled her eyes at him.

"Me, I'm going to a bookstore," Damien said. He eyed Caro almost warily. "Want to come?"

"Depends on what you're looking for." Although that wasn't true. Amazingly, frighteningly, she just wanted to be with him. What the heck was wrong with her?

"Esoterica."

"Count me in."

Damien climbed into the car with Caro and proceeded to castigate himself for stupidity. Even well fed, as he was now, she was still as tempting to him as candy in a store window to a kid. Maybe more so. He just had to remember that a pane of glass lay between them.

If only it were so. At least then he wouldn't have to deal with the aromas as well as the sights. Renewed Hunger pounded throughout him.

Then Caro startled him with a statement.

"You guys seem too normal."

He glanced at her. "Would you prefer it if I flashed my fangs?"

"You have fangs? Really? That's not a myth?"

"Retractable. Of course we act normally. Would you have us skulking around like creatures out of a bad movie?

We were human once. And now that we're not, appearing as human as possible is our camouflage."

"That makes sense."

He almost thanked her sarcastically, then reminded himself he was on edge because she awakened such a powerful need in him. He lived to drink blood and have sex. Sex was his lure, blood his food. Seeming normal was merely survival strategy.

"Do you ever get tired of living so long?"

"Not usually."

"Not bored?"

He rolled down his window a bit in self-defense. "Our experience is much more vivid, much stronger than when we were human. Knowing that you'll die adds the piquancy to your life. For us it is the strength of our experience."

He noticed her hesitation. Then she asked, "In sex, too?"

"Most especially in sex."

"That must make you promiscuous."

A laugh escaped him. "It can." He supposed he *was* promiscuous by her lights. But her survival depended on different things, and that admission probably hadn't helped his case any. Although why he should want to help his case remained a mystery. He was beginning to think Caro could be a danger to his conscience and self-respect. For all he knew, given that her grandmother was a mage, she might even be dangerous to him in ways he hadn't imagined.

Damn, couldn't the traffic move any faster? He was dangerously near the point of finding a dark alley in which he could teach her that sex with a vampire exceeded her wildest imaginings. That would not do.

Gritting his teeth, tightening his grip on the wheel, he sped up a bit—not enough to draw the attention of the police—and tried to get there faster.

He also tried to focus on other things. The night came

alive for him in ways humans couldn't imagine. Distracted though he was by Caro's scents, he was still aware of other things: the hum of tires on the pavement, sounds issuing from apartments around them, the laughter in a movie theater and the amazing, brilliant colors that brightened his nights, colors that made up for the lack of sunlight. More than made up for it.

The moon didn't wash out his world—it brought it to luminous life. Every sense was exquisitely tuned to his existence. All he remembered about being human was how dull the experience had been by comparison.

With relief he found the shop at last, on a dimly lit and quiet side street. It looked innocent enough, with neon signs announcing New Age books and supplies for adepts. He liked the innocuous "adepts." So few really were, but so many tried.

But they no sooner approached the door of the shop than he froze.

"Do you feel it?" he asked Caro.

"What?"

"That energy has pulled back."

She closed her eyes a moment, nodded, then looked at him. "But why?"

"There must be power within this store."

"I wonder if it's what we're looking for? The source."

"I don't know. I'm just glad to know that something can make it withdraw. It's still out there, but not as close. Not nearly as close."

When they opened the shop door, a small bell jingled. The shop itself was crowded with old books, their musty scent mixing with incense. There was barely enough room to maneuver through the stacks, and the wood of old floors creaked beneath their feet.

A woman immediately emerged from a curtained door

at the back. Small and wiry, with long curly hair, beautiful café au lait skin and dark eyes that seemed big in her fine-boned face, she regarded them with a smile.

"What can I do for you?"

"I wanted to browse your books," Damien answered. "Your oldest books."

The woman's eyes narrowed as she studied Damien. "Perhaps something very old?"

"The oldest you have."

"I have a special shelf I don't show many."

"I'd like to see it."

"Not until I know more about you. Some things are meant only for initiates."

He felt Caro's eyes snap to him. She was probably wondering how he was going to handle this. He studied the woman before him a few seconds before he spoke, "I am *mogh*," he said. "And you are an initiate, as well. I could feel the power before I entered. You have a strong spell for protection."

"A thing one too often needs, sadly." The shopkeeper extended her hand, and Damien gripped it palm down.

"I'm Alika. And you are?"

"Damien. Formerly Atash."

Alika's eyebrows lifted. "I rarely meet one who touches such a distant past." She turned to Caro. "And you, too, have the power, although I can see it is not focused. My books won't help you."

Then she closed her eyes, lifted her arms a bit and stood very still. "You come seeking a way to cast off a spell."

Alika opened her eyes and dropped her arms. "It wants her." She frowned at Caro. "Vodoun. Did you anger a bokor?"

"What's a bokor? You mean this is voodoo?"

"In its current incarnation, yes. And a bokor is one

who practices the dark arts." Alika returned her attention to Damien. "Come, I'll show you the books. But I want to hear about this."

"And I want your help. I wasn't aware there were any bokors here."

Alika shook her head. "Sometimes one becomes a bokor temporarily for a reason. Never wise. Never."

"Playing with dark forces is *usually* disastrous. So you have no idea who it might be?"

"None. And if you don't mind, I'd rather not get directly involved." She looked again at Caro. "But why would it be after her?"

Caro answered. "Because I saw what it did."

Caro wasn't allowed in the small back room along with Damien and Alika, but she had enough to absorb from the shelves out front. She dove into a book on Louisiana voodoo and was overcome by the numbers of saints who seemed to have individual powers that practitioners could call on. Most of it seemed benign, though, a fascinating blend of animism and Catholicism.

There was nothing in the book, however, that suggested or even encouraged calling on darker forces. *No help,* she thought as she closed it and tucked it back onto the shelf.

Just then, Damien emerged carrying an old book. "Alika would like us to leave."

"Is something wrong?"

"Apparently she senses we're drawing attention her way." He reached her and took her hand, pressing a small leather pouch into it. "Some gris-gris for you. She hopes it will help. Now let's go before we draw *her* into this mess."

Caro shoved the pouch into her jacket pocket and hurried to keep up with Damien as he sped from the store. She was now so full of questions she felt she could burst.

She saw the trouble as soon as she stepped onto the street beside Damien. A group of five youths were standing around, and they didn't look as if they were there by accident. Their gazes immediately locked on her and Damien, and they seemed to pull together before they even took a step. Then their postures shifted, knives came out of pockets and they stepped forward as a unit. *Just like a gang fight,* Caro thought, and somehow they had become the target. Danger was written all over this, and ordinarily she'd have been reaching for her radio. But she didn't have her radio.

Had the power summoned them? Were they being influenced to make something unnatural look natural? This whole scene seemed off somehow.

"I can handle them," Damien murmured.

Caro might be on leave. She might have even fallen off the cliff of reality, but she was still a police officer. No way was she going to encourage violence and most especially from a vampire who could probably leave these guys shredded on the pavement, if what she remembered was true.

She stepped forward, throwing back her jacket, revealing her weapon and her badge clipped to her belt. "You boys have a problem?"

Behind her, she heard the door of the shop lock. She certainly couldn't blame Alika for that.

And then something shifted. It was one of the weirdest things she'd ever seen. Usually it took time to talk down troublemakers, but this was so different. Their gazes, intense only a moment before, changed. They looked around a bit as if wondering where they were.

She took advantage of the moment. "Just go find legal fun. Okay?"

Then she heard Damien speak in a tone that sent shivers all the way to her toes. "You heard the officer."

As if on marionette strings, the young men turned and walked away together. No hesitation, just instant obedience.

She watched them disappear down the street and around a corner, uneasiness crawling coldly along her spine. Bad enough to face some unseen force, but to see it manipulate others was scary indeed. Damien was counting on keeping her surrounded by witnesses to protect her. Had this *thing* figured out a way around that? By using humans as its tools?

Annoyance, a good antidote to fear, reared up and she turned to Damien. "I could have handled that."

"I'm sure. But how much time do you want to waste?"

"All we seem to be doing is wasting time."

"Time is never wasted in the company of a beautiful woman." Then before she could tell him to cut the crap, he added, "Actually, I learned a few things. My place, your place or Jude's?"

Jude's would have probably been the safest choice, because even though he had sent Chloe home, he was probably still there himself. But all of a sudden she didn't want to be safe. Maybe it was the result of adrenaline, affecting her sense of risk.

Regardless, she knew she needed some answers, answers to questions she should have asked years ago of her grandmother, and questions she needed answered for her own peace of mind.

Then there was curiosity. The kind that made her body shiver. The kind that pooled heavily between her legs. She wanted to know. It was as simple as that, adrenaline or not. If she could get him to promise not to drink from her, how much harm could a fling do? Maybe it could drive away this damn sexual miasma that filled the air around him.

Nothing, life had taught her, was ever as good as you anticipated it to be. With any luck, he'd turn out to be a selfish, lousy lover and she could kick him to her mental curb and get past this.

One thing for certain, she had to get her head clear to deal with this threat. She couldn't afford the continuing distraction of wanting Damien. Not if she had to be around him so much, and considering the limited number of allies she had right now, it appeared she was going to be around him a lot.

"Your place," she said. Then she watched his eyebrows climb in surprise and enjoyed a brief sense of pleasure at having startled him. Small consolation considering what he was doing to *her* mind and emotions.

God, was she really thinking about making love with a *vampire?*

But it wouldn't be lovemaking, she assured herself. Damn, she hardly knew the guy. All it could be was sex. Simple and straightforward coupling. Uncomplicated. Just to get it off the table.

Caro liked to keep her tables clear. It was part of what made her such a good cop and such a good candidate for detective: problems were meant to be solved or dealt with, not allowed to linger and thus cloud one's thoughts.

Dealing with this vampire seemed to have risen to the level of clearing the air or becoming swamped until she couldn't see clearly. While she was distrustful of her ability to keep her emotions out of something like that, she was even more distrustful of her ability to concentrate when she kept getting drowned by the seductive presence of Damien Keller.

Just sitting beside him in the car had her aching with

the anticipation of a teen about to make out in the back-seat for the first time.

Vampires. Damn. Grandma had warned her. Which for some reason made her think of Red Riding Hood and the wolf concealed in granny's clothes. She glanced at Damien as they drove toward his place and wondered if she was planning to get in bed with a wolf. Hell, he'd said flatly that he was a predator, and she was definitely on his menu.

Yet he claimed certain restraints. Well, she guessed she was going to find out. Of one thing she was absolutely certain: he had revealed something when he'd expressed concern about whether she would expose Jude. So he wanted to protect Jude. That meant he wouldn't do anything that might cause her to hurt Jude.

And that, she reasoned, made her fairly safe. He had, after all, backed off like a scalded cat when she had rejected him. Although how she was supposed to protect herself against a creature that could move faster than her eyes could see, she wasn't quite certain.

Somehow she imagined he wouldn't hold still for a wooden stake through his heart—even if that might actually work.

Then the ridiculousness of her own thought processes struck her. She was thinking about having sex with Damien while also thinking about how to kill him. Maybe it was a damn good thing she was on medical leave.

"I'm losing my mind," she said to the night.

"Want to go to Jude's?" he asked.

"What good will that do?"

"Well, I don't know why you think you're losing your mind. I thought you'd decided you didn't want to be alone with me any longer."

"If that were my only problem…." If that were her only problem, *what?* There was no thought to complete. She sat staring into the yawning pit of a world she had refused to believe in all her life, and now she could no longer pretend it wasn't so.

"Hah!" The sound escaped her sharply.

"What?"

"I'm fairly smart. It's not easy to pull the wool over my eyes. I spend an awful lot of time outwitting people who make the mistake of thinking they're smarter than the average cop. It's actually usually easy. Do you have any idea how stupid most criminals are?"

"I can guess."

"The idea of a criminal mastermind is mostly the invention of fiction."

"All right."

"So anyway, I consider myself reasonably smart, street-savvy and not easy to delude. Yet apparently I've been living a delusion all my life."

"Mmm."

That was totally noncommittal, she noticed. It didn't assuage her any. "And I don't even have the excuse of not having been told all my life that there was a world invisible to most of us." She paused gloomily. "Of course, before I became a cop there were other worlds that were invisible to me." The night streets, the gangs, the drug runners, the prostitutes…a whole lot that hadn't crossed her path in the neat little middle-class neighborhood her grandmother had raised her in.

Becoming a cop had been like a bath of cold water, pulling blinders from her eyes as she faced the real sleaziness of the world. She'd dealt with that. Surely she could deal with this.

After she remained silent for a while, he spoke quietly. "Has it occurred to you that that world you just discovered was careful not to reveal itself to you?"

"I suppose."

They pulled into an alley not far from the warehouse district, the kind of place that put her on immediate alert for trouble. Her hand went immediately to the butt of her gun.

"I'm only here for a short time," Damien said. "I had to take what I could find."

"If you keep reading my mind, we're not going to get along well."

"I'm reading your scents. I can't read your mind."

"Neither can I," she muttered, half wondering what her little rant had been about exactly, and mostly paying attention to all the shadows that could hide threats.

But nothing stirred. He turned a corner off the alley into a small parking area and switched off the car. "We can still go to Jude's," he said.

For the first time it struck her that he might be as nervous about her as she was about him. The big, tough vampire who had made a bold pass at her wanted to take her to Jude.

The thought actually made her smile. She'd thought she knew who had the upper hand. She couldn't have been more wrong.

"No," she said, turning that smile his way. "Let's get this settled."

That smile wasn't comforting. Nor were the words *Let's get this settled.* Not that Damien had any deep need to feel comfortable, but he didn't like not knowing what she meant.

He already had the sense that Caro Hamilton could be a formidable adversary. Not only had she been toughened by being a cop, but she was a nascent mage who might at any moment discover the powers she'd been keeping buried in favor of the popular concept of reality. Now that he and that formless energy that pursued her had shattered her concept, something else was going to emerge.

From long experience, he knew he didn't want to get into it with another mage unless he absolutely had to. And the most dangerous mage of all was one whose powers were uncontrolled and unfamiliar.

He grimaced as he led the way to the steel loading doors that provided his protection from the nosy. The building in which he had settled had been abandoned nearly a decade ago, left to rats and insects and rot.

Nothing like his comfortable place on the outskirts of Köln, even though he'd wasted a little time and money to fix it up. Not much, though, since most of the hours he spent here were in the sleep of death. He *had* gotten rid of the rats and bugs.

It wasn't much, and he watched her look around, taking in the mattress on the floor with a quilt covering it, a rickety table with two chairs, and a couple of oil lamps.

"It's cold," she remarked, keeping her coat on.

"I don't feel the temperature."

She eyed him. "Not at all?"

He shook his head. "I'm sorry it's uncomfortable for you here. Let's go somewhere else." How careless of him to have even suggested they come here. He should have remembered she needed warmth. In fact, he rarely overlooked such things, and the oversight was so uncharacteristic that he knew a moment of uneasiness.

He had stayed here too long simply because he was enjoying the company of another of his own kind for the first time in too many centuries. But in staying, he had been reminded that he could no longer run on automatic.

"This is sad," she said.

"What is?"

"That you live like this."

"Trust me, I don't live like this all the time. I have a home I'm sure you would find quite comfortable. This," he said with a wave of his hand, "was intended to be only for a few weeks. I simply lingered longer."

She faced him, standing with her feet apart, firmly planted as if ready for anything, and her question was almost a challenge. "Why?"

Why? Why what? Why had he stayed, or was the question something deeper? It seemed entirely too truculent to be simple curiosity.

Then he smelled it, ambrosia in the air. Her sexual scents overpowered everything else, at least for him. He could no longer smell the dankness of the room, or the lingering odor of burned oil from the lamps. He listened to the throb of her heart, its rhythm of need unmistakable. He could hear the soft swoosh of the blood slipping through her veins, but more important, he smelled the desire in her.

The scent was growing. When she had parted her legs to challenge him, she had freed it, signaling him as surely as if she had spoken.

He hesitated only briefly, aware of what had happened the last time he had approached her. Now he knew what she wanted to settle. She hoped by giving in to the hunger they both felt, she could dispel it.

And maybe she could. There was only one way to find out.

He walked toward her, taking care not to approach faster than she could see. She took one step back until she leaned against the brick wall. Her gaze, though, remained steady, and she evinced no desire to move away.

He preferred better ambience for this, more grace and foreplay, more time to enjoy and savor. That could not happen in this cold, nearly empty room, yet she was choosing here and now.

So she wanted it to be as bald and unadorned as it could get.

He smiled faintly, knowing she was going to get more than she anticipated was possible under these circumstances. With the experience of centuries behind him, he could enter any woman's mood, play any woman's game and delight her in whatever way she demanded.

She was trying, though, to make it as difficult for him as possible. Ah, but for him nothing was too difficult.

When he stood just inches from her, she tilted her head a little to look into his eyes. He read defiance and determination in her face and posture, along with passion.

She wanted a cure. That was one thing he wasn't going to give her.

"No blood," she said throatily.

"No," he agreed. Her game, her limits. To a point.

Then, utterly without warning, he slipped his palm between her legs, drawing it upward until he nearly lifted her from the floor. It was a bold, demanding, controlling gesture, and he half expected her to resist. Instead, all that happened was that a delightful groan escaped her and her eyelids fluttered. Her thighs clamped around his hand, but his strength was such that he could still move his fingers and palm, pressing, stroking, titillating. He used the seam of her jeans to taunt her more.

Even through her jeans, he could feel her damp heat, a pleasure of the greatest kind for him now that the only warmth he could feel came from a human touch. He reveled in it, savoring it, letting her heat flow from his hand, up his arm, encouraging more and more of it with the dance of his fingers.

He could finish her this way. He knew he could. But

why hurry things needlessly? She had other delights he wanted to enjoy, delights she would enjoy, as well.

He pulled open her jacket, pulled down the neck of her sweater and pressed his mouth to the pulse in her throat. He licked her, feeling new shivers run through her with every movement of his tongue. He had promised not to drink but suddenly realized that was going to be a difficult promise to keep. This close to the throbbing vein in her throat, he could smell the perfume of her blood. It filled his nostrils and lungs, and his Hunger grew until it seemed to hold him in steel bands of need.

Just as he thought he might lose control, he snapped his head back. While his one hand continued to torment her below, squeezing, pressing, kneading, he slipped his other up inside her sweater and found her breast.

Her nipple had already engorged for him, feeling huge and hard in his palm. When he squeezed, she gasped, and finally she brought her arms up to grab his shoulders. Now she was participating, at last, holding him so he wouldn't pull away.

He had no intention of doing so. He might be denied his ultimate prize, but her powerful sexual reaction was the next best thing. His own body hardened in response, throbbing and demanding, but he ignored it for now. Instead, he accepted her silent invitation to lower his head and suck and nip at her breast.

The shudders that gripped her as he nipped at her told him she wasn't as far removed from his world as she might like to think. A little pain could amplify pleasure for some, and she was apparently one of them.

Satisfaction penetrated his heat-filled, Hunger-filled mind, and he bit just a little harder. Her response was instantaneous as she groaned and arched into him, and that response felt almost like his own.

It would have been better only if he had drunk from her.

He felt the moment when she crested, and he crested in response, like a snapping bowstring. Dimly, and with no little pleasure, he suspected that nothing she had wanted to settle had been settled at all.

Chapter 5

Nothing was settled. The thought floated vaguely into Caro's mind as the spasms of her climax ripped through her in powerful waves long after she had passed the peak. Nothing.

Because pressed to a cold brick wall, with a vampire's hand between her legs, holding her as hard as a vise, with her breast still aching from his ministrations, she knew she had just gone somewhere she had never gone before. Never had she experienced such a powerful orgasm, and she would certainly never have expected to experience one like this under these conditions. She still wore her clothes, even her gun and badge. And it was not a bed that sustained her as her legs weakened and wanted to give way, but a hand, a single hand, that had elicited pleasure she hadn't even guessed she was capable of.

It appalled her to realize that she'd been settling all her adult life, never dreaming there was so much more to be had.

And it angered her that it had come from a vampire. She had wanted to put an end to this, to clear the air, and instead all she had done was discover something that could only lead to ultimate disappointment when she could no longer experience it again.

She was still trying to catch her breath when he removed his hand and steadied her against the wall by leaning gently against her. Her hands still gripped his shoulders, an unmistakable sign of her weakness, but as much as she wanted to pull them away, she didn't seem able to yet.

He had left her as weak as a kitten. She didn't like that at all.

Yet, whispered some honest corner of her mind, she wouldn't have missed it for anything, although it left major problems in its wake. Now she would forever wonder what delights he could give her if she removed her limitations.

But anger returned her strength, and at last she pushed him away. He slipped back two steps immediately.

"Damn it," she said.

"Did I disappoint you?" But his eyes, not quite golden, not quite black right now, said he knew he had not.

"Shut up, Damien. Let's get over to Jude's and look at the freaking books."

He didn't say another word, merely accompanied her back to the car meekly. *Meek? Hah!* Nothing about that vampire was meek and she had deluded herself right into a peck of trouble.

Well, see if she would let that happen again. She had learned her lesson: no more vampire sex. Ever.

Damien let her be. He'd made his point about how much she wanted him, though why he had he was now unsure. He should have just disappointed her and let her go her way. After all, he had a life to return to in Germany, and he had no intention of hanging around here for long.

Not that that had ever been a problem in the past. The women he shared sex with were women who intended to move on every bit as much as he did. This time he might have made a mistake.

But everything about Caro indicated anger, so that was probably good. If he tried to approach her again, she would probably shoot him, and while that wouldn't kill him, it would certainly dampen his ardor.

The thought managed to amuse him enough to ignore the power her scents seemed to hold over him. He had just slaked one of his needs adequately enough, as he had slaked hers, yet the throbbing Hunger had already returned. That was a different experience for him.

He glanced her way and saw she stared straight ahead, her jaw tightened. Perhaps he hadn't slaked anything for anyone. Maybe he'd just made it worse for both of them.

He wasn't used to that. In the past, when he was done he was done, whether or not he'd drunk from his lover. Never before had the urge returned so swiftly.

Caro, he realized yet again, had quite an unusual effect on him. She had from the very start. His first slip just might have been an aberration, but what had just happened…that was no aberration. He could simply have ignored her scents and taken her out of there. He had *not* had to give in.

What was it about her that was causing him to act so irrationally?

There didn't seem to be an answer, other than that something about her kept pushing him well past caution. Maybe he needed to worry about that a bit. In some way, this woman was dangerous to him.

Worse, he was beginning to realize it wasn't just his

Hunger for her. He liked her strength, her determination, her sense of humor. Perhaps that was the greatest danger of all.

Never had Damien imagined when he'd departed for the bookstore just how happy he was going to be to get back to Jude's office.

Jude was alone, reading a stack of papers at his desk. He looked through the door of his office as the two of them entered. Damien saw his nostrils flare and realized the other vampire knew pretty much what had happened. Jude was suave enough not to mention it, though.

"Blood?" he asked Damien.

"Yes." The need to drink had grown to an overpowering thirst since his encounter with Caro. Since those little nips he had given her had allowed him to taste a single droplet of her blood.

No other blood had ever tasted so good to him.

Making no effort to conceal what he was doing, he bit, fangs extended, into the bag of blood Jude gave him and drank. Let her see. Maybe that would throw up a barrier she would never let him cross again.

Instead, Caro barely spared him a glance and revealed no surprise at all. Evidently she had figured out how he must feed if he wasn't robbing his sustenance from unwilling humans. And evidently, as a cop, it took more to disgust her.

Jude, once he ascertained what they had learned at the bookstore, announced he was going out for a while and taking the car. He didn't say where, and no one asked. The tension in the room was enough to consume them.

Damien tossed the bag into a biohazard container when he was done, then settled at Chloe's desk to read the parchment manuscript Alika had entrusted to him. Caro settled as far away as she could get on the couch and resumed reading her grandmother's journal.

He could smell the anger around her still, along with the remnants of desire. He spared a moment to try to recall if ever in all his centuries he had relied on a human's anger to protect him from his own loss of control.

No. Never. He'd have been amused if it weren't so troubling.

He made up his mind then and there to return to Cologne the instant this matter was resolved. It had been a long time since he'd felt a need for self-preservation, but right now it looked like it might be necessary. The danger of a claiming hovered at the edge of his awareness, a folly he had managed to avoid for millennia. The fact that such a thought even edged toward consciousness was warning enough.

Sometime later, Caro closed her grandmother's book with a snap. "This is no help."

"Why not?" Damien asked.

"Because my grandmother was all about using power for good. All she says about misusing it is a big warning to never do so."

"There's often a price," Damien agreed. "What people these days call *blowback*. Or, as they say, what goes around comes around."

"Yeah, that seemed to be Grandma's view, too." She cocked a brow at him. "Did you never misuse yours?"

"I never called on dark powers. Ever. But I've known some who did."

She leaned forward a bit, sensing deflection. "Never?"

He shook his head. "There are many ways to use power, Caro. Views of right and wrong change with culture. But this I can say with absolute certainty—I never called on dark powers. But this thing that is haunting you—I don't feel it's a dark power. It might have been summoned with a dark wish, but the power is neither good nor evil. It just *is.* I'm beginning to think it's probably an elemental of some type."

"Elemental? As in just a force?"

"Just a force. I feel as if I've encountered this particular one before, but I can't place it. At any rate, there are plenty of these forces around us. They have no mind, they have no intent or thought. But they can be directed by a mage."

"The bokor that was mentioned. Except I'm having trouble with that. I was scanning a book on voodoo…well, actually *vodoun* is the preferred name now, and it didn't strike me as being the kind of thing the movies show. It seemed mostly benign."

"It is. It's a combination of animism with Christianity for the most part, and most practitioners intend no ill. But like any belief, it can be twisted and misused. Animistic religions have one advantage over the mainstream—they believe in elemental powers, and call on them. Variants of vodoun, from Santeria to hoodoo, call on elementals. And anyone, if they get angry enough or feel threatened enough, could turn to one of these elementals for protection. Even for murder."

Caro thought that over, trying to recall anything her grandmother might have said about elementals. Well, maybe she had spoken of them, in terms of nature spirits. More of the stuff Caro had found so hard to swallow. "If you're a mage, why can't you just cast a spell to shut it down? And if it has no mind, why would it follow me?"

"First, I'm not absolutely certain it's an elemental, although I'm inclined to think so. Second, I don't know what summoning was used or for what reason. All of those things matter if I'm to be effective against it. As for why it would follow you, my guess is that it was simply ordered to leave no witnesses. Or it may be that the mage or bokor who summoned it was using his power to watch what it did and then attached it to you. Do you see the difficulty here? Until I know exactly what we're dealing with, I have no way to counter it. Take those youths outside the store. I could cast no spell against the force driving them because I don't know what it is or its purpose. I'd have had to resort to physical action."

That did nothing at all to brighten Caro's mood. Apparently there was a cliff on the edge of reality, and through no fault of her own, she had tumbled over it and was now in free fall, her every attempt to avoid this notwithstanding.

She looked over at the vampire who had done his own part to toss her into the abyss, and she hated him. But even as she hated him, she wanted him. How messed up was that?

To be fair, though, she had to admit she was the one who had wanted to "settle it," and she had achieved exactly the opposite. She almost blushed when she remembered being pressed up against a wall, supported only by it and by the hand he'd so expertly used on her most private of places.

She hadn't thought herself capable of such things. Glancing at him from the corner of her eye, she wondered how much more she might have in her to do. He certainly brought to mind things she'd never really thought about before.

Then she blurted, "What happens when you drink someone's blood?"

He looked up from the parchment pages he'd been reading so swiftly that they seemed to be blown by the wind. "In what way? To a human? To a vampire?"

"I didn't realize it was so complex."

"That depends on how much and what you want to know."

She hesitated, half-sorry she had brought this up but filled with curiosity anyway. Short-term, at least, she had a relationship with this vampire. Understanding was always useful for getting along, and for self-protection. While she mostly believed that Damien wouldn't physically hurt her, there were other ways he could harm her. Best to be prepared and informed.

"Start with threats to me," she said bluntly.

"Ah." The pages had stopped turning, and now he rested one hand on the open book. His eyes seemed to darken, and she made a mental note to ask about that, too.

"Threats to you? None that are serious. I may want to share sex with you and I definitely want to taste your blood, but I wouldn't take as much blood as you'd give as a donation to a blood bank. So, as you see, I wouldn't debilitate you in any way. The only danger to you is one I believe Jude exaggerates."

"Which is?"

"Some people enjoy it so much that they become addicted."

Addicted to having your blood drunk. "That's possible?"

"It is. I have seen it. An unscrupulous member of my kind would take so much and give so much pleasure while doing it that the experience becomes like cocaine. There are people who have become so addicted from a single encounter with a vampire that they haunt the vampire clubs seeking another such experience. Unfortunately, they become victims of the unscrupulous, who take but don't return the pleasures."

Caro was aware of more than one vampire club around

town. "Most of those clubs seem relatively harmless—people just getting off on a fantasy."

"Most of the time that's all it is. They play little games and pretend."

"It bothers me that some of the people pretending to be vampires actually drink blood, though."

He lifted a brow. "Why, if it's by mutual consent?"

"Because I can't imagine a normal person wanting to drink blood."

"Ah." He thought about that. "The world is full of kinks, isn't it? But for me this isn't a kink. It's reality. Blood repels you?"

"In and of itself, no. But I know I couldn't drink it without getting sick."

"I suppose that would be a common reaction among humans."

Then she snapped back to what she had originally been trying to understand, and it wasn't how some humans could drink the blood of another. She understood enough about the range of kinks from her job. She had seen far more dangerous ones than simply allowing someone to poke you or give you a minor cut to drink a few sips of blood. Worse than wanting to drink blood or give blood to someone who did, some fetishes were absolutely deadly.

"So the only way you could harm me is to make me addicted to you?"

"Not the only way. But I'd get no pleasure from having you addicted. I'd regret it. So far I've managed never to do that."

"But what is so good about it?"

His gaze darkened even more. "I can't really explain. You'll have to take my word. There's a place between life and death where only a vampire can take you, a place so full of ecstasy that words simply aren't enough to describe it."

Ecstasy. He said it with such calm assurance that she found it hard to argue. What was more, the way he said it made her tingle and throb again. The experience he had given her such a short time ago had awoken cravings in her entire body. If he could give her even more than that...

But she shied away from the thought, hating that he had the power to evoke such a strong response. And it was indeed power. She loathed feeling that someone could control her being so easily.

Angry with herself, she spoke acidly. "I suppose you vampires just walk away untouched by all this havoc you wreak on humans."

"No." He sounded annoyed and his eyes grew as black as a moonless, starless night. "It would help if you understood something. If I drink from someone, they become an everlasting part of me. I may not ever see them again. I may not even care to ever see them again. But they become part of me, whether I choose it or not. Thus I am careful in my choices. I don't want to be populated by the demons of others, their aches and pains and griefs. Minor though they may be, just imagine how they could accumulate over the centuries. At least bagged blood carries none of those risks because it is basically dead. For me anyway."

That was an appalling thought, but she wasn't quite ready to give up her anger, because it helped corral her chaotic emotions and protect her from him. "Well, then, I guess you should choose only empty-headed bimbos. That leaves me out."

His laugh astonished her, but laughter or not, his eyes remained black. "No. I choose those I find sympathetic or compatible. That way, not only can I give them unparalleled pleasure, but they give me something, as well."

"So what is it about *me?*"

Much to her pleasure, he appeared to be at a loss.

"I'm not sure," he said eventually. "Perhaps it would be best if we never found out. You may think I'm dangerous to you, Caro, but to be perfectly honest, I suspect *you're* a danger to me."

With that he lowered his head and resumed reading, making it utterly clear that he was done with this conversation.

A conversation that had done little to settle Caro's mind. How could she possibly be a danger to *him?* She had even waved her service pistol at him and he hadn't seemed the least fazed by it.

"How could I endanger you?" she asked, not caring if she interrupted his reading.

She heard a faint sigh, and then he was leaning over her, so fast she hadn't seen him move. There was *that* little problem, she thought sourly. How could you shoot something that moved faster than sight? How did you protect yourself? Danger to him? *Hah!*

"You play with fire, Caro," he said softly.

"Yeah?" She could feel her chin thrust forward, defying him. "What kind of fire? And just how do *you* get singed?"

He shook his head a little. "Another time. It may not even be a real danger. I just know I feel these little warnings."

Then, without so much as a by-your-leave, he reached out to touch her hair, then ran his fingers down her cheek to her throat, then lower still until they brushed the peak of one breast.

Instantly she was on fire for him, and if there'd been any blood left in her head, instead of all of it pooling between her legs to create a hard, heavy, damp ache, she might have blushed.

But her blood had already pooled down there, enflaming sensitive tissues, making everything else fade to insignificance. She wanted to hate him for that but couldn't manage it. She also wanted to hate him because she saw the flicker of awareness cross his face as he smelled her reaction to his touch.

From somewhere came the wild thought that she wished she could plug his nose just to maintain her privacy.

But it was hopeless now. He knew. Her body couldn't decide whether to clamp her thighs together or let them fall open to invite his touch. Right now every ounce of her being was centered between her legs.

"Damn you," she managed to whisper.

Instantly he reappeared across the room, but he didn't look amused. "I might say the same to you," he remarked. "A willing woman responding to me the way you do is one thing. Unwilling is another. Damn you, too, Caro, because I feel the same desire."

He felt the same desire? Really? Surprise filled her, causing her to realize for the first time just how much she needed that kind of reassurance. Control was an important part of her self-image, and she had never thought herself needy in the least way. But here she was, needy and relieved to know she wasn't the only one feeling it.

He closed the book he'd been reading with a definitive snap. "I need to get out of here. You perfume the room with enticing scents. Fresh air is the only answer."

He rose, then paused. "But I can't leave you alone."

"What difference does it make?" she asked, swamped both in the desire she felt and in the inevitable fear she felt about being alone right now. It wasn't an overpowering fear—she wasn't certain she was capable of that—but it was uncomfortable nonetheless.

"Difference?" he repeated. "It might make the difference about whether I pounce on you. As I recall, you're distinctly opposed to pouncing."

Any other time, this might have been an amusing conversation. *Pounce?* Why did that sound like such a funny yet good word all of a sudden?

"Pouncing aside," she said, "you *do* remember those guys outside Alika's shop? They weren't there by accident. I probably could have handled that group, but what if this power sends something else? Witnessing may not be enough to protect me, so I'd rather have backup alongside."

The corners of his mouth tipped upward. "Backup? You mean you'd rather have my strength, my powers and my ability to kill at your side?"

The cop in her rebelled at the part about his ability to kill, and then she wondered why it should. Didn't she always hit the streets with an armed partner? And this one seemed better armed than most for the threat they were facing. Guns clearly weren't going to cut it unless to kill humans who were under some outside control.

"Can I be frank?" she asked.

"Of course. I'm frank with you. To use Jude's phrase, I want you like hell on fire. I admit that phrase has always perplexed me, but it seems to convey the meaning adequately."

Now she flushed a little. "Pull in your fangs and your pheromones, or whatever you're using on me."

"Trust me," he said bluntly, "I'm using none of my wiles on you. They clearly don't work. In this particular situation, *you* seem to have all the wiles."

Now *that* made her feel good. A different kind of warmth settled in her. As she'd discovered, not too many men were interested in an armed woman, except possibly for her handcuffs. "Let's get back to my point."

"Certainly. Something about killing, I presume."

"Actually, yes. The thing is, Damien, I don't want to kill people who are being controlled by that elemental, or whatever it is. I really don't. If they're acting under the influence of something they don't understand and can't control, why should they pay with their lives?"

He tilted his head. "Moral questions used to be so much simpler."

"It's called social evolution," she said tartly.

A chuckle escaped him. "Point taken, though I don't always agree. All right. You want any pawns to be removed from the table alive."

"Yes."

"I can promise to try. But there is your so-called doctrine of self-defense. I might also point out that you carry a gun, which speaks volumes about how you yourself might respond to some threats."

That disgruntled her a bit, because it was true. "Okay. But here's the thing. I was taught to try to defuse situations rather than escalate them. So if you use your powers, try that weird persuasion thing first."

"The Voice," he said. "It works perhaps ninety percent of the time. Not on you, evidently."

She wasn't so sure about that as she recalled how his command to those youths had seemed to tingle its way through her body. She hadn't felt controlled by it, but she had certainly *felt* it.

"So," he said, "do we take a walk or do I sit here trying to concentrate on a book that I can barely read because of the distraction your scents provide?"

"Some help you're going to be," she retorted.

"It's my nature." The words were in no way apologetic.

"Let's go for a walk. Weren't there some other stores to visit?"

"Moving from one confined place to another with you

is hardly going to help," he grumbled. "No car. Jude probably took it. Which may be the only thing that saves me."

"How does it save you?"

"Good heavens, woman, have you no idea why I keep rolling down windows?"

The frustration he expressed, combined with finally understanding why he kept freezing her in the car, made her giggle.

"You think this is funny?" he demanded.

"Kind of," she said, still giggling. "I just hadn't thought about why you kept rolling down the windows."

"Now you know. I really own no desire to turn you into an icicle. You're driving me insane, so show a little pity."

The idea of him wanting her to show a little pity amused her and kept her secretly grinning while she bundled up for the cold winter night. While the daytime heat from the sun, buildings and cars had melted away almost all the snow, at night chilly winds blew in the canyons between buildings, icy enough to be threatening.

But Damien donned no extra clothing. He hadn't taken off his black leather jacket when they'd come inside, and he added nothing to it as they departed.

"You really don't get cold?" she asked as she jammed her gloved hands into her pockets and bent into the wind.

"No. I don't get hot either. At least in the traditional sense."

That brought another secret grin to her lips. "Why not?"

"How should I know? I don't even know how I exist. Of course, you really don't either, if you want to get down to the nitty-gritty details. But to answer your question, I don't feel temperature at all unless it comes from human contact. Hot or cold makes no difference to me. I could walk naked in Antarctica for a week and return to tell you how lovely it was."

The idea both amazed and saddened her. "Don't you miss it? I can't imagine not feeling warmth, especially on a night like this."

"You could give me warmth. As for missing it…" He shrugged a shoulder. "We're adaptable, just as you are. We get used to it. The only time I think about it is when I'm touching a human and feel it again. Then it becomes so pleasurable, I ache for it."

She fell silent, scanning the streets out of long habit, hunched within her jacket, the hood drawn tight. "I guess," she said finally, "I don't think about it much. The weather is the weather. When it's cold, I turn on the heat. When it gets too hot, air-conditioning. But I can't imagine not feeling it at all. Especially a good hot shower."

A half laugh escaped him. "You humans spend a lot of money and effort to make sure you live in an unchanging temperature environment. You prefer not to notice the cold or heat. I simply can't."

That was an interesting way to think of it. But there were good things, too, like coming in from an icy day and warming up with a mug of coffee or hot chocolate. Feeling your cheeks and toes burn a bit as they revived. Minor things perhaps, but she doubted she would want to give them up—even though she sometimes came home from a shift feeling like a miserable icicle, or like something that had been steamed for too long.

"How far is this place we're going to?"

"It's over on West Bolger."

She pulled up her mental map of the city. "If we walk we're not going to have a whole lot of time to get you back before dawn, especially if we stay too long at this place."

"Well, I could make it all happen faster, if you'd allow me."

"How so?"

"I could carry you. You'll get colder, but we'll move faster than the wind."

She had no doubt of that, having seen him appear to disappear and rematerialize out of thin air. But to have him carry her? Being that close to him was dangerous to her peace of mind. Worse, letting him carry her would leave her with absolutely no control of anything.

On the other hand, the streets were getting colder, the walk would be long and time consuming, and it seemed really pointless to waste all this time if they didn't have to.

"So you don't have a car?" she asked.

"No, I'm on a visit. I came because Jude needed help."

"Help for what?" She was stalling and knew it, but she was curious, too.

"You may remember a few months ago there was a rash of what were called animal maulings?"

Her heart quickened. "We never got an answer to that. It just stopped. What was it?"

"A bunch of vampires. They want to rule the world, keeping humans as chattel. They were particularly angry at Jude because he drove them from this city and has driven them from others. He even formed a coalition of us who feel we can live in harmony with humans."

"Wow," she said, trying to absorb all this.

"It's a long story, but Jude and others had to fight them off. To protect you and your kind. I came to help but arrived just as the battle was wrapping up. I should have gone home but was enjoying the company of Jude and his friends, so I lingered. Thus I am still here."

Talk about tipping over reality's edge. "A battle between vampires?" *Unreal.* Yet she remembered the terror that had gripped the city before the killings suddenly stopped. "I never imagined."

"We never wanted you to."

She had a lot to mull over and would have liked to do so, but then she spied something that awoke the policewoman in her, distracting her.

They had reached a corner, and a car sped by, too fast. Farther down the street she saw a group of boys or young men, out too late to be up to any good. How much did she want to deal with right now? They were most likely gang members and things could get real ugly, real fast if she tried to intervene solo or get past them.

"I'll opt for vampire transit," she said, making the decision abruptly.

"Wise decision. I smell trouble wafting this way. Drug-energized trouble."

"You can smell when people are on drugs?"

He didn't answer her, instead drawing her quickly around the corner out of sight. "Hang on" was the only warning she got.

The next instant she had been tossed onto his back and was clinging for dear life to his shoulders and hips as the world spun dizzily by, leaving her with no impressions but flashes of light and shadow. After only a few moments, she closed her eyes to keep from getting sick and pressed her face against his back to keep it warm as the wind chill seemed to drop close to absolute zero.

She guessed that must be why vampires couldn't feel temperature. None of them would be able to move fast for very far if they were susceptible to heat and cold.

Her mind rebelled at how fast they reached West Bolger. When next she could see something, Damien lowered her to her feet and she looked around, recognizing the neighborhood. This area was at the outer reaches of her precinct and the kind of place cops expected to have trouble.

Damien's hands lingered as he lowered her, but she

didn't brush the importunate touches away. Feeling a little dizzied, she focused on getting her bearings.

Trouble, she had learned, accompanied poverty like fleas on a dog. It wasn't that most of the people here were bad people. But it was a neighborhood full of despair, and despair created plenty of desperation and resentment. Fertile ground for gangs who could see no way out by remaining law-abiding. The Police Athletic League was strengthening its involvement here, trying mostly to attract youngsters to safer outlets for their time. Another organization had recently joined in to provide tutoring and other aftercare in the same building. Still, it would take years to fully win young minds and start the "upward and outward" movement that was the ultimate goal. Caro donated a lot of her free time to the effort.

But, she had to admit, this neighborhood seemed a lot safer by daylight than it did right now. Instinctively, she felt for her holster, then dropped her hand.

All of a sudden, she realized Damien was staring at her. "What?"

At least half the streetlights were broken, and the remaining few offered little light, but even so she could see the intensity of his look. A shiver, whether of apprehension or anticipation she could not tell, ran through her.

"Nothing," he said abruptly. Turning on his heel, he headed across the street to a shop.

"It's late," she remarked. "We probably wasted this trip."

"Some shops do most of their business during the midnight hours. Others never really close. Given the type of business this shop does, I suspect they answer their bell at any hour."

She couldn't ask why he suspected that as she was too busy racing across the street after him. Boy, could that vampire move. But she supposed she'd get her answer if the door opened.

He had to press the button twice, but finally there was some noise from within the tiny shop. Then a curtain twitched aside, behind a barred window, and an eye peeked out. For long moments it seemed they would be ignored, so Caro lifted her jacket, showing her badge. Fortunately, most people would open their doors to a cop rather than risk having it busted down.

The eye disappeared, and then she could hear dead bolts turning. Finally the door opened a crack, although it was still guarded by three chain locks.

"What do you want?" a wizened man demanded.

"Help," said Damien.

"I don't squeal." The door started to close.

Damien's voice changed, assuming that timbre that made Caro shiver. "Open the door. We mean you no harm. The information we want is in your books."

The air seemed to change. Without further protest, the old man opened his door and let them in. As he made way for them and locked up behind them, he looked mildly confused.

But whatever control Damien's voice had had over the man wore off quickly. "Better spend some money," he grumped. "This place isn't a library."

The owner was not only wizened but thin and stooped, as well. He looked as old as Methuselah and hobbled his way behind a tiny counter that held an ancient cash register. There he perched on a stool Caro could barely see.

Dusty, dingy and right now the place was poorly lit, as well. At the moment it would be impossible for her to find a book or anything else by sight.

But Damien seemed to have no such problems. He wandered along a shelf of old books, running a finger along them as he surveyed titles. "Do you know anything about elementals?"

To Caro it seemed the man behind the counter stiffened. "I don't dabble in what I sell," he said irritably. "Fools mess with what they don't understand."

"I agree with you," Damien said pleasantly. "But I need to learn about elementals, and you must know if you have any books or monographs dealing with them." He turned from the shelf and faced the man. "Even if you don't dabble, you surely must hear a great deal from those who do."

For some reason, Caro felt compelled to take a step backward. It was as if some invisible force tugged at her, but it was not the power that had been following her. After that one step back, however, she forced herself to stand still. What was going on here?

"I hear all kinds of things from idiots," the shopkeeper said. "Look around you. I don't even go for the incense and crystals some hang everywhere. I sell the books. That's it."

Damien nodded. "So you've heard nothing about a bokor?"

At that the man stiffened. "No. Have you?"

"It's been mentioned. And since a bokor may be troubling a friend of mine, I'm naturally looking for information."

"Of course," the man said. "Look, I'll be honest with you. I don't hold truck with most of this stuff, but it makes a living. Everyone wants some crazy knowledge these days, as if getting a little religion wouldn't be enough."

"It's alternative religion," Damien remarked.

"Apparently. But if you believe this crap, why would you want to get involved?" He shook his head. "I get lots of people, but most of them probably couldn't manage to perform a ritual well enough to raise any kind of Cain."

"Most likely not. But what if someone could?"

The shopkeeper leaned forward and arched his back as if stretching a painful muscle. "If someone could," he said, "then I guess we're in deep shit."

"Any idea who it might be?"

A shake of the head. "I keep as far away from people who claim to be adept as I can. There are other stores like this, and some of them are run by people who buy their own sales pitch."

"Meaning?"

"They believe, or say they believe in this New Agey stuff. Maybe some of them actually practice Santeria or hoodoo. I keep clear, and I don't want to know."

Caro spoke. "I've answered complaints about Santeria in this neighborhood."

"I don't doubt it. But what can you do about it? It's not illegal to sacrifice a chicken anymore, although you'd think folks around here couldn't afford the chickens."

"They eat them afterward as part of the ritual."

"So I hear. Which makes it no different than a creepy kind of slaughterhouse. I can live with it. I'm no vegetarian."

"So you have practitioners in the neighborhood."

The shopkeeper sighed. "Yeah. From what I've heard, nothing bad comes out of it. It's a religion, and everybody says it's about doing good. God knows, folks around here need something to keep their spirits up."

Caro couldn't argue with that. She also couldn't escape the feeling that this man wasn't going to tell them a thing. She could understand that. Living in this neighborhood was difficult enough without being under suspicion.

Then Damien spoke. "Do you ever get bored enough to read your own books?"

The man cocked an eye at him. "I don't believe this shit, but I'm also not stupid enough to read about it. On the off chance there's something to it, why do I want it in my head? What if just reading those things could make something happen?"

Superstitious, Caro thought. Another thing she could well understand, although even a few days ago, she would have denied it.

"Then we come back to my original question," Damien said. "Do you have any good references on elementals?"

Grunting, the man slid off his stool and came around to the tumbled and dusty stacks. "Like I said, this isn't a library."

"I'll pay. Just get me your best ones."

"You're looking in the wrong place," the guy muttered. "I *do* have some organization." He disappeared around the corner of the floor-to-ceiling shelf and came back a few minutes later with two thin, tattered volumes. "Not a popular subject," he remarked. "Twenty dollars each."

Neither book looked worth that much to Caro, but Damien paid without complaint. "Are there any more of them?" he asked as he slipped his wallet back into his hip pocket.

"Not much call for elementals these days. People want bigger deals. Nasty deals. Not enough to call up a wood sprite anymore."

Damien's tone changed subtly, seeming to charge the air a little. "Then people don't know what real power is."

The man froze again, then closed his cash register. "Maybe so. The less I know, the better."

The man wrapped the books in brown paper and tied the parcel with a string. Caro was charmed for a moment because it seemed so old-fashioned.

Then she and Damien were on the icy street again, listening to the door lock behind them.

"What do you think?" Caro asked him.

"Later. Let's get away from here as soon as we can."

They walked down a dark alley, then he put her on his back again and the night sped by too fast to see.

Chapter 6

Garner was at the office when they returned, and he made no secret of his impatience to talk with Jude.

"Where *is* he? He sends me out to do things, and now he's not even answering his phone? What's the point of always being in touch, like he demands?" Garner waved a phone. "Radio phones in case someone gets in trouble. His idea. And then he doesn't answer?"

Damien stilled. "He didn't say where he was going. Did he tell you?"

"Of course not! He never lets me know anything. I feel like a dog. Go here, Garner, go there, Garner. Cripes."

Damien ignored the complaints. "What has you so worked up?"

"There's been another murder!"

Now it was Caro who froze. "Who? How?"

Garner, clearly glad to at last have someone to listen, leaned forward. "That guy whose entire family was killed last week? The one you came here about? His brother-in-law bit the dust. But that's not what's so interesting. What's interesting is that he lived alone, that he was inside a locked condo and that there's a lot of street talk about how it could have happened. Where the hell is Jude?"

"Wait," Caro said. "Did he have any relationship with the Pritchetts other than the marriage?"

"I don't know. All I know is that the only reason they found him was because some friends started to get worried when he disappeared for three days and didn't return calls. That's why I need Jude!"

"Relax," Damien said quietly. "Jude can't answer his phone if he's traveling fast."

"It's been a half hour. He can cross this entire city faster than that. It's irrelevant anyway. I don't see his car out there."

Damien exchanged looks with Caro. "He *did* drive."

"Yes." Tension was winding her tighter than a spring, the kind of tension she felt when walking into a potentially deadly situation.

"Can you find out anything on the computer?" Damien asked her.

"I'd need a case number."

"No way to get it?"

She jammed her hand into her jeans and pulled out her cell. She dialed a familiar number and heard a familiar voice. "Pat? I need some help. I hear Andrew Pritchett's brother-in-law was found dead."

Pat asked her to hold a minute, and shortly thereafter Caro could tell from the change in sounds that Pat had moved to a bathroom. When she hung up, she was able to answer Damien's question.

"They don't know if the death is associated. No information on how it occurred but Pat said the guy looked as if he'd been scared to death. That might indicate a weak heart. Regardless, she's going to text me the case number."

"Then you can get the reports?"

Caro hesitated. "It won't exactly be legal, but yes."

"In the meantime," Damien said, turning back to Garner, "see what you can find on that machine about associations between Pritchett and his brother-in-law. Maybe they were in business together."

"Why me?" Garner asked, regarding the computer as if it might explode. "Jude will have a fit if I mess something up. Why can't you do it?"

"Because I've never bothered to master a computer. What would I need it for?"

"Plenty, apparently," Garner muttered. "Imagine that. Thousands of years old and no computer experience."

"Try this," Damien said a little acidly. "Thousands of years old and only in the last few decades of that time have computers become meaningful at all to ordinary people."

At that, Garner smirked. "Time to catch up, vampire."

"I rarely waste time learning skills that are utterly useless to me."

"Oh, cut it out," Caro said irritably. "I'll see what I can do as soon as I get the file number."

"I'm still worried about Jude," Damien said. "I wish he'd given us some idea where he was going."

"Maybe," said Garner, brandishing his phone, "he's just not answering because it's me calling."

Damien lifted both brows but then pulled out his own phone and put it to his ear. "There you are," he said after a moment. "Garner is having kittens because you're not returning his calls."

He listened a moment, then laughed. "No, you can tell him that yourself. Caro's about to use your computer if you don't mind. Really? All right, I'll tell her."

He disconnected and looked at Caro. "Jude said to wait. Terri is examining the body and he's already been to the crime scene. He has information."

"All he had to do was tell me that," Garner observed morosely. "Then I wouldn't have had to worry."

Nobody answered him.

Caro started to remove her jacket as the chill from riding on Damien's back began to slip away. Coffee. Hot chocolate. Then her hand found the stitched pouch she'd been carrying.

She pulled it out of her pocket and held it up. "Something affected me tonight when we were in that bookshop. Something made me step back from that man, and it didn't feel like that thing that's been following me. Could it be this?"

"It could," Damien said. He took it from her hand. "I wonder if I was too trusting."

"In what way?"

"Alika said you need protection. You do, but how can I be sure this will provide it? Maybe it's not for protection at all."

"Lovely," said Garner.

Damien barely spared him a glance. "So now we have two questions. Did Alika give you this for real protection? If so, was it this that made you back away from that shopkeeper tonight? If not, why did you back away? Did you sense something wasn't right about him?"

Caro racked her brains trying to figure it out, finally admitting, "I don't know."

"Great," muttered the never-silent Garner. "Either one of them could be involved in this."

"Or neither," Caro said sensibly. "Don't put on blinders, Garner. It limits investigations."

"We still have more places to check out, too," Damien

added. "But I really want to know how the brother-in-law might be involved in this, and whether his death was from natural causes."

"That's important, all right," Caro agreed. "If there's one thing I've learned, it's that coincidences do happen."

"Maybe in *your* line of work," Garner argued. "In mine there are fewer coincidences."

"So what are people saying on the street?" she asked to divert him from his irritability.

"Woo-woo stuff, which is only woo-woo if you've never seen it in action. It probably doesn't mean much really. At least in terms of anyone knowing anything. So the condo was locked. Anybody walking out could have ensured it was locked up. The only mystery was that when the cops arrived, the door chain was still hooked up."

"Really." Caro sat on the chair beside Chloe's desk. "No disturbed windows? Nothing?"

Garner shrugged. "I couldn't get near the place. The only thing I was interested in was that this guy was related to the Pritchett family."

Damien spoke. "Did you sense anything?"

"I sense things all over this town. There are enough nuts to supply a factory. All that matters is a scent I'm supposed to pick out. This one *might* have had the lingering odor of whatever was around Caro the other night."

"Was?" Damien repeated. "Is it gone now?"

"It's not here. That's all I can tell you."

Damien held up the small pouch. "Maybe it *is* protective." Then he frowned. "And if so, how would Alika know exactly what you needed to be protected against?"

"It was clear she's sensitive," Caro reminded him. "She knew when trouble was approaching and shooed us out."

"So logical," he remarked, but there was a gleam in his

eyes that said he knew when she could be utterly illogical. She glanced away, hoping she didn't blush.

That was a memory she wanted to bury in a deep hole. Of course, memory was never that cooperative. Nothing like saying, "Don't think about an elephant."

Jude arrived at last, bringing cold air into the room with him. It clung to him as if he were frozen, sucking heat from around the room. Caro pulled her jacket over her shoulders, wondering how long it took a vampire to reach the ambient temperature. She hadn't noticed it with Damien, most likely because she'd been nearly as cold herself upon their return.

"It wasn't pretty," Jude remarked. "But I got the important information, at least what's available for now. Terri says the guy's heart exploded. She was quite clear he didn't have a vessel rupture or a collapse in the cardiac wall. His heart literally exploded."

Caro felt tension squeeze her own heart. "That's not possible."

"In theory. There wasn't a mark on him either, and the rictus of his face could be either pain or terror. No way to tell."

He popped into his office and returned with two bags of blood. He tossed one to Damien, then bit into his own and began drinking. For the first time, Caro noticed that their eyes changed color as they fed—from black as night to golden.

A few minutes later, when they were done feeding, Jude took the bags into his office, then returned without them. "Okay, we missed something in the background check. I'm not going to call this a coincidence. No way. Not from Terri's description of the guy's heart. We now have six impossible murders, and every one of the victims was related to the rest."

Caro's phone buzzed, and she pulled it out. "Pat texted the case-file number."

"Forward it to me," Jude said. "I'm going to spend the rest of tonight researching." Then he looked at Damien. "Take Caro home until dawn. This place is about to become a beehive, and she looks exhausted."

"I can help," she objected.

"Tomorrow. When you have some rest. I need everyone in top shape. That means you, too, Garner. You get back here in the morning to help Caro and Chloe. I'll leave a list of what I learn and questions to be pursued."

They took Jude's car and Caro was grateful not to be out in the biting wind, moving at nearly supersonic speeds. Damien rolled down his own window a few inches, but this time it amused her because she understood why. Her scents drove him crazy. She'd never enjoyed driving a man crazy before, and she rather liked the illusory sense of power it gave her. She knew it was illusory, though, because she had no doubt this vampire could overpower her in an instant if he chose.

"Are you scared?" he asked.

"Do you care?"

"Actually, yes. There's a great deal I can protect you from, but unless I figure this out I may be no protection at all. And that scares *me*."

"I'm touched."

He snorted. "Seriously, Caro, you ought to be afraid."

"I don't seem to scare easily. I have to be *in* a situation, not thinking about one. And then after the first burst of fear comes, adrenaline kicks in and I'm one of those people who gets the fight rather than flight response."

"Just as well. From this thing there is no flight."

"But Garner said he couldn't sense it around me. So I

don't need protection, do I?" Although, strange as it would have seemed only a couple of days ago, she didn't want this vampire to leave her alone.

"I take Garner with a grain of salt. He's not perfect. And not sensing that thing around you at that moment doesn't mean it won't come back."

She felt a trickle of uneasiness then. She really didn't want to feel that thing watching her ever again. *Think of something else.* Like her irritation at not being able to work the case because Jude had sent her home to rest. Like whether Damien had any feelings beyond lust.

She turned a little in her seat, studying him as light from streetlamps flashed across his face. "Does anything frighten *you?*"

"Something bad happening to you on my watch." He pulled into a parking place near her building and switched off the ignition.

"Cut the crap, Damien. I mean what *really* frightens you?"

"That was it." He turned, putting his arm over the back of the seat. "As for other things…" He shrugged. "I don't fear death. A vampire dies every morning. I don't fear never resurrecting, because I'll never know. I don't fear pain because I heal so fast."

"What about other things? What about your heart?"

"You mean my feelings?"

"Yes."

He hesitated. "Long, long ago, after I entered the priesthood, I had to make a choice. I chose to serve even though it cost me the woman I loved. I was never permitted to see her again. It was a long time ago."

"I guess. So you never loved again?" That seemed sad, but then she reminded herself that she'd given up such things for her job, too. At least for now.

"I never permitted myself to. Look at the way I live, Caro, and ask yourself how many would want to share my life except briefly."

Before she could answer, he climbed out of the car and came around to open her door for her. One look at his face was enough to tell her that the subject was closed.

All the way up to her apartment, she puzzled the question. He seemed content enough with his life. In fact, he had told her it had benefits that made up for the sacrifices. So why did he feel it was so unlikely that anyone would want to share life with him?

"What about other vampires?" she demanded when they were inside her apartment. "Couldn't you find someone who already lives your life?"

One corner of his mouth lifted. "We're territorial. Finding two of us together is rare. That includes males and females. A few manage, and all of us can manage for brief periods. But for eternity? That's rare indeed."

She guessed she could understand that. "I've read that many human marriages start falling apart by the eighteenth year."

"Thus you make my point. And for us there's an additional complication."

"What's that?"

"Just get your sleep. I'll wake you before dawn and we'll go back to Jude's."

But she stood stubbornly still. "Are you saying you can't divorce? Why would that be?"

"It's not about divorce." He sighed, and for the first time she saw him run his fingers through his hair in a sign of true exasperation. "Maybe you should know," he said finally. "I keep telling you we're playing with fire but then I only tell you half of it."

"I'm not planning to play with fire again," she said firmly.

At that he actually smiled. "Plans. Yes. They so often work."

"Stop it."

His smile remained, and she was quite certain he'd smelled the scents of her desire for him off and on all evening. If she were to be honest about it, the only time her body wasn't demanding more of him was when she could keep her mind distracted enough, and even then there was an edgy sort of yearning between her legs. Desire seemed to have a mind of its own. Since meeting him, there seemed to be a part of her that was always ready, always aware, always wanting.

Frankly, that sucked, but nothing seemed to stop it.

"There's an addiction that vampires experience," he said, his smile fading. "I've managed to avoid it for millennia, and I'd like to continue to avoid it."

"Like crack addiction, what you said I might feel?"

"Worse. The only cure is death, or sometimes vengeance."

She caught her breath. "Whose death and whose vengeance?"

"Ours. We call it claiming. An innocuous word for something so dangerous. If a vampire claims someone or something, it's beyond obsession. For example, were I to claim you, you'd never be able to leave me. You might run to the farthest end of the planet, and I would follow and find you. I wouldn't be able to prevent myself except by ending my own existence. And were I to claim you and you died, I would have only two choices—to avenge you or die to break the claiming."

"Wow," she whispered.

"Judging by what happened to my friend Luc after his

claimed mate died, I'm not so sure that vengeance is a cure either. Most of us attempt to avoid claiming, although it's beginning to seem to me that it's not something that happens by choice. Jude claimed Terri, and that's the third case I've seen since coming here."

"But…she's not a vampire. So what happens when she dies?"

"Exactly what I told you. Thus Jude will have a decision to make eventually. Terri wants him to change her so she can fully share his life. But he's reluctant because he knows how painful the change is and knows there's no way back once it's done. But at some point or other, he's going to have to decide whether to keep her by changing her or face her eventual death, and his own as a result."

Caro tried to imagine it. "I've heard of heartbreak, but this is beyond anything I've ever heard of. Well, not true. Some humans become that obsessed."

"But obsessed in a different way usually. How many cases have you seen in your career where a human would rather kill the object of his obsession than leave it?"

"Too many," she admitted.

"Our kind…we kill ourselves rather than those we've claimed."

Her eyes felt strangely hot as she looked at him. "That's scary."

"It is," he agreed. "So we avoid it if there's any way we can. You'd better get some sleep. Dawn will come all too soon."

She turned toward her bedroom, not because she wanted to obey him, but because she felt a need to think over what he'd said. But just before she entered, she looked over her shoulder to ask, "Isn't there anything good about claiming?"

"I wouldn't know from personal experience. But Jude seems happy with it."

She carried that to bed with her, trying to imagine what he'd said and telling herself that being stalked by an obsessed vampire was not something any woman could really want. She'd seen enough obsessed people and it had never struck her as a healthy state of affairs.

But it wasn't claiming she was thinking about when she finally slipped away into sleep. It was the thing stalking her and the sense it was coming closer somehow, and growing more dangerous.

In her dreams, it dogged her heels as she tried to run—she was never able to see how close it was or what it intended.

All she knew was that somehow Damien was there with her, encouraging her, promising to place himself between it and her.

She didn't want to wake. A half hour before dawn, Damien tried to get her up and out of bed, but she'd finally reached a point of exhaustion where nothing short of a fire in the house would get her moving quicker than a snail's pace.

She heard him moving around her room as sleep tried to cloud her brain again, then felt him lift her in his arms as easily as if she were a child.

And for some reason, she didn't mind that he carried her down the stairs, put her in the car, buckled her seat belt and drove off with her.

Vaguely she knew she was too groggy, that she never had this much trouble waking up, but she didn't care. She was asleep again as they pulled away from the curb, and she stirred only when they jolted to a stop in front of Jude's office.

One thing she did notice: the sky was lightening with the first rosy tinge of dawn. "Light," she said, unable to form a more coherent sentence.

"It's all right," he murmured. Then strong arms lifted her again, and she retained only the merest memory of being carried inside to the office and laid on the sofa.

As sleep started to claim her again, she heard Damien say, "Something's wrong. I can't wake her."

Then she slipped over the abyss into the nightmares and darkness again.

Damien and Jude gathered in his office where, with the door closed, no light could enter. There they could postpone the sleep of death, but only for a little while.

Neither of them felt they could simply let their own deaths take over when Caro couldn't wake up, yet Damien knew the prickling on the back of his neck was painful and would soon become utterly distracting. In fact, soon he wouldn't be able to avoid the sleep of death at all.

"Maybe she'll be safer here," Jude said. "I've got a lot of wards on this office."

"I'm worried about when neither of us is awake. Who is going to watch over her and ensure this sleep doesn't turn into something else?"

Jude's frown deepened. "How can we be sure what's going on here? How can we know how to counter it? I'd suggest you keep her in my office with you throughout the day, but…"

"But," Damien agreed. "But I'll be virtually useless unless she tries to wake me. If she opens the damn door to get out I'll be cooked, and she could die right beside me without me ever knowing. No solution."

The burning on the back of his neck was beginning

to feel like hot coals. Soon he wouldn't be able to avoid dying any longer.

"We need to get her attention," Jude said. "Wake her enough to get it through to her."

"All right, I'll try."

Jude stopped him before he turned. "I don't think you can go out there now."

The flames that seemed to be licking at the base of Damien's skull would seem to agree. "Then what the hell are we going to do?"

"Chloe." Jude picked up the phone and punched in a number. "I need you over here now. Something's going on with Caro, and we're not sure what. Regardless, neither of us is going to be awake for more than a few minutes. You're going to have to keep an eye on her. We can't."

Silence, followed by "We can't seem to wake her up completely. If anything changes, you're going to have to bust into my office and get me and Damien. And you're going to have to find and put up those blackout curtains for the outer office because it's too late for us to do that."

When he disconnected, he looked only mildly irritated. "Like I have time to answer a million questions right now. Okay, I'm going to bed with Terri. She's waiting for me. And you sleep here in my office. It's totally blacked out, as you know. Once Chloe gets the blackout curtains up, the outer office will be safe, too. Then if anything happens..."

"Something is already happening," Damien said tautly. But they both knew that. Never in all his centuries had he damned the sleep of death as much as he did right then. Caro might need him desperately, but he was going to be virtually beyond reach. There was not one damned thing he could do about it.

Cussing, as darkness began to grab him, he dropped to the floor, unable to resist his curse any longer.

* * *

Caro heard a lot of fussing. She reached toward it, desperate to escape a suffocating darkness that seemed to be squeezing her chest, trying to pull the very air from her body.

She struggled toward the sounds, and gradually they dragged her from the depths of sleep, and she pushed herself up on one elbow. She had only the dimmest memory of how she had arrived here, but she knew where she was. Turning her head, she saw Chloe standing on a chair and pinning a black curtain around the room's one barred window.

"What's going on?" she asked groggily.

Chloe glanced over her shoulder. "You," she said. "The guys were worried because they couldn't wake you up, so I'm vampire-proofing the office in case we need to go shake them out of their coffins."

"Coffins? Really?"

"Hardly. Vaults more like. I just like to call them coffins."

"They can wake up?"

"Resurrect," Chloe said as she drove another tack in the wall. "Please. It's resurrection, according to Jude. They don't sleep, they don't dream. Gone, poof, like the dead."

"Oh." Caro managed to sit all the way up and rub her eyes. "I feel hungover."

"Something got to you, all right. Jude has enough wards around this office that it's possible whatever hit you may have been forced to withdraw."

She jumped down from the chair. "Are you awake enough to do something for me?"

"I think so. Just don't make it complicated."

Chloe flashed a grin. "I'm going to take a flashlight

outside. I want you to come over here and check to make sure absolutely no light is getting past this curtain."

"In a minute. I think I can manage it in a minute."

"I made tea, but if coffee would be better I can make you some."

"Tea will do fine. Caffeine, right?"

"Plenty. I like it strong and black."

When Chloe returned and gave her a hot mug of steaming black tea, Caro asked, "What happens if light gets through the curtain? Poof?"

Chloe shook her head. "Not likely. But they'd get severe burns wherever the sun touches them."

"I don't want to see that."

"Me either."

Chloe perched beside her on the couch. "You're taking this whole vampire thing awfully well."

Caro rubbed her temple with her fingertips, trying to ease a dull ache. "Chloe, you're talking to someone who saw a man levitated and impaled by nothing I could see. Who is being followed by something I can't see. Who had a grandmother who claimed to be a wi—okay, a mage, and who taught me about things like this. Of course, I didn't believe her. It had to hit me between the eyes like a two-by-four."

"Some things have to do that," Chloe agreed. She sipped her own tea, then placed the mug on a small octagonal table in front of the couch. Curling up, she tucked her legs beneath her and studied Caro. "I figured it out pretty fast one night when Jude saved me from some guys who intended me no good. He swooped in like a superhero and saved the day. Of course, he'd get mad if he heard me say that. He doesn't like me to make him sound extraordinary in any way."

"But you think he is? Apart from being a vampire?"

"Let me put it this way, and you can laugh if you want, but I'm serious." Her expression changed to reflect that. "People are always looking to movies and books to see a story about the battle between good and evil and the triumph of good."

Caro nodded. "There's a lot of that."

"Well, the fact is, there *is* an ongoing battle between good and evil. Jude fights evil. He fights the kind of evil most people don't even recognize exists. And for all I give him a hard time, I like being part of that. I *really* like it. So yeah, to me he's a superhero."

"And Damien?"

"He's a trifle arrogant, but he's part of the battle, too. I'm not sure what he does in Cologne, but he was one of the few who answered Jude's call for help when we were fighting the rogues—did Damien tell you about that?"

"A bit."

"A bit is all you need. There were dozens of them and only a handful of us. Damien only came for a brief visit to help Jude with a problem, but he's stayed and is continuing to help with you."

Caro nodded, not sure how she felt about knowing that her problem was the reason he stayed. "How long have you worked for Jude?"

"Six years. Long enough to know what kind of person he is. Well, what kind of vampire." She gave a little giggle. "He's willing to risk everything to protect others. Even permanent death. So yeah, I have a lot of respect for him. Few of us humans will ever know how much safety he provides in this city."

"I'm starting to get an inkling."

"But only an inkling. You protect the city from human threats, and that's great. But Jude's more of a supernatural cop. He protects us against the things we can't see."

"Like the mystical murderer of an entire family."

"Like that," Chloe agreed.

"Does Pat Matthews know?"

"She knows he handles stuff the police won't. She does *not* know he's a vampire."

Caro smiled wryly. "I don't think she'd be comfortable knowing that. But she's a lot more broad-minded than most I work with. Everyone was trying to shut me down about what I saw. She told me to shut up about it at work and get over here."

Chloe nodded. "That's how we get some cases. It's a working relationship. We take what the police can't handle."

"Why are you trusting me so much?"

"Because Pat trusted you and mostly because you're still here working with us. For Jude, it's not so much trust as taking care of a problem. He never leaves an important problem alone, no matter the risk to him."

Then Chloe rose. "Feel up to seeing if the flashlight comes through anywhere on the window?"

The tea had helped, and the feeling of being hungover had begun to fade. Only as she was rising did she notice that some of her own fresh clothes were neatly folded on the chair beside Chloe's desk. "Where did those come from?"

"Damien brought them along with you last night. We have a shower you can use before you change." Chloe sniffed. "Only took me five years to get Jude to put in a water heater."

"That long?"

"Jude doesn't feel the icy water. Or did Damien neglect to tell you they don't feel temperature?"

"He mentioned it. I just hadn't extrapolated."

"Trust me, it extrapolates to showers, as well. I used

to find every excuse to go home to shower, and it wasn't easy in the middle of a fast-moving case."

The blackout curtain proved to need only one more tack, largely because it was so much bigger than the window that it did a really good job.

Now it was night inside even though it was broad daylight outside.

Chloe brought out some bagels she had purchased on her way in along with some smoked salmon and cream cheese. Caro realized she was famished and helped herself liberally. "What kinds of wards does Jude use?" she asked.

"The kind he grew up with—holy water and sanctified oils. Sometimes he has me put up my own wards."

"Which kind are yours?"

"I'm sort of Wiccan, but since I started working with Jude I've learned a whole lot about all kinds of other beliefs." Chloe made an impish face. "You could say I've developed my own methods."

"I admit I don't know much about it," Caro remarked as she ate. "My grandmother called herself a witch, but Damien says she was more of a mage."

"Really?" Interest was written over Chloe's face. "I think he meant that your grandmother may have had very strong powers?"

"Evidently. I'll be honest, Chloe. I'm pretty much at sea with all of this." In fact, she seemed to be sailing farther from the shores of reality with every passing hour. "I didn't really pay attention to Grandma because I didn't believe in much that I couldn't see."

"I imagine that's been busy changing."

"Obviously."

Chloe forked another sliver of salmon onto her bagel. "Well, Wicca is what Jude insists on calling an emergent religion. By that he means we don't have one single act together, and I guess he's right about that. We disagree on a lot of things and agree on a lot of others, and we all call ourselves Wiccan."

"So how do you decide?"

Chloe shrugged. "I take what suits me and make the rest myself, basically."

A few minutes later, she paused as she ate and looked directly at Caro. "What do *you* believe?"

"Right now I'm undergoing a radical transformation." A truth that didn't sound nearly as bad as it sometimes felt.

They worked all day, exploring the detailed back-grounds of all the murder victims. At this point, Caro was ready to bend some rules, and she accessed case-file interviews with everyone who knew the family. Chloe even taught her a few things, such as how to hack into so-cial networks to see things that only the account holder was supposed to see.

She was so absorbed in finding information and mak-ing notes that she was startled when Jude and Damien emerged, signaling the end of daylight. There had been no cues, of course, with the office sealed up against light, but it was still hard to believe so many hours had passed.

Damien scanned her. "You look much more awake."

"No kidding," Chloe responded. "I was banging around in here for nearly an hour before she opened her eyes."

Ignoring the others, Damien came to squat beside Caro where she sat at the spare computer, which Chloe had placed on a table for her. "How do you feel?" He contin-ued to appraise her, his eyes filled with concern.

"This morning I felt hungover, but I'm fine now. For a while I dreamed a darkness was squeezing my chest and sucking all the air out of me. It was so hard to wake. I'd like to know what happened."

"So would I." He reached out to touch her hair and cheek with such gentleness that her heart squeezed.

She had not expected him to be gentle. Nor did she want her heart responding to him in any way. Despite her reluctance, however, she couldn't bring herself to pull away from his touch. She needed it, needed it so she wouldn't feel quite so alone while she faced this evil killer she couldn't even see. Needed it because her heart ached for it. Needed it because she had suffered so many shocks in such a short time that a kind touch could feel like a lifeline.

"I'm not sure you should leave this office until we learn more."

Nothing was better guaranteed to raise her determination. "I am *not* about to become the prisoner of fear!"

He smiled and stood. "There's my Caro," he remarked. "Nonetheless." He looked at Jude.

"I agree, at least for now. We need to feed the ladies. Chloe, why don't you join me? Let's go out and get some real food. Terri will be joining us soon, and she doesn't have to go to work for a few hours yet."

Chloe jumped up. "Real food? As long as I don't have to cook it. But I don't want anything we can have delivered. I want something different. Caro?"

Caro shook her head. "Anything is fine. I'm not picky."

Terri's voice drew her attention to the doorway of Jude's inner office. She was dressed for work already, to judge by her neat slacks suit, and was smiling. "I already put in my vote for seafood. Are you allergic, Caro?"

"Not at all."

"Then the three of us will be back shortly with loads of shrimp, lobster and crab."

Caro watched the women pull on their winter coats and leave with Jude before she said to Damien, "We were obviously excluded from that outing. Or I was."

"I don't mind," Damien said. "Do you?"

Before she could answer, he reached for her hand and drew her to her feet until she stood only inches from him.

Once again he raised a hand to caress her hair and cheek lightly with his palm.

"When I resurrected tonight, the first thing on my mind was you. How do you do that to me, Caro?"

She wished she knew the answer, because he affected her the same way. Throughout the day her thoughts had turned to him, and when she had taken a nap under Chloe's watchful eye so that she could stay awake longer tonight, he had been waiting for her behind her eyelids and in her dreams.

Hot, sizzling dreams, the kinds of things the mind could only spin in unguarded moments. One in particular made her almost want to blush, and she might have if not for the fact that no one but she knew what it was.

She had dreamed that she stood before him in a dimly lit room, while he used that voice that made others obey him but that only made her tingle.

But in the dream it had made her obey him as it could not in the waking world. He had simply smiled and said, "Strip for me."

And she had. She could remember every aching moment of it as desire, anticipation and nervousness had filled her. What if he didn't like the way she looked? What if he never touched her at all?

Never in real life had she done that for a man, and it almost shocked her that she could have such a wish, even in her dreams, to display herself that way.

In the dream, she had stood naked before him, following commands to turn, bend over, part her legs, until she had felt so incredibly exposed, knowing he was looking at her sex while she couldn't see him at all.

At the order to spread herself more, she had obeyed, experiencing an even more agonizing need to be touched and reassured that he desired her.

In the dream she had felt so deliciously helpless and enthralled, so free and yet so oddly inhibited.

The only thing she wanted was for him to do whatever he wished with her.

Finally, finally, she had felt the soft touch of his fingers on her exposed petals, stroking, separating, exploring…

And just as she thought she would explode, the dream had vanished.

Standing before him now, she was very glad he couldn't read her mind.

But he could read her scents, and as she peeked up at him, she saw knowledge in his gaze. At least it wasn't arrogant knowledge, or even self-satisfied knowledge. He seemed perplexed, actually.

"Somehow," he murmured, "we are going to have to find time to settle this matter between us. Safely. For both of us."

At least he was frank. She appreciated that. Most of her experience with dating had been of the kind that involved dancing around, a lot of pretense and even some outright lies. In fact, she had reached a point where she believed the words *I love you* were one of the biggest lies in the English language.

At least he was calling this what it was: raw desire. She was also somewhat reassured by his description of claiming. It meant he potentially had as much to lose as she did.

She felt breathless, though, as he lowered his head and nestled his mouth against hers. Cool lips, soft lips. Not cold. Nothing about him was as cold as she would have expected.

Then he drew back, trailing his hand over her throat

and breast before quite suddenly reappearing across the room. "But not now."

Definitely not now. Not with Jude, Terri and Chloe likely to walk in at any moment with dinner.

"Soon," he promised. "Very soon."

She actually hoped so. She had to get this vampire out of her head and out of her dreams. She struggled for a coherent thought, something else to talk about before she ceased to give a damn if someone walked in.

"Why was I so sleepy?"

"I don't know and that worries me. It definitely wasn't a natural sleep."

"It didn't feel like one. I felt drugged. But when I took a nap this afternoon, that was normal sleep." Well, normal except for her dreams. "Do you think that energy was doing something to me?"

"That's my guess."

"But it killed the others. It hasn't killed me."

"Perhaps because of that gris-gris Alika gave you. Or perhaps because we got you back to Jude's office before it could finish its work. One thing I've decided is that if you want to go back to your apartment we need to make sure Jude wards it thoroughly."

"Okay, I'll agree with that. But we've still got to figure out how to deal with this elemental."

"I'm beginning to think the only way to deal with it is to find the person who summoned it."

That didn't cheer Caro at all. Millions of people in this city. Thousands who could be dabbling with occult powers. Finding the one responsible for this sounded a whole lot harder than finding a human murderer. "You know, when the police hunt for a killer, we usually have a clue or two. Some indication of a troubled relationship. Fingerprints, other physical evidence. There's no evidence in this case."

"You were the one who cautioned us not to narrow ourselves too much. A wise caution. But it remains that elementals don't kill people for their own reasons. They kill because people set them the task by creating a curse that calls them. So we still have the clue of motive to guide us."

"And any one of thousands of people who might have done this. Unless we find *the* motive."

"You found nothing today that stood out?"

"With all Chloe and I did, we came to the realization that this guy was a developer and landlord with his fingers in so many pots around the city that we might be able to narrow our suspect list to a few thousand rather than tens of thousands."

"Great." He sounded as unhappy as she felt.

The others returned with steamed crab legs, boiled shrimp and some lobster tails. The women gathered around a folding table to eat while the two vampires sat farther away.

"So," said Chloe, as she forked some threads of lobster from a tail and dipped them into drawn butter, "Caro and I spent our entire day trying to sort through Pritchett's dealings. It would be only a small exaggeration to say he was involved in about fifty percent of what goes on in this city, from real estate to development to belonging to the boards of banks and other companies."

"In short," Caro said, "he was probably a huge target in a lot of ways. You don't get to that level without making some enemies."

"What about the rest of the family?" Jude asked.

"Kids had no reported problems at school," Caro answered promptly. "The police interviewed their friends and school officials. Nobody was aware of any troubles."

"The brother-in-law?"

"He just started working for Andrew Pritchett a couple

of months ago. That's the only association we could find other than the marriage."

"What did he do?"

Chloe and Caro exchanged looks. "We don't know," Caro said finally. "We only know when he went on the payroll."

"What did he do before that?"

Caro's heart accelerated a little and she leaned toward Jude. "He worked for the city-planning department."

"Ah…" The sigh seemed to emerge from both vampires at the same moment.

"It could just be a coincidence," Caro reminded them. "He did his job okay, according to everything I could find. Pritchett might have hired him to make his wife happy."

"Or something else could have been going on."

"Agreed."

Damien spoke. "We need to look much closer at that. "While I'll be the first to allow that life has plenty of co-incidences, this one seems just a bit suspicious. We need to look more closely at what Pritchett was doing over the last six months and why he might have found someone from city planning useful."

Then he swiftly changed the subject, turning to Jude. "I want you to put wards on Caro's place. Something got to her last night. In her home. From what she said of her dreams, it may have been trying to kill her in her sleep."

Jude's smile was almost wry. "I thought you were the mage."

"I'm taking a refresher. Regardless, Caro came out of whatever was being done to her after she got here. So there's some protection in your spells."

"And Chloe's," Jude remarked. "All right. When I take Terri to work, we'll all go and try to make Caro's place safe."

Chapter 7

They all piled into Jude's ramshackle car and dropped Terri at the morgue. Then Jude and Chloe warded Caro's apartment and Jude gave her some holy water and a tiny vial of sanctified oil. "Carry them with you," he suggested. "You never know."

But after they'd returned Jude and Chloe to the office to do more research on Pritchett's background, Damien and Caro took the car to go visit some more shops that catered to the adherents of alternative religions.

"I really hadn't realized how many of these shops there are," Caro remarked. "And I thought I knew this city, being a cop."

"I imagine they keep a fairly low profile. Most would tend to have a small, select clientele, and they wouldn't want problems with mainstream religionists."

"I guess. It just seems odd I've never really noticed them before."

"Why? Because of your grandmother?"

Caro glanced at him. "Maybe I didn't notice *because* of my grandmother. Out of sight, out of mind."

"Ah." He let that lie, giving her space to work it through if she wanted.

It was then that she remembered another dream from her nap that afternoon, one that had nothing to do with her incredible desire to hop in the sack with a vampire.

Her grandmother. She had been sitting on her grandmother's lap in the old rocking chair that creaked with every movement. Grandma had been telling her another of her fantastical stories—or had she?

Dreams were elusive at the best of times, and since she'd already almost forgotten she had had this one, it was a struggle to remember much more than how good she'd always felt sitting on Grandma's lap.

How safe. How cherished. A lump rose in her throat.

You have the gift, sweet child. I feel it in you. It's a greater gift than mine, perhaps as great as my grandmother's.

What had that meant? Had her mind made it up? But no, something deep within her felt convinced that her grandmother had said that. A great gift?

She closed her eyes and tried to pull more of the memory or dream to mind, sensing it might be important in some way, whether her sleeping brain had manufactured it or whether it was the result of something she recalled.

Feel within yourself. It's sleeping now, dreaming of great things, but you can wake it at any time, my darling Caro. Belief is the key.

Belief? All her life she'd refused to believe in much beyond her five senses. Yes, she had a certain psychic skill, but sometimes she even convinced herself she was just good at reading people.

Even though she never quite believed that.

"Damien?"

"Yes?"

"When you were a mage—well, I guess you still are—but back when you practiced all the time, what did belief mean to you?"

"In what way? What I believed in? What I believed about myself? How I used belief?"

She hesitated, partly because the question wasn't really clear to her. "I think my grandmother once said that belief is the key, and I think she meant to my power."

"That would make sense. Do you want to stop for some coffee before we go to the first shop? You look cold."

Well, of course she was cold, she thought wryly. He was protecting himself against her scents by keeping his window rolled down again. If she had to ride in the car too often with this guy, she was going to need better winter clothes.

But coffee sounded good, as did a brief break before they met another enigmatic shopkeeper who would seem determined to tell them as little as possible.

He pulled over and parked in front of a nearly empty diner. She noticed as they walked in, however, that Damien didn't go unnoticed. Eyes immediately looked his way, and then almost subtly, people seemed to pull back a little as if they sensed something. It amused her to see people react so unconsciously to a man who appeared perfectly normal. She wondered what they were sensing.

When he looked around for a waiter, though, a middle-aged woman came hurrying over as if commanded. Could his glance do that, too?

"Two coffees," he said, then turned to Caro. "Do you want dessert? You didn't eat all that much."

The thought of something sweet with her coffee sounded

very good now that he mentioned it. She grabbed the plastic menu and scanned quickly. "Cheese Danish, please."

When the woman walked away to get their order, she leaned toward Damien, who sat across from her. "Can you drink coffee?"

"I can drink and eat. It just doesn't please me anymore. Most things taste about like dirt."

"Oh." She wasn't sure she'd want to give up the joy of eating lobster or a pastry. "Do you miss it?"

"Never. Most of what you humans enjoy so much didn't exist in my human lifetime. I ate a lot of lamb, fish, flat breads, fruits, figs and olives. And everything was full of sand."

She laughed. "Sand would kind of kill it for me."

"It was part of life. I didn't think about it then." He was smiling, though. "So I've never tasted most of the culinary delights you humans so enjoy now. How could I miss them?"

"Good question. I hadn't really thought about it."

"When I served at temple and someone brought me a plate of figs or olives, they always poured water over it to rid it of the sand. Hopeless enterprise for the most part, but a nice gesture."

"But I thought it was the fertile crescent, so full of plants and gardens."

"Part of it was, although not all of it. We had swamps, too. But the winds would blow and the dust would come from elsewhere. Even today you get the Saharan dust on your East Coast at times."

She nodded. "I've heard about that."

"Usually not enough for you to notice. Being closer to the deserts, we experienced more of it."

"You still haven't answered my question about belief."

Just then the waitress returned with their order. He

waited until the coffee and pastry were served and they were alone again in their corner of the diner.

"Belief manifests in many ways and can be used in many ways. Often, as a priest, I played on the beliefs of our adherents. You see that often in religions even today. Your priest or minister says something and the congregation believes it as an article of faith. Things don't have to be explained. Nothing is questioned."

"Did you believe in what you were doing?"

"Of course. I became a priest."

She nodded. "Okay, so you believed along with your adherents. But what else? What could my grandmother have meant?"

"Belief is indeed a key and not just to the minds of others. If you are a mage, as I am, it's necessary to believe in your own power, Caro. You have to *believe* in your gifts to unlock them. You have to believe that you can repel a demon or cause a mountain to move. Whenever you wish to do something you can't do by ordinary means, you have to believe you can do it by extraordinary means."

"Belief is a difficult thing."

"Very, if you weren't raised to believe something. Jude's wards are the ones he was raised to believe in—holy water and chrism, the sanctified oils. But ask yourself what empowers water that contains a bit of salt or olive oil into something that protects against evil."

She nodded, swallowing pastry. "Belief."

"Exactly. Jude is open-minded enough to take advantage of the wards that Chloe has learned. *She* believes in them."

"So belief is the key to accessing power?"

"In a way. Belief is also what makes things powerful. I'm not going to say that forces don't exist apart from belief, because they do. But to harness them, you must both believe in them and believe in your own ability to do so."

"But I never believed in this thing that's attached itself to me."

"Until you saw what it did to that man."

He had a point. She definitely believed the evidence of her own eyes and that there was a man lying on a morgue table that Terri had said couldn't have been impaled that way by ordinary means unless he'd *fallen* on those horns. Had that helped make her aware of this force that watched her? Helped her to believe it was there? Was she making it more powerful by believing in it?

Damien spoke again. "Belief sometimes comes from experience and sometimes from learning. Sometimes it's almost inherent. But no spell I ever worked as a mage worked if I didn't believe it would."

Caro ate another tidbit of pastry while she thought about that. "Did your belief grow with every experience that worked?"

"Of course it did. It's a bit like a hump you have to get over."

"So my grandmother was telling me something important."

"She was telling you something *essential.* Two people can use the same spell. One merely hopes it might work. The other absolutely believes it will. Same spell, different outcomes. The person who *hopes* will probably see little result compared to the one who believes."

Caro thought about that for a few minutes. "I'm a great believer in hope," she said finally.

"Hope is what keeps us going. But belief, as your grandmother said, is the true key to our inherent powers."

"Well, since I believe that thing exists, I ought to believe in my ability to send it away."

"You should." His smile was kind. "But the two are not necessarily interchangeable."

Okay, she thought as they drove to the next shop, she certainly believed that force had killed at least five people and possibly a sixth. She certainly believed it had been dogging her heels since she had seen it in action.

So how great a leap should it be from believing in *it* to believing in her own power to drive it away? But she had to admit, it was a heckuva leap, right across a chasm she'd been avoiding all her life.

Rage had probably been the motivating factor in summoning the elemental, if that's what it was. So how about she start with a little rage of her own in place of the fear and uneasiness she'd been feeling? Hadn't her grandmother said something about fear feeding other powers?

It was one of the reasons, she was sure, that she'd grown up to be relatively fearless. Heck, she wouldn't be able to do her job as a cop if she were constantly afraid of what might happen, and while a little fear could be a good thing in a bad situation—self-preservational, even—she wasn't sure it was always the most useful response.

It didn't seem like a useful one now. She wasn't yet scared enough to reach the flight-or-fight response of adrenaline, which in past dangerous situations had made it possible for her to confront her fears. What was different this time?

The fact that she couldn't see the threat? No guns were being fired? Or maybe the lingering belief somewhere deep inside that something intangible couldn't really hurt her.

Maybe that was the hardest bit of all to swallow. Maybe she needed to swallow it, and quickly.

Something had certainly put her into an unnatural sleep early this morning, haunted her dreams, fed on her fears.

So it could affect her. Maybe the only reason it hadn't killed her was that Damien had gotten her to Jude's, where the spell or effect had worn off.

Or maybe it had something to do with the inherent power her grandmother had always claimed she had.

"Damien?"

"Yes?"

"If I have power, can you teach me how to use it?"

"I can help you start," he said slowly. "But how far into this world do you want to go?"

"I think I'm already into it up to my neck."

"That's debatable. Other people can fight it for you."

"No. I've got to play a part in this. I have to be able to live with myself, you know."

He didn't say any more until they were parked in front of the Candlelight New Age Shoppe. "All right," he said. "We'll start small because I'm rusty and need to practice, and because if we try anything really big, you're apt to grow doubts rather than belief."

"Fair enough."

As they stepped into the shop, Caro was struck by how different it was from the previous two. This owner believed in light and cleanliness and space. It might have been a large, traditional bookstore except for the heavy scent of incense and the candles burning in sconces. The crammed rows of jars behind the counter made the shop look like an old-fashioned apothecary.

The lady who greeted them apparently didn't feel her job called for any theatrics. She looked like a middle-aged businesswoman in a hot-pink suit that flattered her coloring. Her graying hair was so perfectly coiffed that Caro almost reached up to pat her own dark hair into place.

The woman's smile was warm and inviting. "Can I help you with something? I'm Jenny Besom, the proprietor."

Caro immediately reached out to shake hands. Damien, she noticed, hung back a little, and that was so unlike him Caro felt her alert level rise just a bit.

"We're doing some research," Caro said when Damien didn't launch into the matter. "We're curious about elementals."

"Elementals?" Jenny sounded surprised. "I don't get many people asking about that." She gave a little laugh. "Most want to know how to cast a circle or how to invoke a healing. Or, of course, whether there's such a thing as a love potion."

Caro smiled, glancing at Damien, wondering what had made him stay in the background. Damien was never in *anyone's* background. "No, not in the market for spells—just some understanding."

Jenny looked past her at Damien and seemed to do a double take. Her smile faded a bit. Caro immediately wondered if Jenny was seeing his aura or sensing something else. In the diner she had certainly seen people's body language express some uneasiness as Damien passed.

Then Damien spoke, and Caro heard that tone again, the one that evoked obedience. What in the world had set him off?

"Elementals," Damien said. "Do you have any personal experience of them?"

"No." The smile had faded from Jenny's face.

"What powers do you use?"

"I invoke powers to heal and help."

"And nothing else?"

"No, never."

"But help can be interpreted in various ways, can't it?" Jenny nodded.

"I thought so. Have you sensed something going on in this town?"

"Yes."

"Do you know who is behind it?"

"No."

"Are you *sure* you haven't heard anything at all?"

"Nothing."

He pulled out one of Jude's cards and placed it on the counter before her. "If you hear anything about someone using power for ill, call this number and report it."

"Yes."

"What will you do?"

"Call and report it."

"Forget I was ever here. You can talk to this lady now. She's the only one who came in."

"Yes, the only one here."

With that, Damien turned and the only sign of his departure was the sound of the door.

Caro stood looking at Jenny, wondering what the hell she was supposed to do now.

Then Jenny seemed to shake herself. "Sorry, I was woolgathering. I spend so much time alone I'm used to wandering in my own thoughts."

"No family?" Caro asked sympathetically.

"Never had one. Most of the time I think that's a good thing," Jenny said. "I have friends, of course, but I'm still alone a lot in this store."

"I'm sure."

Jenny picked up the card on the counter. "I should call if I hear about something bad going on?"

"Please, anything at all.

"Of course." Jenny became brisk. "I'm sorry I don't have anything on elementals. My customers don't get far into the weeds on these things. In fact," she added almost humorously, "they dabble around and come back in a month looking for something else to play with."

Caro laughed. "Thanks for your time, Jenny. It was a pleasure to meet you."

"Come back sometime. In fact, on Thursday nights I have a medium who comes in. Whether she's gifted or not I don't know, but she sure is fun to listen to."

"Thanks. I might do that."

Outside, Caro found Damien already in the car. She climbed in beside him. "What the hell was that all about?"

"Let's go to your place. Or Jude's. Whichever. Some things need to be talked about inside protected space."

Puzzled, but wanting familiar space and a few of her own personal comforts, she told him to take her home.

It was a quiet drive, and for the first time she felt waves of uneasiness radiating from Damien. He always seemed so confident, so comfortable, but right now he was almost jangling.

The result was that she was pretty well jangling, too, by the time they entered her apartment. Nor was she comforted when he asked for the holy oil and sealed her door again by dabbing it on the lintel.

"What is going on?" she asked.

He put a finger to his lips. Watching in amazement, he went to get the box of salt from her bedroom. He sprinkled it around the room in a large circle. All the while he chanted something she couldn't make out, in a language she had never heard. She sat in the middle of the room, waiting until he had closed the circle and joined her.

"What the hell is going on, Damien?"

"I just made a protective circle."

"I *know* that," she said sarcastically, then paused. "What were you chanting?"

"A spell from ancient times, one I used often and still recall. It strengthens the circle and keeps out all uninvited powers."

"And we need that why? What happened with Jenny at the bookshop? Why did you use that voice on her?"

He cast off his leather jacket and sat on the floor, facing her. "I sensed something."

"I could figure that out, too. Details, Damien. Try some details."

But he asked a question instead. "How did Jenny strike you?"

"As a modern businesswoman. Friendly. Welcoming. Not very into the stuff she carries at her store...." Caro trailed off. "That's not very likely, is it? She'd have to know her subject or she'd soon have no customers. And she did mention healing spells."

"Exactly. All the while she was pretending to deal only with dabblers and dilettantes, I got the feeling she was hiding something."

"But you used the Voice on her. It worked. I saw it work. She said she didn't know anything."

"The Voice worked on her. But something else was working on her, too. I could feel it."

Caro chewed that over. "It's possible," she admitted. "She struck me as so out of place in that store."

"There's a reason you felt that way. Work on it. All I know is that she responded to my questions in a way that she was *allowed* to respond."

"How can you tell the difference?"

"Centuries of practice. Take my word for it. I didn't get the whole truth. What's more, this ordinary modern businesswoman picked up on the fact that I'm not exactly human. She may not have identified what I am, but she definitely sensed it."

"Alika identified you as a mage."

"Yes, but it doesn't make me happy to be identified as something *other* by someone who is pretending absolutely nothing out of the ordinary goes on in her store, her circle or her life."

"You've got a point."

Caro still hadn't shucked her jacket, but as she did so now, she felt the pouch of gris-gris Alika had given her. She pulled it out and held it palm up. "I wonder if I should trust this. How do I know it's for protection?"

"Close your eyes and concentrate on it. Remember what your grandmother said. You have the power, and the key is belief. Believe you can tell whether it's for good or ill."

"Can't you?"

"It wasn't given to me. I might not sense it in the same way. Besides, for days now I've been so aware of that force hovering in your vicinity that I'm not sure my senses aren't dulled when it comes to you."

She hoped *all* his senses about her weren't dulled, but she pushed the thought away to try to do what he asked. Closing her eyes, she told herself that she absolutely *could* tell if that pouch protected her or did something else. That shouldn't be hard.

"Just let your mind wander if it wishes," Damien murmured. "Follow where it leads and don't fight it. The same power that allowed you to see my aura and sense other things is there. When it is ready, it will answer your question."

Sounds of a lullaby her grandmother had often hummed to her wafted up from the deep recesses of memory. Thoughts of the mother and father she had never known rose up along with it, reminding her of loss and, worse, a long-buried feeling of abandonment.

But she hadn't been abandoned. She had figured that out a long time ago. Her parents hadn't chosen to be killed by a drunk driver.

Ah, but if they'd had those powers her grandmother kept talking about, they could have saved themselves.

She gasped, dragging in air as if she were drowning. Where had that come from?

"Caro? Caro?"

Damien knelt before her but didn't touch her. As she opened her eyes, still gasping, she realized that hot tears were running down her cheeks.

"Caro? What happened?"

She hurt so much she couldn't prevent herself from blurting the source of her pain. Brokenly, still breathless from the way her diaphragm had cramped with agony, she told him. "My parents died in a car crash before I was a year old. If my grandmother was so damn powerful, Damien, why couldn't she save them?"

Then he did touch her. He sat close to her on the floor and lifted her onto his lap as if she weighed nothing at all. She still clutched the pouch, but he pried it gently from her hand, then began rocking her slowly.

"Mein Schatz," he said quietly, "some things are ordained. No power can prevent them."

She hiccuped. "Are you going to tell me the murder of the Pritchett family was *ordained*?"

He sighed quietly, his breath cool as it trickled over her cheek. "There are mysteries. There will always be mysteries. Among them is a greater power than any can imagine, the power that set the universe in motion and gave birth to all things. There are plans and fates and probabilities that we can't control. The overall arc of our lives is beyond that. We have lessons to learn and journeys to take."

"But what about the Pritchetts?"

"They were murdered," he said. "We know that. The murder was wrong. There are times and ways we can twist fate, but somehow it always snaps back to where it will go, with us or without us."

"I don't like that."

"I doubt many do. But I am not dismissing the murders. I'm not saying they weren't a crime. Of course they were. But in some way, the greater power will balance out and adjust for it. In your life, perhaps part of your arc was to lose your parents. Regardless, there are some strands in the universe we simply cannot bend to personal will."

"If my grandmother had the power, if my *mother* had the power Grandma said she had, she should have been able to save them!"

"Perhaps she didn't have time. Perhaps it all happened too fast." He cradled her closer and dropped a kiss on her forehead. "And perhaps it was meant to be. But now I understand why you resisted your grandmother's teachings so much."

She couldn't deny it. How could she believe what her grandmother said when her mother, who had supposedly possessed the power, too, hadn't been able to avoid one drunk driver?

As the question settled into a hidden, hollow place inside her, another understanding hit her like a gut punch. "I blamed my mother for not saving them."

"Of course you did." He shifted a little, then turned her face up so that he was gazing into her eyes. "That was a natural response to your grandmother talking to you about a mage's power. So first you blamed your mother, and then you decided such power couldn't exist or your parents would have still been alive."

He lifted his finger from her chin and gently wiped away her tears. "Whatever happened, for some reason it was beyond your mother's power to control. No mage is omnipotent, Caro."

She closed her eyes, letting the emotional earthquake roll through her. Fault lines, covered over by years of denial, ruptured and settled into a different geography.

And with that shift, she saw her entire life in a new light. Why she had become a cop. Why she had resisted senses and skills that might rightfully be her own. Why she had fought so hard to maintain a life of ordinary reality and battled the suggestion there were things she could not detect with her five senses. Things that were as real as the vampire who held her now.

Then, startling her, Damien said, "I can't do this."

An instant later, she was sitting all alone and he had backed to the farthest edge of the circle.

"Can't do what?" she asked, totally at sea.

"I can't act normal. I'm not normal. I'm a damned vampire and there's just so much *ordinary* I can give you."

Damien's eyes burned in a way he couldn't remember feeling since his change. His entire body was overloaded with the hungers she woke in him. His blood pounded in his ears. His Hunger had pushed him to a brink where he felt he might snap. The ache to taste her blood, to lose himself in the ecstasy that sex with her would be, had reached phenomenal proportions, agonizing in their intensity, all the more dangerous now because he was aching for her pain. An emotional connection threatened him far more than a physical one.

And she sat there, uninitiated human, looking so shocked and, damn it, *wounded* by the way he had withdrawn so suddenly.

But it had either been that or give in to the tsunami of need that hammered him, that tried to sweep him away on its roaring waters to places Caro didn't want to go, might never want to go.

His basest instincts raged, demanding satisfaction, and the little voice in his head that was trying to remind him of all the reasons that wouldn't be wise was almost drowned by waves of need and Hunger.

Every single instinct he possessed demanded that he pounce and pounce now. He couldn't remember the Hunger ever being this strong, except in the days right after his change, when the temple had kept him well satisfied with willing food.

Wisdom dictated he should get out of here before he did something Caro would never forgive. Wisdom also reminded him that he couldn't leave her alone. Not yet. Damn, never in his many centuries could he recall having felt so torn by competing needs. Willing women had always been easy to find. Always.

But while this one might be showing signs of willingness, there was still resistance. And worse, somewhere deep inside he feared that he might become the one addicted.

He'd always avoided that. What the hell was he doing here? He should just turn her over to Jude and get back to Cologne.

A wildness filled him as he realized he was trapped. This woman was trapping him as surely as if she had chained him out in the sunlight.

He looked at her and saw not only the object of his desires, but also the biggest threat he had *ever* faced.

"Damien?"

He couldn't even speak. How could he possibly begin to explain what was tearing him apart inside to someone who had no such needs.

"Hush," he said, and closed his eyes. Not that it helped much. He could still smell her. The gods had never created a better ambrosia than this woman's scent.

"What am I doing wrong?" she asked.

His eyes snapped open. "You exist."

He was surprised she didn't leap up and flee across the circle. Instead, her cheeks still tear-stained, she simply looked at him.

"You can leave if it would make you feel better."

"Leave? Really? I can't leave you alone with whatever this threat is. I'm a better vampire than that. Besides, you haunt me even when I'm not with you. If I could still dream, I'm sure you'd be there, too."

Astonishment washed over him as he saw one corner of her mouth crook upward and a faint blush come to her cheeks. "You certainly haunt my dreams."

That was something he did not need to hear. She was a witch all right, although not the kind her grandmother had meant. She had ensorcelled him, wrapped him in the spell of her scents, his needs, her temptations. A Siren. A real Siren, not some creature of myth.

Her faint smile faded, and her expression became damnably earnest. Then her words told him that she was pained for him, as well. "You said you could drink from me without hurting me."

"No, Caro. No."

"You mean you can't?"

"I can, but it's dangerous."

"I'm willing, if that's what you need."

"You didn't just go there." He closed his eyes again, as once again powerful needs surged, trying to break the fragile leash that controlled them. "Just stop it. Don't provoke me. Don't tempt me."

"You look like a man in agony." Her voice had grown tight with a deep caring he could actually smell. She hurt for him. For *him!*

A man. For the first time he wished he *were* just an ordinary man, one whose hungers couldn't turn him into a ravening beast. He'd been content with what he was for a long time now, and it shocked him to realize he could actually wish for the days when he'd been an ordinary mortal.

She was doing that to him. Had he been able, in the maelstrom of conflicting emotions, he might have added hatred to the storm.

Except he could not hate her. Nothing in him would allow that.

He studied her gloomily. "You don't get it and you can't get it."

"Then try to explain it!"

"I have. Apparently the words don't explain well enough, or you simply can't understand, being a mortal."

"Then try again. Please."

"You've never been an addict, have you?"

"No."

He waved a hand. "Then you can't begin to understand."

"Try anyway."

A burst of anger filled him, and in one fluid, invisible instant he attained his feet and loomed over her. "Listen very carefully, Caro. Accept that I am not exaggerating."

She nodded, looking a little uneasy. Of course she looked uneasy, but she had asked for this.

"There are delights no mortal can imagine until they are experienced. There is a place where vampires can take their mortal lovers, a place between life and death where *ecstasy* becomes a pale word to describe what happens. I can lift you to heights of satisfaction and completion you will never find any other way. If I drink from you, you'll get just a taste of that ecstasy. More than one human, after experiencing that, has gone on a lifelong hunt to experience it once again. To use your analogy, like a crack addict."

"How can it be so good to be drunk from?"

"It just is. How in the world do you think we've survived for so many centuries? If we had to kill everyone we drank from, we'd all be dead, or you'd all be dead."

"Oh." She barely breathed the word, and he could see she was trying hard to understand. "But there's more, isn't there?"

"Of course there's more. I told you about claiming. Maybe you don't really believe it. But if I were to claim you—and I'm not at all sure that is something I have the power to decide—I'd follow you to the ends of the earth or beyond. The only way I could stop would be to kill myself. You don't want to risk that, nor do I."

"Just from drinking from me?"

"Drinking from you and making love to you at the same time. Thank goodness it can't happen from just one or the other separately. Not for vampires. Not as far as I know. But drinking from you could make you addicted. I won't hurt you like that."

"You don't know for sure that will happen."

God, she was driving him to the edge of madness. It would have been so easy just then to swoop and take everything he wanted and then, when she looked at him with hazy, amazed and satisfied eyes, tell himself that she had asked for it. Because she *was* asking, whether she realized it or not.

"You're playing with fire," he said sharply. "You have absolutely no idea how badly I want to taste you. No idea of the Hunger that is pushing me to do it. Imagine if you had been starving for weeks and suddenly someone offered you food. Would you be able to say no? This is as bad or even worse, because that rotgut canned blood Jude insists on serving may keep me alive, but it doesn't satisfy my *real* needs."

She looked down, gazing at her twined fingers. He

wished he knew what she was thinking, because a few choice thoughts might be enough to yank his leash back into order.

But when she looked up, she appeared sad. "So offering comfort to me is painful to you."

"Beyond painful."

"I'm sorry. I won't let it happen again. But one more question."

"What?"

"Would that change if you could drink from me?"

Damn, she was determined to push him over the edge into madness. There could be no other explanation. None. She couldn't be this dense. No, she was far too bright for that.

So what was she doing? Trying to provoke him into tasting her blood? Or was this a genuine attempt to understand the parameters of what he was trying to explain?

Did it matter? Either way she was seriously testing the limits of his self-control.

"You're afraid," she said quietly. "Afraid that one or both of us might become addicted."

"Basically, that's it in a nutshell."

"It would be bad if only one of us became addicted."

"Extremely bad."

She nodded slowly. "I can see that. So my question is this. You said you could drink just a little from me without addicting me. Would you still be at risk for addiction?"

"Stop thinking. You're not making *my* thoughts any clearer."

She smiled faintly. "I'm glad to know I'm not the only one who has been screwed up by your arrival in my life."

"What's that supposed to mean?"

She stood up. Now they were only inches apart. "You've turned reality on end for me."

"I thought witnessing an impossible murder did that."

"By now I might have been able to convince myself I'd had a temporary break or something. Witnesses are notoriously unreliable, you know."

Where the hell was she going with this?

"Damien, I can't stand this. My very presence is causing you agony."

He couldn't deny it.

"So I suggest you sip a bit of my blood, get it out of your system and maybe we can move on."

"You used that argument once before," he reminded her. "It didn't exactly get anything out of either of our systems."

But there was nothing as seductive, he thought irritably, as the appearance of perfect logic. Sip a little of her blood and get her out of his system? It was possible, of course. But not entirely. Never entirely, because tasting human blood was a primal imperative for him, and hers smelled sweeter than any meal ever served to him.

"You don't know what you risk," he said hoarsely.

"I think I do. You said it was possible to leave me unaddicted. The only one with anything to fear, according to you, is you. And if we leave sex out of it, you shouldn't get addicted either."

Flawless logic. Enticing logic.

"Are you afraid?" she asked.

It wasn't a dare, but it came across as one, and when had he ever been able to resist a dare? Or fail to answer a taunt, even though he was quite certain she hadn't meant it that way?

"What are you thinking?" he demanded even as he closed the last few inches between them.

"Some things need settling. There's a threat out there and both of us are distracted. We need to clear our heads somehow. The easiest way to clear yours is to let you drink from me."

"And you?"

"The last time I tried that, I just got more confused."

In spite of his heightened predatory state, and the feeling that he could lose it at any moment, a crack of laughter escaped him. "So you *do* recognize the dangers, *Schatz*."

She shifted from one foot to the other. "Well, yeah, but...this is nuts, Damien. I've got a little blood to spare. I'm tired of torturing you without intending to. So have a little drink on me and then we'll get back to business."

He hoped it would prove that easy because he could no longer resist. She was so close, and she turned her head a bit, pulling back the neck of her sweater to reveal the veins that throbbed so enticingly in her throat.

Not there, he warned himself. *Too much too fast, less control.* He drew a deep breath, filling himself with her scents: the perfume of her blood, the delightful aromas of human, the dizzying scents of her tamped-down desire for him. A saint couldn't have refused this offer, and he was no saint.

Seizing her hand, he drew her down on the floor beside him so she was sitting beside him, a much safer position for them both. He looked deep into her warm eyes and saw determination and a hint of fear. The fear might have turned off a mortal man, but he was no mortal man. That fear was as aphrodisiacal to him as it was to any predator.

"Whatever you do," he said deep in his throat, "don't move. Do not move."

"Okay. But why?"

"I'm a predator," he reminded her. "If you move I may mistake it as struggle, and I'm not going to be thinking all that clearly for the next few minutes."

Her eyes widened, and for a moment he thought she

would withdraw her offer. Instead, she closed her eyes, sighed and said, "Okay."

Carefully, he tugged at the neck of her sweater when all he wanted to do was rip it off her. With sensitive eyes, nose and fingertips, he found a much smaller, safer vein below her collarbone, above her breast.

Bending his head, he licked her there gently, numbing her skin with the special saliva that came only when he extended his fangs.

He heard her sigh but he was already lost.

Chapter 8

Caro didn't feel his bite. She had steeled herself for pain, at least as much pain as an injection, probably more. Instead she felt no pain at all.

In an instant, her world changed. All of a sudden she felt two hearts beating, his and hers, and with each passing second they settled steadily into synchrony. At the same time, pleasure began to flood her, almost orgasmic in its intensity. She felt the blood pound in her own veins, and with that pounding came a clenching between her thighs, sweet, sweet clenching that kept time with her blood.

She dampened in response, wanting touches, wanting to hold him, but only his dimly remembered warning held her still. She could not move. She must not move.

But oh, how she wanted to. Upward she flew, everything vanishing except the soaring feeling that swept her away to a place she had never imagined, a place where nothing existed except her body, a body that ached and yearned and filled with joy at what was happening.

They united. They united more surely than if their bodies had melded sexually. She felt him, felt his pleasure, felt how it equaled her own, and thus multiplied her own.

Oh, heavens, it felt so good!

The last wisps of thought floated away. Never had she imagined such ecstasy, as if her entire being dissolved into the most passionate of delights, all the greater because she could feel his, too.

She hovered at the brink of satisfaction, suspended in pleasure almost too great to bear. Helplessly, she reached for him, wanting to press his face even closer, to keep him drinking until she tumbled over the pinnacle into ultimate release.

Then he was gone.

Drowsy, sated but unsated, she came back slowly from that faraway place. Reluctantly she opened her eyes to see him across the room.

"I told you not to move."

Oh, lord, she had ended it herself. The realization struck her so hard it hurt. If she had just not moved… But it was too late now.

Her heart was hammering, her body still throbbing with need, and she wanted so badly to finish it. But the way he stood told her it was done. He was stiff, almost angry.

"I'm sorry," she managed.

"Don't be sorry. I'm glad you moved. It reminded me of the danger just in time."

Danger? He was right. She'd have happily gone on until she hadn't a single drop of blood left. She closed her eyes, willing her body to calm down, willing her brain to return to the real world. Little by little, the ache eased, the need passed.

"That was incredible," she murmured finally.

"And now you see why I'm worried about you becoming addicted."

"It doesn't seem like such an awful addiction."

"It would if I left you to the mercies of others to get what you want."

Ouch. She almost winced, but had to acknowledge the justice of what he said. Even though it felt like a knife wound. "I'm stronger than that," she said, choosing anger over pain.

"I hope so."

Though her legs still felt a bit rubbery, she rose to face him. "You may have taken me to the moon, Damien, but you sure as hell didn't take me to the stars. I can live without it."

"Good." But she noted he didn't exactly look either relieved or happy. *What now?* she wondered. They'd gotten absolutely nowhere with the looming threat or solving the murders, so it wasn't as though they could go their own ways. Not yet.

Well, she'd wanted this issue settled. She was sick of feeling as if she were a constant thorn in his side, and sick of wondering what it would be like to give him what he wanted. She already knew he was practically unparalleled in his sexual skills. Now she knew that being drunk from by a vampire was at least as good as any sex she'd ever had.

Where did that get them? Nowhere, except maybe *he* could relax a little around her, which would make it easier for her to relax.

What a mess. "Look," she said a little sharply, "we need to get back to work on identifying this elemental and who summoned it. Before I get killed. Unless you *want* to spend the rest of my life guarding me. For my part, I'd like to be able to get back to my regular life as soon as possible. I'm a cop, for God's sake, not some woo-woo mage. I want to get back to the real world."

At that, his stony facade cracked a bit. The corners of his mouth tipped up, and he relaxed visibly. "So you want to get back to the *real* world?"

She didn't like his sarcasm, but she couldn't blame him for it. *The real world?* She wasn't sure anymore that she even knew what it was.

He bent and picked up the talisman Alika had given her and held it out. "Figure out what this is, cop. Focus everything you've got on it. Once we know what it is, we'll know something about both you and Alika."

"How so?"

"We'll know some of her intentions. We'll also know what she thinks she was protecting you against. Or what she was trying to draw toward you."

She accepted the pouch gingerly. "What are you going to do?"

"I'm going to sit here and remember. My skills may be rusty, but they're not completely forgotten."

She sat cross-legged on the couch, closing her eyes as she held the pouch. It occurred to Damien that they had shared an awful lot of intimacy for two people who had never gotten as far as removing their clothes. Not that his imagination failed him. It was easy in these modern days to imagine what lay beneath a woman's clothing, and he had little trouble imagining Caro naked. He had no doubt he would find well-toned perfection. For just a short while, he let his imagination travel that path.

He waited a few minutes, then settled himself on the arm of a chair. He had to admit, drinking of her had settled his impulses down, although it hadn't killed them. The taste of her lingered in his mouth, and he wanted more of it, but for now those clamoring desires were quiet enough to let his mind wander elsewhere.

And wander it did, over roads trodden centuries ago, over rites and rituals he hadn't needed in a long time.

He was sitting in one of the temple gardens in the shade of a tree, reclining on pillows, thankful he could no longer feel the heat of a Persian summer night. A woman walked toward him, clad in the loose white gown of an offering.

Once such women had brought him plates of figs and olives, or succulent bits of fish or lamb. Now they brought themselves, prepared to serve him in any way he chose. Once they had seen him as a powerful priest. Now they saw him as a god on earth, filled with powers and strength they could not comprehend. They feared him, but once they had served him, they yearned for him always.

Such was his power.

But he had other powers as well, powers that went beyond being undead. He could feel that power tingle in his fingertips, and when he allowed it to build, the tingling filled him until he could cast bolts of lightning, or make things levitate, or even kill without touching.

That was one of the reasons the priesthood had changed him—to take those powers and put them in an undying body. He sometimes wondered if the spells he chanted actually worked, or if it was merely a way of focusing some ability he had that most of the other priests did not.

But he rarely entertained such thoughts because there were so many delights to enjoy, and so many things the temple demanded of him.

Sometimes he felt caged in his priesthood, in the way he existed to serve his masters when he knew full well he could destroy them all and rule the temple alone.

But he never gave voice to those thoughts. They were

evil thoughts, and he more than anyone realized how important it was that he never be without constraints.

The things he might do....

Like a kaleidoscope, memory took him down the paths of centuries, through changing times where adaptation had required other things of him, when his powers had been useless or even dangerous to himself.

All the way to the present day.

Damien's eyes snapped open. He saw Caro across from him, either asleep or still concentrating on the gris-gris pouch. No, he didn't smell the hormones of sleep around her, so she must be doing as he asked.

Then he looked down at his own hands and examined them, noting that they tingled faintly as they had not in so long a time. Had the spells and rites really been necessary? Or was his power inherent?

Given the times and how long it had been, he didn't know. He wasn't sure he should trust something he hadn't used in so long. Would he have the focus to control it? Could he summon it without remembering the right incantation? Damned if he knew, but he didn't want to discover his limits at exactly the wrong time.

But the tingling felt good, like the embrace of an old friend he hadn't seen in forever. Cautiously, he focused on it and tried to strengthen it.

It grew. Just a bit, but enough to bring back all his old questions.

He glanced again at Caro, inevitably remembering the gift she had just given him. Once such gifts had been meaningless to him because they came by order of the temple authorities. When times had changed, he had changed with them, learning new ways to entice willing donors.

But since coming to this town and staying with Jude, he had for the very first time developed a true appreciation for the kind of gift a woman bestowed upon him by sharing her blood.

Especially this woman. With his needs temporarily quieted, but not at all somnolent, he studied her, thinking about what his attraction to her meant. That she was attracted to him wasn't the question. Nor, except for that first night, had he tried in any way to seduce her, and her reaction then had set him back on his heels.

But it had started something between them, something that disturbed him deeply. He should be able to walk away from any woman, and he couldn't blame his inability to walk away from Caro entirely on their current problems.

No, she called to him in a way no one ever had. Through all his centuries, no one woman had ever meant more to him than a delightful feast for the senses, pleasant to dally with but not missed once they left at the end of the night. Delightful creatures, but he had never felt any desire to stay with even one of them. They satisfied his needs, sometimes repeatedly, and then he let them go. A few had tried to linger, but he had never permitted it.

So what was it about Caro?

Even as he asked the question he knew there was no answer. As he had said to her, there were cosmic mysteries beyond understanding. The only thing he could be certain of was that he needed to be careful. He sensed danger, the danger of involvement.

Perhaps even the danger of a claiming. Wouldn't that be ugly, because he was quite certain she had no wish to spend the rest of her days with a vampire. She might be drawn, she might feel sexual desire, but none of that was enough to ensure a long-lived relationship.

A sigh escaped her and he watched while she opened her eyes and sought him out.

"Anything?" he asked.

"I'm not sure how to interpret it. I've never done this before."

"Go with your feelings. Just tell me what it makes you feel."

"I don't feel any threat."

"That's a good start."

"But…" She hesitated, biting her lower lip. He closed his eyes for an instant, resisting the urge to bite that lip himself. How quickly she roused the Hunger in him.

He waited, knowing this all had to emerge in its own time. Just as the tingling in his fingertips remained faint, nowhere near any level of true power.

"This is going to sound crazy," she said.

"I doubt it. You're talking to a mage. Go on."

"I feel… It's like it makes some kind of bubble around me. Nothing I can see or feel. Something I just sense."

"That sounds like protection. Maybe that's what pushed you back at that second place."

"So that would mean the old shopkeeper is the problem?"

He shook his head. "I can't say that. Not based on a single feeling you had. The elemental may have gotten too close to you."

"Oh." She looked down at the bag in her hand. "I guess this is safe to keep with me then."

"It would seem so. But stay in tune with it in case something changes."

"How do I do that?"

"Just do what you've been doing. With practice it'll take less effort."

She nodded, then stretched to put the pouch in her jeans pocket. "Now what?"

The answer was there in the prickling of his neck. "It's getting near dawn. I need to go to ground soon, so I suppose I should get you back to Jude's."

"But he warded this apartment."

"I don't want you to be alone, Caro. At all. It's better where you can wake us if something happens, where Chloe can help keep watch."

"Well, at least there I can keep working the case."

He waited while she packed some more clothes, then he bundled her into the car and drove her back to Jude's.

Sometimes the limitations of being a vampire got to him. Not often. But tonight they were driving him crazy.

It didn't help to remind himself that an ordinary man would need sleep, as well. Yes, he could wake in an emergency, but for how long? Probably not as long as a mortal could if necessary.

The sleep of death, which for him passed as if it never happened, suddenly seemed like the worst of curses. He needed to protect Caro, yet for hours he would be almost useless to her.

In that alone there was plenty to regret.

At Jude's office, they found things hopping. Garner, mostly. He could barely hold still, and his excitement seemed almost triumphal.

The blackout curtain still covered the window of Chloe's office, so the two vampires could manage awhile longer. Jude leaned against the edge of Chloe's desk, arms folded. Terri, looking tired herself, sat on one end of the couch. Caro joined her. Chloe sat behind her desk, frowning. Damien took up station near the door.

"Settle down," Chloe snapped at Garner. "I'm up too early. You're giving me a headache."

"You're just jealous that I found something out."

Jude spoke. "We're still waiting to hear what exactly you learned. How about getting to the point and saving the parade until later? Do you know what time it is?"

Garner froze, looking momentarily crestfallen, but then his high spirits resurged. "It's Pritchett."

"We know it's Pritchett," Chloe said sarcastically. "He's dead."

"That's not what I mean. You know he's a big deal in real estate."

"That wasn't hard to learn," Jude reminded him.

"I know, I know. And all these years he's been making his money from rents. But about six months ago, something changed. He's spread out into redevelopment."

Silence greeted the words.

"How exactly?" Damien asked.

"He was planning to tear down some of his older buildings and replace them. That's why he needed his brother-in-law. The guy apparently went to bat for him at the planning office. But the point is this—some people are going to lose their homes. And some of them are seriously unhappy about it."

Caro's heart accelerated. "That could explain a lot. Did you find out which buildings? Who's unhappy?"

Garner shook his head. "I figured that would be easy for you guys to find out. I'm just passing along what I learned on the street. I don't know how many people are going to lose their places, but apparently eviction notices went out to some of them just two weeks ago. And more are or were on the way. A lot of people who haven't gotten evicted yet were wondering when they'd get a notice, or even *if* they'd get a notice. So you could say the guy made himself a target."

"Obviously," Jude drawled, but his expression didn't match his tone. Indeed, his frown deepened.

Caro glanced around at all of them. "That would do it," she said. "I'd almost be willing to bet the buildings he's planning to tear down house the poorest people for the most part. Isn't that always the way?"

"Usually," Jude said.

"How very odd," Damien remarked.

Caro looked at him. "How so?"

"In my country renewal means fixing what we have, not tearing down the places where people live. I live in a building that's nearly three hundred years old. It's been refurbished many times."

"But you have to understand the calculus here," Jude said. "If he tears down low-rent tenements and replaces them with something much more modern, he can charge more rent and make more money. Lots more money."

"Then where do the people go?"

"Exactly." Jude sighed. "It's getting to be time. Chloe, see what you and Caro can learn about Pritchett's plans. At least then we can focus in on some particular neighborhoods."

"You got it, boss. Although if you ask me, hunting demons is easier."

Everyone looked at her.

"Well, it is," she insisted. "They leave their stench everywhere, and Garner can usually suss them out in no time at all. This whatever-it-is doesn't seem to be leaving a trail. At least not one that leads directly back to the persons who called it."

"It will," Jude said wearily. "It will. One way or another." Then without another word, he reached for Terri's hand and led her into his bedroom in the back.

Damien straightened to follow. "I'll be in the inner office," he said. "Wake me if you need me."

That left Caro, Chloe and Garner alone. Chloe sighed. "That's a vampire for you. Leave a bunch of orders then hit the vault. Sheesh."

Caro had to sleep. No escaping it. She took Chloe's offer of the cot in a tiny room off the outer office and fell into a deep sleep that seemed empty of dreams.

Her cell phone ringing woke her sometime around noon and she answered it sleepily, glad to hear Detective Pat Matthews's familiar voice. Only as she heard it did she realize how cut off she'd been feeling from her life, her habits and her friends.

"So how's it going?" Pat asked. "Is Messenger being any help?"

"Actually, yes. Is Malloy missing me yet?"

"Not really. Not with two cases he can't explain. He's looking a little grayer these days. But it definitely would *not* be a good time to come back, Caro."

"Why not?"

"Because some other people are muttering that something weird is going on here. If you show up, Malloy will probably blame you for the whispers. You don't need that. Just stay out of the way for a little longer."

"We're working on solving these cases," Caro reminded her.

"I know. Don't give me any details. There are some things I simply don't want to know."

After she felt sufficiently caught up on the news from the precinct and her friends there, Caro disconnected and sat staring at her phone.

There was one problem here, she realized. One that nobody had mentioned and one that was going to drive the cop in her nuts.

Even if they found the person who had set these murders in motion, there was no way they could bring him to justice. The crimes would remain unsolved. The perp would never be punished.

"Damn," she said. "Double damn."

"You okay?" Chloe called from the office.

"No."

Caro jumped up and hurried to dress and brush her hair into some semblance of order. Then she stormed out to confront Chloe.

"Why are we doing this?"

"Doing what?"

"Hunting for the person who caused these murders?"

"To protect *you*," Chloe reminded her. "Remember? That's why you came here in the first place. Something is following you. Something that probably wasn't too happy about having a witness."

Caro sagged into the chair beside Chloe's desk. "I haven't exactly forgotten that part."

"Then what's the problem?"

"If we find the person who caused all of this, there's nothing we can do about him. No arrest, no trial, no punishment."

Chloe rapped her pencil eraser on the desk in a short tattoo. "Have you considered that some crimes never reach that kind of resolution? That most of what Jude deals with he considers settled if he can just send it back to hell? Not everything in this world fits cop definitions of justice."

Caro put her chin in her hand. "So we just stop this and it's over?"

"That may be all we can do. People don't go to jail anymore for practicing witchcraft."

The answer left Caro unsatisfied, but she couldn't argue with it. She certainly wasn't about to advocate vigilante justice.

"You find anything?"

"Yeah, I've been pulling up the development plans. Apparently Pritchett had just started to really roll on this. He has about six approvals for eviction and demolition. But you know what?"

"What?"

"I'm wondering what else is going on here."

"Why?"

"Because," Chloe said, "that man got more approvals for demolition in the last few months than this city has seen in over five years."

Caro sat up straighter and met Chloe's gaze. "You think he was into something?"

"Some kind of bad mojo, you mean?" Chloe nodded. "I'm starting to wonder."

"So maybe it rebounded on him."

"Well, maybe. Except there'd be no reason for it to come after you." She leaned forward, looking almost excited. "What if he was up to some spell-casting himself? And what if he ticked off someone else with the power?"

Caro almost gaped.

"Think about it," Chloe said. "The guy pulls off the near impossible with these demolition permits. That brother-in-law of his wasn't all that powerful. More like a pawn. What if someone else didn't like what Pritchett was doing?"

"Clearly someone didn't," Caro agreed. "But, Chloe, this sounds like a bad movie."

"When you've worked with Jude long enough, bad movies start to seem real."

Caro had to admit she'd seen things backfire on people before, things that had nothing to do with magic or mystical powers. The more you did bad things, the more likely you were to become someone's target—or get yourself into hot water up to your neck when it was discovered.

"Okay," she said slowly, "I'll admit the possibility here. Pritchett may have been dabbling in some black arts. It could have rebounded. God knows I've seen enough criminals screw themselves up in ordinary ways."

"Aha, you're getting it."

"But by the same token, I've seen others get into plenty of trouble because they ticked off the wrong person."

"It could be one. It could be both."

"You should be a cop, Chloe. That's some devious thinking."

Chloe grinned. "You'd have thought of it if you weren't still balking at magic."

Possibly true, Caro admitted to herself. That side of this whole affair was still troubling, still making her hesitate as she waded into this strange world. Maybe it was time to stop hesitating and just dive in with both feet.

Hell, she was walking around with some kind of talisman in her pocket and locked into some kind of sensual dance with a vampire. Why stick at a little black magic?

"I'm going out," she announced.

"Oh, no, you're not!" Chloe jumped to her feet. "The whole reason I'm here is to make sure you're not alone because Jude and Damien have taken a notion that this thing that's after you doesn't want to be witnessed, and that's all that's protecting you. Are you insane?"

"No. Listen, Chloe, out on the daytime streets I won't be alone. There will be dozens of people out there. Plenty of witnesses. How likely do you think it is to act?"

Chloe sank slowly back into her chair. "Even in a busy city it's possible to be alone some of the time."

"How about if I promise to avoid that?"

Chloe's expression turned glum. "Do you really believe that thing couldn't make your heart explode in public like it did to Pritchett's brother-in-law? Everyone would think it's a heart attack."

"Then maybe having witnesses isn't protecting me at all."

Chloe shook her head. "Then what *is?* If you had some idea, I'd feel better. Maybe the point is having witnesses who would know what's happening. Like me. Like Jude and Damien. People on the street wouldn't know, would they?"

Caro had to admit Chloe might be right. But the need to act in at least some way was beginning to overwhelm her. Sitting here all afternoon speculating about what might have caused all this was apt to drive her to distraction.

"I'm going to need a straightjacket," she muttered. "I can't stand being constantly cooped up this way."

"I don't blame you. But that doesn't mean you need to take this on alone. What could you learn out there anyway?"

"What people are talking about in the vicinity of the buildings that are scheduled for demolition."

"Nice idea, if folks will talk. You think they want to talk to a cop?"

"Not in some of those neighborhoods," Caro admitted. "But I won't be going as a cop."

"Then what? A social worker? Get real. You cops don't realize how obvious you are to people even in street clothes. Especially in places they don't like cops."

"Give me the addresses, Chloe."

"No. I happen to like this job and I want to keep it."
With that Chloe pointedly turned off her computer.

"You're gonna make me mad," Caro warned her.

"You can't arrest me for that. Garner told us what they
were talking about anyway. Wouldn't it make more sense
for you to find out if there's some voodoo queen out there
in the locales? Some weird kind of church maybe."

"Voodoo isn't weird," Caro said. "It's an established religion, unlike some. Why did you pick that in particular?"

Chloe shrugged one shoulder. "I don't know. Too many
movies, maybe. But one thing I know for sure—we ought
to be searching for something very different from a traditional religion. Something that could and would call down
a curse."

Caro gave in. Chloe was making sense, and her desire
for action was getting in her way. Didn't she want to be
a detective? Yes. And what did detectives do most of the
time? It sure wasn't cops and robbers. It was research and
questioning. Questioning in those neighborhoods would
meet a lot of resistance. That meant she needed to skip the
action and do the mental legwork.

She sighed. "Can we at least get out of here for a walk?"

Chloe chewed her lip. "Well, if you promise it's just a
walk, and not very far, I'll admit I could use some sunshine, too. But it's cold out there."

"I spend a lot of time on the streets. I don't mind. Just
bundle yourself up. Say just for a walk around the block."

"This isn't one of the best parts of town," Chloe reminded her.

Caro patted her belt holster. "How often do you have
an armed escort?"

At that Chloe giggled and bounced off to find something warm to wear.

Not that a gun would do much against the threat they

were worried about, Caro thought. But God, she needed some sunshine. Living like a bat might suit vampires, but not her. Checking her pocket, she felt the talisman again and closed her eyes. She could still sense the invisible bubble it seemed to wrap around her, and she wondered if it would extend to Chloe, as well.

While she waited, she reached out, trying to sense even more. Little by little she picked up on things. The vampires and Terri sleeping in the next rooms. The wards Jude had put around this place. In fact, the more she concentrated on the wards, the more they became visible until they nearly glowed.

Oh, wow! She could see those invisible marks of chrism, and some of the things Chloe had spread around, as if they were lit from within. Inevitably, she pulled the talisman out and looked at it. It, too, seemed to glow, though differently. Not bright and white like Jude's chrism, but more of a lavender. A different kind of power?

Trying to reach out even farther, she found herself blocked by the wards, as if they created an impenetrable shield she couldn't see beyond. That was interesting, she thought. Now she wondered what might happen out on the streets where there were no wards. What she might see and sense apart from the auras she had for so long tried to ignore. What if she could read those auras? What if she could sense other things about people, as well?

All of a sudden a desire to know her own inherent powers burst to full life within her.

She definitely had to get out for a walk.

"What's going on?" Chloe asked.

Startled out of her concentration, Caro took a moment to connect. "What do you mean?"

"You looked funny. And I felt something."

"I was just trying to…" She hesitated, wondering how

much she should say. It wasn't as if she'd talked with Chloe about this much before. On the other hand, she figured that nothing happened in or around Messenger Investigations that Chloe didn't know something about.

"I was just testing my senses. My grandmother said I had some kind of power, but I've never really used it. Damien's been encouraging me."

"Oh, girl," Chloe said cheerfully, "do we have stuff to talk about now. Come on!"

They emerged onto the street to find some snow had fallen since sunrise, just enough to make the world sparkle and look fresh under a blindingly brilliant sky.

"Gawd," Chloe said, pulling a pair of sunglasses out of her purse, "there really is a daytime world!"

Caro had to laugh. "Come on, you must get out during the day sometimes."

"I do," Chloe admitted with a grin. "But when things really heat up, I generally go home at dawn and come back around sunset, and in between I'm usually asleep or trying to wake up. Sometimes I don't get out of the office at all for days on end." She shrugged, stuck her hands in her coat pocket and started walking. Caro strode beside her. "Most of the time I don't mind. It's exciting. But every so often I snipe a little about it."

"I can't imagine never seeing the sun again."

"Neither can I, honestly, although Terri seems to be adapting pretty well to Jude's hours. I don't hear her complaining anyway." She glanced at Caro. "What about Damien?"

"What about Damien?"

"I can see that vampire has a big case of the hots for you, and you don't seem exactly unhappy about it. If you really can't live without the sun, maybe you'd better be careful."

Caro tried to shrug it off. "It's just a passing thing."

"Maybe." Chloe surprised her by letting the subject drop. "So what's this about having powers? I've been trying to develop some of my own, but I haven't been having a whole lot of luck. Mostly I can do a few protective spells that seem to work. Are we talking about spells here or something bigger?"

"Something else. I don't know if you could call it bigger. My grandmother told me I had inherent powers, but I never really wanted to listen to her about it."

"So you became a hardheaded realist, namely a cop."

"I guess so."

They reached a corner and turned to circumnavigate the block. Even though this wasn't the best part of town, there were plenty of people out and about. Only a few of them made Caro's hand itch to touch her service pistol.

"So Damien's helping?" Chloe asked. "Because Jude said he used to be some kind of mage."

"He's trying, I guess. Trying to get me to focus on things I sense by other than usual means. It's working a little bit. For example, today I could actually see all the wards in Jude's office. Even the chrism seemed to glow."

"Oh, man, that would be so cool. Anything else?"

"I couldn't see beyond the wards. That's one of the reasons I wanted to get out here. To see what else I could sense."

"Then I should shut up and let you sense. Just promise to tell me what you pick up."

The quiet was welcome and pierced only by the crunch of feet on the fresh snowfall and an occasional voice. With a sigh, Caro let go of some tight restraint within herself, opening a place she usually kept fairly shuttered. The world was suddenly alight with the auras of the people they passed. Beautiful auras for the most part, although the colors in some made her uncomfortable, and others worried her a bit.

That woman might be sick. That man is thinking something ugly. The rainbow colors seemed to speak to her at a level below conscious thought. But how could she be sure her interpretations were correct?

Prodded to find out, she walked over to the woman whose aura dimmed in the region of her heart. "Ma'am, are you feeling all right?"

The woman, who appeared to be about fifty, seemed startled, then said, "Actually, I'm not really feeling well. Do I look sick?"

Caro hesitated only a moment, then took the risk. "You look ill. Can you get to a doctor? Do you need me to help you?"

"I'm awfully tired," the woman said with a wan smile. "I feel as if I'm walking uphill. I think I'll just go home and rest."

But having gone this far, Caro decided to let her view of the woman's aura guide her. "I think I should call an ambulance."

At that the woman panicked. "I don't have insurance. I can't pay for that! No, don't call anybody. I'll just go home and rest."

She hurried past Caro, but as Caro watched, she could see that after a few steps the woman started lagging again.

"What's that about?" Chloe asked, keeping her voice down.

"Something in her aura. I don't know if it's her heart or what, but something's not right."

Chloe looked after the woman. "I wish I could see that. But if she won't take help, what can you do?"

"Nothing without a reason," Caro admitted. More than most people, she was aware that even touching another person was battery, and if she called an ambulance and the woman objected, nothing would get done anyway.

"But you're worried," Chloe said.

"Very. I just wish I knew exactly what was worrying me." Then she had an idea. Shoving her hand into her pocket, she pulled out a ten-dollar bill. "Do you have any cash?"

"I think so. What for?"

"Maybe she'll let us call her a cab to take her to Mercy. Their E.R. treats everyone whether they have insurance or not."

Chloe brightened. "Great idea." She snatched the money from Caro's hand. "Let me do it. I think you weirded her out enough for one day."

While Chloe ran after the woman, Caro stood waiting and watching. She probably *had* weirded out that woman, she thought. In a major way. If it saved her from a serious health problem, that was okay, but what if she was misinterpreting the woman's aura? Regardless, she hadn't managed to learn a thing about her powers yet. Nothing she could begin to rely on.

Then in a single instant, two things happened. First she realized she was suddenly all alone on this street. Chloe disappeared around the corner after the woman and there wasn't another soul in sight.

Then her skin began to crawl almost as if it were covered with ants. She wasn't alone, for all she couldn't see another soul. Something was there, watching, threatening.

And it seemed to be touching her.

A momentary panic fluttered her heart, but years as a cop had told her how to take that and turn it into something useful. She stood frozen, perfectly still, and since she didn't know what else to do, she used every ounce of will she had to drive the sensation away.

Despite the chill, sweat broke out on her brow as if she were making a huge physical effort. Willpower. She was accustomed to using it to make herself do difficult things, but she had never thought of it as something capable of driving away an external force. But what else did she have as a tool?

She envisioned her will as a tangible thing, to be focused on and strengthened with every bit of her being. Driving away all other thoughts, she focused on the strength within her and used it to send a mental blast: *get away!*

Instantly, the crawling sensation vanished, although not the feeling of being watched. Before she could test what she had accomplished any further, she heard the rapid pounding of footsteps and Chloe calling out, "Are you all right?"

She opened her eyes and saw Chloe racing up. "Fine. I'm fine. Just for a minute there I felt…attacked. How's the woman?"

"She took the cab to the hospital. I made the driver promise not to take her anywhere else. But…I felt something, too, Caro. What was it?"

"I don't know. That elemental maybe. I pushed it back."

Chloe's dark-rimmed eyes widened. "You did?" Then she let out a yip. "Yes!"

Caro almost smiled. "Hold on there. I'm not sure I did it."

"I bet you did!" But then Chloe's grin faded. "We have to go back now. Frankly, I don't want to face either Jude or Damien if anything happens to you. You got your test run—now be sensible."

Caro couldn't argue and, truthfully, she didn't want to. She'd learned something out here, and now she needed time to think about it and try to figure out what it meant.

Clearly out here on the street, gris-gris notwithstanding, she was subject to at least minor attacks.

Nodding to Chloe, she turned and they took the shortest path back to the office.

Chapter 9

"You did *what?*"

Caro faced Damien, her feet firmly planted, and thrust out her chin. "We went for a walk. I can't stand being caged. Besides, I wanted to try out my so-called powers."

"Something may have attacked her," Chloe said unhelpfully. "But she fought it off."

Damien unleashed a string of what sounded like German, and it certainly sounded like a bunch of curse words. One or two of them, Caro thought she almost recognized. Like *Scheisse* or something close to it.

"Relax," Jude said, sounding amused. "She's still with us, isn't she?"

"Relax?" Damien thundered. "After what happened to the Pritchetts, how am I supposed to relax? She could have died while I was dead!"

The statement struck Caro as absurd. *Died while he was dead?* It sounded so ludicrous that she couldn't quite stifle a giggle. He glared at her.

But even as part of her recognized the absurd in his statement, another part of her realized why he was so frustrated. He'd devoted himself, willingly or not, to protecting her, and during the hours when he'd been unable to do so, she'd taken a huge risk. Of course he was angry. But she suspected the anger was self-directed at his own helplessness during daylight hours.

That understanding made her feel bad because it was something she could easily identify with. One of her biggest frustrations as a cop was being unable to prevent things from happening. She spent her life dealing with the aftermath of events that shouldn't have happened.

She stared at Damien, taking in his explosive frustration, and offered all she could. "I'm sorry. I won't do it again."

"You'd better not. Damn it, I'll handcuff you to me while I sleep if I have to."

She believed him. But instead of getting angry at the threat, she felt an entirely unexpected shiver of pleasure, as if some part of her responded sensually to the idea of being cuffed to him.

Where had that come from? Never before had she felt the least inclination toward kinkiness. Except now she seemed to be involved in the kinkiest relationship possible, one where the drinking of her blood caused her extraordinary pleasure. What was a handcuff in the face of that?

Damien took a few steps, moving almost too fast to see, then he stopped and faced her. His expression had softened a bit, and he no longer looked furious. "My life has limitations. I'm sorry they cause you so much difficulty."

"No!" She was horrified that she had made him feel that way. So what if he needed to sleep during the daylight? She needed to sleep herself. Nobody could be there all day every day. "You're not causing me difficulty. Damien… everybody needs to sleep sometime."

At that a harsh laugh escaped him. "You needn't be kind to me. But please understand. If something had happened and you were here, in this office, we could have wakened to help you, however difficult it would have been. Just as you can wake if you're needed. For you to be out on the street alone… It doesn't bear thinking."

"I was there," Chloe pointed out sharply. "Sheesh, I'm not nobody. And Caro evidently learned a lot that she needs to learn. How was she supposed to do that with you hovering around like an avenging angel?"

That drew a bark of laughter from Jude. "I don't know about you, Damien, but I don't think I've ever been likened to an angel before."

"Least of all an avenging one," he agreed, but the fury appeared to have seeped from him. His gaze returned to Caro, and he frowned faintly. "We have to work this out somehow, in a way that doesn't endanger you."

"Haven't you been listening?" Chloe said tartly. "*She* drove the thing off *herself!*"

"I at least pushed it back," Caro said hesitantly.

"Do you remember how?" Damien asked. "Do you think you can do it again?"

"I think so."

At that, Damien smiled. "So, you made a big step."

"Maybe."

"Pushing it back is not the same as getting rid of it," he agreed. "Nor is it a guarantee of protection. For one thing, it was daylight, a time when many powers are weaker. We still have to find the source and get him or her to call this thing off."

There was still that, Caro thought glumly. Now it was night again, when foul things evidently came into ascendance. "I guess it's not just the human inability to see well at night that causes us to fear the darkness."

"Not entirely, no," Damien agreed. "I wish I understood the connection, because it would be a useful tool. But I can tell you that in all my centuries I've noticed that something happens after darkfall. As if some kind of constraint is eased."

Chloe spoke. "I suppose that's why ghost hunters are always hunting ghosts in the dark."

"Partly," Jude agreed.

"Partly?"

"Well, there are fewer distractions in the dark, for one thing. Fewer things that can be misinterpreted. But Damien's right. I've noticed it, too. The witching hour really is the witching hour."

"I've wondered," Damien said, "if this doesn't happen because humans are at their most unguarded and weakest during those hours between midnight and dawn."

"It wouldn't surprise me," Jude agreed.

"Whatever the reason, we still have some more places to check out, Caro and I. You have that list of proposed demolitions, Chloe?"

"I'll take some of them, too," Jude said.

So a little while later, filled up on the sandwich she and Chloe had shared, Caro left Messenger Investigations with Damien.

This time he didn't want to bother with the car. "It'll slow us down, and right now I feel this matter is dragging on entirely too long."

"Any particular reason?"

"Yes. The longer it goes on, the harder it will be to repair whatever gateway was opened."

"Gateway?"

"Later. Zip up. I'm carrying you on my back."

She didn't mind that at all. She enjoyed the sensation of flying, even though she couldn't see a darn thing, and she especially enjoyed being wrapped around Damien this way, even if it was from behind.

What the hell, she thought. She might as well admit she had a serious case of the hots, as Chloe would say, for a vampire. She wanted him, wanted to go all the way with him, at least short of that claiming business that worried him. It was kind of ridiculous to realize they'd been so intimate on a couple of occasions yet they'd never lain naked together. How odd was that?

But he'd already shown her he could take her to places she had never imagined. While she didn't think she was addicted or would grieve for the rest of her life if she could never visit them again, she was certain that she wanted to experience more and go further with him.

She hoped the wind of their passage was blowing away her pheromones because with his hips so snug between her legs, she felt heavy heat pooling between her thighs, a longing that made her tighten her legs around him. Every movement of muscle rubbed her most sensitive nerves through her jeans, heightening her desire.

She pressed her face against Damien's back to protect it more from the cutting wind and experienced a moment of instant clarity. What the hell was she thinking? A short time ago she hadn't even believed in vampires, and now she was almost out of her mind with hunger to have sex with one. How did that fit in the world of Caro Hamilton, cop?

It didn't. But Caro Hamilton, cop, had seen her world change in an instant when a murder victim had gone flying through the air, propelled by an invisible force. She would never again be the woman she had once been.

But if she had to be attracted to someone, why a vampire of all things?

God, the world had spun at least ninety degrees. Nothing looked the same anymore. Crazy with desire for a vampire and now discovering powers she had denied her whole life long.

She had definitely fallen down the rabbit hole and couldn't figure out how to put the brakes on.

They alighted finally on a rooftop in the southern end of the city, the oldest part. Urban renewal had been proposed here more than once and had always failed. At least until Pritchett had become involved.

She rubbed her cheeks to warm them and looked around. "What now?"

"This is one of the buildings he got permission to demolish. Do you suppose if we wander up and down the stairs here we might meet some people who will talk to us?"

She glanced at him. "You can make them talk, can't you?" Her watch told her it was still early enough for people to be out and about. Not everyone would be home for the night. "Let's go."

He opened the roof access door as if it wasn't locked. Perhaps it wasn't. Most threats in this city didn't come from the tops of buildings.

Inside it was warm. Heat had risen along the stairwell, and as soon as it met her cheeks, they began to sting.

"I'm going to have to get a ski mask if I keep traveling by vampire."

Damien cracked a laugh.

At least they descended the stairs at a reasonable speed, a human speed. Unfortunately Caro had been wrong. They didn't encounter anyone on the stairs except some kids running up, and they were too young to talk to.

Finally they reached the street and stepped outside. And right next door was a bookshop called Books, Bells and Candles.

They exchanged glances and without a word headed for the door.

Like many such places, it looked old and as if it were operating on a shoestring. Caro wondered if she would choke on the dust if she moved a book. A wall of candles, most of them looking religious, filled the back of the store. Behind the counter were sets of things like tarot cards and the *I Ching*.

A tiny woman, who looked like a dried prune, sat in a rocker next to a space heater. She greeted them with a smile. "Come to throw me out?"

"Why would we do that?" Caro asked.

"Well, they gave us all eviction notices. Next month, they said."

"The man who was planning that is dead."

"I know. Sad thing. His family, too." The woman shook her head, *tsk*ing quietly. "Now, who would want to harm children, I ask. Makes for some very bad juju."

"It does," Caro agreed. "No, we were just wondering what folks here were planning to do now. Have you all found someplace to go?"

"Didn't get a whole lot of notice. Folks are mad."

"What about you?"

The woman shrugged. "Does it look like I have anything to worry about? I was thinking of moving to Seattle to live with my daughter anyway. This place barely makes the rent every month. You get old, you get set in your ways, but sometimes you have to change."

"But others are angry?"

"Of course. They've lived here all their lives, just as I have. The place may be ugly, but it's still standing. Can't figure out why folks need to move. I'm not even sure how you could make this place any better. You looked around the neighborhood? Tell me what high roller would want to live in the middle of this."

"That's a good question," Caro admitted. "But I don't know what the man's plans are. I was just disturbed because I figured folks here would be upset by this."

"Damned upset," the woman agreed. She peered at Caro. "You some kind of social worker?"

"Of sorts. I'm just trying to figure out how everyone's handling this."

"Some is mad, like I said. Some might even want to get even. Kinda late for that, since the man is dead, though. Worst they can do is damage a building that's going to be blowing up anyway."

"That could change now," Caro offered again.

The woman snorted. "Rich men have big companies that keep on even after they die. Not like my little business."

"I can check into that for you."

"Won't make no difference. Somebody did something bad. Imagine killing a whole family like that." The woman shook her head.

Damien spoke for the first time, and his voice shifted to that timbre that Caro had come to recognize. "Do you know anyone who might be into casting spells to hurt anybody?"

The woman's eyes glazed. "There's talk. There's always talk. But you need a bokor for that. Look for a bokor."

"Where?"

"I don't know. I hear whispers, but they don't tell me." She lifted a hand, touching a crucifix that hung around her neck. "No truck with the dark powers. Not me. I value my soul."

"Any ideas who might be involved?"

"Not me, and I don't want to know."

Outside on the street, Damien paused and Caro watched as he closed his eyes. He drew several deep breaths through his nose as if testing the air. Then he astonished her.

Holding out his hand, palm down, he moved his fingers a bit as if feeling the air. Caro's jaw dropped at what she saw next. There was a sparkle, a faint blue glittering around the ends of his fingers, and she could have sworn she saw a crackle of electricity pass among them.

As soon as he dropped his hand and opened his eyes, she demanded, "What the hell was that? What did you just do?"

"You saw?"

"I saw. Electricity around your fingers."

"Amazing."

"Damien!"

He smiled faintly. "Things are coming back to me from my distant past. I was feeling the air for powers, sending out my senses in a quest. That thing is still hovering nearby, but nothing else. Nothing that would lead us to its source. It's not here. We need to keep looking."

"So what's new," she muttered as she followed him into a deserted alley. He hoisted her on his back, and the crazy roller-coaster ride started all over again.

Now she had to deal with what she had just seen him do, and she had a million questions that were clearly going to have to wait.

Just what kind of powers did he have that he could make sparks like that with his fingertips and be so certain that the source of the evil pursuing her was not there?

Oh, she was going to give him the third degree when she had a minute. A police officer knew how to question.

Caro's powers were growing as were his own. Damien could feel it. He wondered if that was because they were both trying, or if it was a growing reaction to the elemental that hovered near her most of the time.

Wondering didn't change it, however, nor did thinking about it answer the question. Probably a combination of both, he decided.

He was having trouble keeping his focus, though. Having Caro so tightly wound around him was delightful, and although the wind spared him her mesmerizing scents, he picked up a faint whiff every time they stopped. Her blood, her delicious blood, surely the finest of champagnes. Her desire, waves that always seemed to be there, sometimes ebbing but never gone.

The Hunger in him, also never gone, tried to rise and dictate his actions. It wanted him to lay her down on one of those icy building roofs and take her thoroughly and completely, entering her and drinking from her at the same time.

The woman was going to drive him mad.

For centuries he hadn't really thought about it. Certainly not when he'd lived in Persia and tempting delicacies had come to him willingly, making offerings of themselves. He'd made a kind of peace with the changing times and had learned to find his quarry in ways that harmed no one.

But he'd never really thought about the deep grip of the Hunger on him. How it affected him. How it could cloud his thinking. How it could dominate him.

Mainly because there'd never been a reason before. Now there was, and that reason was Caro. Simply Caro. He thought he'd tested the dimensions of his Hunger before, but he was learning he hadn't even come close.

Those dimensions were dangerous. Not just because of the possibility of claiming. After all these centuries he had begun to believe that he was immune to that problem, although Caro made him wonder.

No, the danger resided in distraction and inattention. He had to focus on the threat, not on his Hunger for Caro. He didn't need his instincts clamoring for satisfaction when it might cost her her life. He'd never forgive himself if something went wrong because he failed to control the constant, hammering, throbbing, demanding need he felt for her.

But the Hunger wasn't entirely amenable to control. He could no more entirely quash it than he could prevent the sleep of death. It was as essential to his existence as food was to any being, and it would not be denied for long.

He could drink gallons of that rotgut Jude purchased from a blood bank, and it would only briefly ease his nature's demands. Caro roused those demands to heights he couldn't remember ever having experienced except as a newborn. He wanted her. He wanted her in every way a vampire desired prey, in every way a vampire desired a lover.

Cut it out, he ordered himself as he leaped to a new rooftop. This was not the time. He had Caro's life to consider.

Wrong time or not, however, with her wrapped around him it was impossible to fully suppress his yearning. So close and yet so far.

It was almost a relief to reach their destination so he could put her down, put even a few inches between them. He was careful to stand upwind so he wouldn't get a noseful of her enticing scents. Oh, he could still smell her, but at least it wasn't hitting him full-force in the face.

"Are you okay?" he asked as he watched her rub her cheeks.

"No, I'm not okay," she said querulously. "How many more places do we have to visit to hear exactly the same thing, which is nothing?"

He wondered what had made her so irritable. Then he

smelled it, sweet and enticing, and knew the ride had been as much torment for her as for him.

He couldn't quite hide a satisfied smile. Ungenerous perhaps, but there was something good about knowing he wasn't alone in his torment. Perhaps he could do something about that, for her anyway. Later.

For now he stepped to the side so that her alluring scents didn't reach him as strongly.

An image flashed across his mind's eye, an image of her naked and writhing beneath him, begging him to take her and drink.

He sighed.

"I'm going to do this differently," he told her. "You reach out with your senses and see what you can detect. I'll do the same. Talking to people seems to be getting us nowhere."

"I'll second that. Okay, I'll give it a shot."

He watched her close her eyes and almost smiled again as he saw her stiffen with effort. "Just relax," he said. "Sometimes trying too hard just blocks it all."

She obeyed him, relaxing herself in stages until she looked more comfortable.

As soon as he was sure she wasn't trying to force herself, he stretched out his own hand. No one on the street would see it, but he was still surprised that Caro had been able to. The hum of power, so long unused, felt wonderful. His fingertips tingled and sparkled with energy, and little blue streamers of electricity arced between them.

Let it build, he told himself. *Just let it build.* It had been so long, and he had missed it so much.

It grew until he felt it humming up his arm, then into his entire body. He felt alive with the power and wondered why he had abandoned it so long ago. Times had changed, forcing him to be far more discreet and cautious than in his temple days, but maybe he had sacrificed too much to caution. Way too much.

He watched his hand begin to glow blue with the power, a glow that was probably starting to surround him from head to foot. So much power, but it had to be directed.

He thought of the threat, reached out to sense it hovering nearby. When he found it, he extended his power outward toward its source or summoner.

As soon as he touched on it, it snapped back, but as it instantly dissipated, he caught a general direction. It wasn't as good as an address, but at least he knew which parts of the city he didn't need to check out.

Unless, of course, the bokor moved.

He let the power seep away, then waited for Caro's reactions. When she opened her eyes, they seemed darker than usual. "I felt it," she said. "But then it snapped away. You?"

"Me, too."

She turned slowly and pointed to the west. "That direction."

"That's what I got, too."

"Then let's go."

He reached out to grip her arm. "Wait."

"Wait?" Her irritation was unmistakable. "Wait for what? I'm tired of this thing stalking me. I'm tired of never feeling alone even when I'm in an empty room. I'm tired of wondering if it will somehow slip by you or other witnesses and do the deed anyway. And I'm worried that it might go after someone else, too. Like Pritchett's brother-in-law. That thing is murderous and it has to be stopped."

"I absolutely agree."

"Then what are you dragging your heels for?"

"Are you ready to face a bokor?"

"Isn't that what we've been looking for?"

He shook his head slightly. "We've been looking for information. I'm not ready for a confrontation with a bokor and neither are you."

"But you made that thing snap back."

"For now. The bokor will know it. Now he has a measure of my power and yours. That doesn't work to our advantage unless we prepare."

"Why not?" She sounded impatient. "If we wait, we give him more time to prepare, too. Maybe come up with a stronger force or more of them."

"That's possible. Possible but unlikely."

"You'd better explain."

"Let's go back to your place. Your lips are turning blue. Then we'll talk."

She grumbled a bit, but she allowed him to carry her home. Such sweet torture.

Once inside her apartment, he waited for her to wash up and change and get herself a hot drink. Then he made another protective circle around them so they could sit in her living room and talk.

"So explain to me how we gained any advantage by not going after the guy right now."

He liked the feisty set of her jaw, and the way her gray eyes snapped at him. He tried to remember the last time any woman had ever stood up to him this way, and he couldn't. Times had changed indeed, but even so Caro was a force to be reckoned with.

"He'll know his elemental was detected and deflected, but that's all he knows. That could have happened in a number of ways. By not following, we leave him to think it may have been purely accidental."

"But what if he doesn't?"

"We still have to prepare. Caro, there are simply some battles you can't wade into without adequate preparation, and magic is one of them."

"What kind of preparation?"

He put his hand over his mouth. He didn't want her to see the smile twitch his lips as he anticipated her explosion. Because she was going to erupt.

Then he wondered why he was even considering mentioning it. She would definitely erupt, with some justification because his proposal was going to seem so out of line to her, and then where would they be? Worse off than right now.

"Damien? Just get on with it. What kind of preparation?"

He picked his words with care, feeling as if he were tiptoeing between rays of sunlight, which for him were the equivalent of mines. "In my tradition…"

"In your tradition what?"

"In my tradition we practiced certain rituals to enhance the power of the mage. Rituals of great focus, power and intensity."

"And they were?"

"Sex."

Her mouth hung open. She shook her head a little. The expected eruption didn't happen. Instead she almost squeaked, "Sex? A ritual?"

"Very much so. Can you think of anything that embodies the life force any better?"

Her mouth closed, then opened again. "Life force. But you're *dead!*"

"Not exactly," he reminded her. "Undead, not dead. I straddle two worlds, which makes me more powerful. But I can still focus the life force. And so can you."

"Sex," she repeated. Then the eruption came, clearly because she didn't like the *way* he was proposing this. A seduction was one thing, but a ritual? It must sound like an excuse to her. "What is this? Some new kind of pass to get into my pants? Are you that desperate?"

"I'm desperate all right," he admitted frankly, "but not enough to lie to you. What I'm telling you is true. Lots of people believe in the strengthening powers of sex, that it unleashes the hidden powers in all of us, however temporarily. If you know what you're doing, the powers aren't temporary."

"And I suppose you know what you're doing," she said acidly.

"Of course. I was a temple priest."

Again her mouth opened and closed. While this was nowhere near as bad as he'd anticipated, he expected more. This wasn't her culture's way of looking at sex. In fact, there was hardly a group on the planet more prudish than her culture, although there were probably some. *The Brits,* he thought with a flicker of humor. All that Calvinism and Puritanism had found a great home here.

"Sex," he said when she offered nothing more, "is a joyous celebration of life. Properly practiced, it's purely good."

"You'll have to excuse me, but I'm a police officer. I've seen it used in a very different way too often."

"I'm sure you have. There are always abusers of gifts. People who use them as weapons. Like the bokor we seek."

She sighed. "Point taken. So what do you expect me to do? Get naked with you on the floor?"

He bridled a moment, then reminded himself this concept was utterly alien to her. "I'm not trying to take advantage of you, but to explain a ritual. The occasion requires considerably more ceremony and thought than that. It requires a certain amount of devotion."

"Devotion sounds good," she admitted. "Let me think about it."

He could only wonder at her thoughts because she didn't share them. Not that he had expected instant capitulation. While he could see, smell and nearly taste her desire for him, she probably wanted something a little more romantic, or a little more spontaneous.

He suspected the whole of idea of making love as a ritual was what was setting her back on her heels. It did sound a bit clinical if you weren't used to the idea.

Her gaze tracked back to him and it was now suspicious. "Did you just make this up?"

"Absolutely not."

She shook her head a little. "I don't know about this. It sounds so cold."

"It's anything but." Yet he could understand her feelings. Most women preferred to be wooed.

"What exactly would be involved?"

"I'd make love to you and try to bring us both to the highest pitch of completion possible."

He saw her eyes darken, smelled the scents of her desire. His own arose in response, and he knew he was halfway there.

"What else?" she asked.

Now came the part he was sure was going to upset her. But there was no way around it.

"I'm a vampire," he reminded her. "My predatory instincts must not be wakened."

"So…I'd have to hold still?" She looked as if that didn't exactly please her.

"More than that," he admitted frankly. "I'd have to tie you up."

Chapter 10

Tie her up? The words caused a windstorm of reactions in her, ranging from anger at the mere thought of being constrained to an amazingly powerful shiver of longing.

She closed her eyes, knowing she couldn't conceal her scents from Damien but hoping she could keep her eyes and expressions from giving away more.

"I could tie you up," she pointed out tensely.

"You could. But there are two problems."

"And those are?"

"You don't know the ritual, and if I become predatory, there are few bonds that could hold me."

"Lovely." Sarcasm dripped from the word.

But she wondered what her real resistance was. She couldn't deny the way her body had clenched at the thought of being tied up and loved by him. Never had she suspected she might have a hankering to be bound like some kind of sexual conquest. Undeniably, however, the urge was there. At least with Damien.

Now that the image had been planted, she couldn't escape it. Instead, her mind wandered around the notion of being both helpless and exposed while he loved her in whatever way he chose. Another pulse of desire tightened her core, making her ache so hard.

She knew where he could take her even fully clothed. She had been longing for more ever since. What was she afraid of?

Being helpless? Of course. She hated being helpless. Even as her libido responded powerfully, some part of her resisted. Why?

Because she suddenly felt incredibly and uncharacteristically shy. The notion of helplessness and being fully exposed made her feel like an inexperienced schoolgirl who had never before been touched, who had never before been naked with a man in even the smallest way.

"You have to take charge?" she asked quietly.

"Yes."

"And I'm supposed to just let you tie me up and use me in whatever way you choose?"

"I would be a tender lover, *Schatz*. The point of this is pleasure, not humiliation or bad feelings. That would subvert the ritual."

Her eyes snapped open. "I'd feel a whole lot better about this if I thought you gave a damn about me."

He appeared astonished, which gave her a small measure of satisfaction. "I don't call anyone else *Schatz*."

"What's that mean, anyway?"

"Treasure."

Oh, man, he knew exactly how to slip past her defenses. *Treasure?* That word hit her right in the heart like a warm dart. She bit her lip. "I need to think about this, Damien. It's not like we ever really made love before. You're asking a lot."

"I know. But I could, right this instant, come to you and love you in all the ways I want, ways that you want, too."

"As long as I don't move."

He nodded. "It's not that I fear hurting you. I fear forgetting myself and drinking from you at the same time."

"So I'm still just a food group?"

"You're far more than that or I wouldn't even suggest this. Would it make you feel better if I come to you first as an ordinary lover?"

Would it? She didn't know anymore. How could she when she'd had such an unexpectedly strong response to the idea of being bound by him? "Will it affect the power of the ritual?"

"It might," he said slowly, almost reluctantly. "These rituals are usually performed by two people who have never been together before."

"And that enhances the power for both of us? Or just for one of us?"

He shook his head a little. "*Schatz,* I can't be certain. My experience in this was always with women who had no powers. You have powers yourself. Why should they not be enhanced for you as they will be for me?"

"Well, that's the question, isn't it." Her voice had grown tart again, tasting almost sour on her own tongue. "I've got to think about this, Damien. I feel like I just got sideswiped. And I need to know more."

"I understand. Perhaps you should do some research on this. But I offer you one warning."

"What's that?"

"Your culture tries to make things like this sound bad. Don't take their word for it. I know from experience just how empowering this would be."

"In other words, just take *your* word for it."

He gave her a lopsided smile. "Yes. I wish you would."

"Do we need anything for this ritual?"

"I need to find a few things, yes. The bonds must not hurt you. I need to dress you in such a way that you feel comfortable with every step."

"You need to dress me? Why?"

"Because trying to do this with you in your usual garb would be impossible. A robe. I need a robe for you. And for me. And silken bonds."

"I have no idea where to find those." Although in truth she did. Being a cop had taken her to some interesting places. She just wasn't sure she wanted to shop in them. "I still need to think about this."

"Of course. I can go out and gather the items we need while you do research at Jude's if you like. Or we can gather them whenever you are ready. It's up to you."

Up to her. That was the damnable part. As much as her body was shrieking yes to the whole idea, her brain was turning traitor and wishing it had no decision to make at all.

Utterly unlike her, she told herself scornfully. Then she wondered if she had ever really known herself. Because here she was, wanting to be tied up by a vampire.

Oh, that really made sense, didn't it.

She sighed and rubbed her eyes and wished away the edgy nervousness that had filled her ever since he'd brought this up. It was what she had been wanting since she'd met him, wasn't it? To find out what it would be like to make love with him?

And the little experiences they'd had together had already shown her that he could take her places she had never imagined existed. So why was she being difficult? Why was she fighting what she had wanted?

Simply because he called it a *ritual?*

What was wrong with that? she asked herself. She'd had a few boyfriends in her time, and sooner or later the sex had become almost ritualistic anyway. The same things, the same way, every time. Once, she'd tried to change that and had lost a boyfriend, who felt she was insulting his skills as a lover.

"What steps are involved?" she asked, hearing a thickening in her own voice, undoubtedly another response to the fires he had stirred in her. She wished she thought he couldn't hear it, but what the hell. Every time she got wet for him, he knew it. Heck, every time she felt the least arousal he smelled it. She had no secrets. He probably knew exactly how strong her response had been to the idea of having him tie her up. At least so far he had respected her wishes even when they were in conflict with the hormonal flags she must be wearing.

Life used to be so much easier. Having secrets could be a good thing, but it had been stripped from her by a vampire's knowing nose. Damn it.

"I prepare the space," he said quietly. "Candles, incense, no distractions. We must be totally focused on one another."

She couldn't imagine that that would be a problem.

"We take a ritual bath. It should be together, but we can do it separately if you like. We must cleanse ourselves."

"Okay." She envisioned them standing naked in her shower together. No way could the tub hold them both at once.

"Once we are clean of all the lingering detritus of the world, we go to the chamber. There I will make love to you with every bit of skill and power and caring I possess, transporting us to ecstasy, to a place that can be reached no other way. Our gifts will join as our bodies join. And afterward, I shall hold you until the sun makes me go."

That didn't sound too bad, she thought. In fact it sounded rather delightful. "Is there a time length or anything?"

He smiled faintly. "If it doesn't take several hours, then I haven't loved you properly. Each gift must be cherished, every instant enjoyed."

Oh, wow. From past experience, she would have thought an hour tops. How could he spend so long loving her?

She realized then that she very much wanted to find out.

"Okay," she said.

"Tomorrow night," he answered. "I need to get some things. Let me take you to Jude's so you'll be safe while I go out."

She looked around her small apartment, sensing that just beyond the circle he had created that thing was hovering again. "It can't hear us?"

"The elemental? Not within this circle. And the wards Jude put here should keep it under control."

"I can back out at any time?"

"If you wish. Of course you can. You may be bound, but this must not involve force of any kind."

Maybe she could live with that. If she had to agree to everything...

The thought was interrupted by an unexpected surge of wildness in her, as if she were ready to jump off a cliff to see if she could fly. Cautious, ordinary, sensible Caro vanished as another part of her nature emerged. As a cop she often took risks, but they were part of the job, and she always tried to manage them as carefully as she could.

This was a different kind of risk, and she thirsted for it. Like the thoughts she had once talked herself out of about trying a fire walk at one of those self-improvement seminars. She sensed, though she could not be sure, that on the other side of this would lie freedom. Freedom from what, she didn't know. She just felt a sudden certainty that she would be tossing aside shackles she hadn't realized she wore.

"Let's go," she said. She still had another day to change her mind, after all.

It was a day that proved excruciatingly long. Damien had returned with large parcels in the early hours, then had excused himself to go sleep.

Caro wondered what was in those parcels, but they were in the inner office with him, and she simply did not want to open the door and risk any possibility that he might inadvertently receive some exposure to light. She didn't entirely trust that blackout curtain.

She tried sleeping on the cot in the room just off the front office, then tried again on the couch. The night ahead loomed before her, alternately filling her with anxiety and eagerness for the passion he had promised.

She was a mess. She *had* to sleep, to be ready for the night's mysteries, for they would certainly be mysteries, beginning with the fact that she had never really made love to Damien, and ending with the fact that she honestly had no idea what to expect.

This approach to sex struck her as artificial, yet she had indeed checked online and discovered just how old and widespread was the belief that sex could unleash powers, sometimes just naturally, but often as part of organized ritual.

God, she felt like a virgin on her wedding day, with absolutely no idea of what was to come. Knowing the basics wasn't enough. Damien had thrown a lot of other things into the hopper with his talk of rituals, bindings, increasing power…a whole bunch of mysteries and things to get edgy about.

Things she had never done before, things she had never considered before, all of them looming. It was no help to remind herself that he'd said she could back out at any time.

Chloe was busy at the computer, and busy being her watchdog. That felt silly, too. She'd pushed the thing away herself, hadn't she? So maybe she had little to fear from it.

Regardless, she was going stir-crazy, locked up like this under constant watch, and sleep was so elusive she wanted to scream. She needed to be in top form for tonight, whatever it held.

And she *did* want tonight, she finally admitted to herself. She'd been wanting it one way or another almost from the instant she had set eyes on Damien. She couldn't remember the last time simply looking at a man had aroused her, and she couldn't be anywhere near Damien without her thoughts turning to the sexual.

So tonight she would find out if it was as good as her body wanted it to be. The more she thought about it, the more she even liked the idea of being bound, of giving up all responsibility. There was something enchanting in that notion, the notion of just experiencing without having to do a damn thing except enjoy it.

Heat pooled between her thighs. She had never had a purely selfless lover, one who would take his own pleasure from hers. Not that she had ever expected one. Sex should be a shared giving and taking. But suddenly she was being offered something she had never imagined: a lover who would expect nothing from her but her own pleasure.

Wow.

A smile came to her face, just a small one, and her internal struggle settled down. This was an experience she simply could not pass up. No way.

With that, drowsiness claimed her, carrying her away into dreams of a candlelit room where a vampire hovered over her, learning her most intimate secrets with his hands and then his mouth.

Unfortunately, she didn't stay asleep. Maybe an hour before darkfall, she woke suddenly. Not even a lingering bit of drowsiness slowed her down. She sat up, hearing running water, and realized Chloe had gone to take a shower.

She wondered if everyone knew what was going to happen tonight and therefore expected some big deal, or if Chloe had just thought Caro was safe within the shield of wards and could take a moment to freshen up.

Either way, Caro seized the opportunity. She had to get out for a walk. She wasn't used to all this confinement. She was used to being out and about most of the time, whether in a patrol car or just strolling the streets and window-shopping. Inactivity didn't suit her at all.

Grabbing her jacket and zipping it up tight, she left a note saying she was going for dinner. Then she headed out for the late afternoon streets. As soon as she stepped out of the office, the feeling of being watched returned, but she reminded herself that there were plenty of people out and about on the street, and it still wasn't dark.

The icy air nipped her cheeks. The remnants of the last snowfall had ceased to sparkle, having melted a bit and picked up the city's grime, but there were still places where the lowering sun struck and turned it golden in stark contrast to the bluer shadows.

It was a beautiful late afternoon, with twilight just around the corner and calm, still air. It was so rare among the buildings to have no breeze at all that she noticed the quietude of the air.

People passed, some of them nodding and smiling, others totally ignoring her. She walked swiftly, stretching her muscles, bringing up her heart rate.

She wouldn't go too far, she told herself. Just up a couple of blocks in a straight line so that if Chloe looked out for her she would be visible.

But damn, it felt so good to be out and moving again.

Even here in this poorer part of the city there were plenty of shop windows to glance into. Occasionally she paused at a display of exotic foods. One of the things she liked in this city was the blending of so many cultures. Here a Korean food store, there an Indian food store. Tiny little hole-in-the-wall restaurants scattered along the street issued enticing aromas of foreign dishes.

The farther she walked away from Jude's office, the more the place felt like a real neighborhood. Most of the shops and restaurants were at or just below street level, with apartments rising over their heads. She began to hear different languages along with the different aromas.

This was one part of the city she had never worked, and she began to think she had missed something very special.

She had walked only a few blocks, though, when the sense of being watched turned into a strong sense of presence. Looking away from lighted windows, she realized that twilight was coming on faster than she'd anticipated. Either that or she'd lost track of time.

Turning, she started back to Jude's office, reaching for whatever power she had used yesterday to keep that elemental away.

For a little while it pulled back. But then she felt it move in again, and the sensation was so strong that she quickened her step.

God, it was getting dark fast. What had she been thinking?

The urge to run was growing in her, but she forced it

down. Whatever this force was that was coming after her, some instinct told her that fear would only feed it.

Instead she clung to that willpower she had found only yesterday, concentrating her thoughts on forcing the thing back. It gave a little, allowing her to breathe more easily.

Just another block, but night was almost here. She judged by the light that the sun must have nearly finished setting. Soon the shadows between the buildings would become inky.

Almost as soon as she had the thought, they did just that. At the same time, the watcher returned and her skin began to crawl. It was there—it was close. She willed it away, but this time it failed to yield.

Half a block to go. She gathered everything inside herself and envisioned herself sending out a blast of light against the elemental. This time it barely hesitated before it was on her again.

Her chest began to hurt. She felt cold all the way to her bones where only moments ago she had been warm enough. Panic fluttered in her, demanding she flee, but how could she flee this thing?

She could see no one else on the street. Where had everyone gone? She hurried her pace even more, while imagining her body growing warmer, her chest easing. A few moments of success...

Then she felt as if the wind had been knocked from her. She couldn't catch her breath at all. Weakness poured through her, causing her legs to give way. Her diaphragm seemed to have frozen, and no matter how hard she tried to draw air into her lungs, it wouldn't come.

She was going to die right here and now, and her mind fought back darkness, seeking something, anything, to push that elemental away before it was too late.

The night dimmed even more and she realized she was blacking out. It was over. She made one more monumental effort of will to drive that thing away, to gather one more breath.

She failed. Darkness moved in, claiming her and she had one last conscious thought: *I've been such an idiot.*

Just as the last of the world seemed to fade, she heard Damien shout, "Caro!"

An instant later, steel arms surrounded her and lifted her. Like a newborn baby, she gasped for her breath. This time her lungs filled.

Safe now, she let go, let darkness claim her, a darkness that wasn't supernatural at all.

Damien, torn between fury and fear, put the unconscious Caro on the couch. Terri immediately knelt beside her to check her out.

"What the hell were you thinking, Chloe?" he heard Jude demand.

"She was asleep. How was I supposed to know she'd leave because I spent ten minutes in the shower. I thought she knew better than that."

Damien didn't care about Chloe's failure, didn't care about anything except seeing Caro's eyes open again. He couldn't remember the last time he'd been beside himself with fear, but he was now.

"Get a blanket," Terri said. "She's too cold, but she's breathing all right."

Chloe raced away and returned with a heavy comforter. Damien insisted on covering Caro himself and tucking it around her. For the first time, he wished he had some excess body heat to offer, but he knew he didn't. Not one iota. Awake, his body was just above room temperature, not enough to act like a heater.

He was not accustomed to cursing the fact that he was a vampire, but he cursed it now. He seldom had cause to think about the ways it made him useless or helpless, but Caro was constantly reminding him.

Yet he had to face the fact a mortal man could do little more at this point. If she was going to go out on her own, she'd do it, and so what if he couldn't wrap himself in that comforter with her right now and warm her?

At least she was still alive. He wondered if he would ever tell her what he'd sensed when he'd seen her on the pavement, how he could feel that elemental surrounding her and consuming her. How he had sensed her very life force draining away. How he had nearly panicked about losing her.

No, probably not good to tell her all that, and certainly not before he sorted out his own feelings. Vampires had strong emotions, but panic usually wasn't one of them.

Jude touched his arm. "She'll be all right. You said you had something to do tonight?"

Damien had to shake himself back to the present from the moments just passed on the street.

"Yes. Caro and I were going to try to enhance our powers."

Jude lifted a brow. "Yours are coming back? I thought you feared you'd lost them."

"I had, but believe me, they're coming back. Maybe it's the proximity to this elemental stirring up things that have slept for so long. I don't know. I just know that I'm finding some of them again, and to meet this bokor I need every bit possible at my disposal. I don't even want to attempt to find him until I'm ready."

"Which puts Caro in danger longer."

"Not much longer. Although we're going to have a serious talk about this tendency of hers to go walkabout."

A quiet chuckle escaped Jude. "Good luck. How often do you think Terri listens to me?"

Terri, still perched beside Caro, looked up. "I listen to you all the time!"

"When it pleases you, madam."

Her blue eyes twinkled a moment, then she returned her attention to Caro. "She's going to be fine. She's warming already. And I need to get to work."

She rose and went to kiss Jude. "You stay here. You might have to do some hunting tonight."

"Me? For what?"

"Maybe you can locate that bokor for Damien. Just be careful."

"I am always careful," he drawled.

"Sure. I've seen it. Turning yourself into a torch is very careful." She cupped his cheek. "Behave for my sake."

Then she grabbed her coat and left.

Damien squatted and touched Caro's cheek. He could feel warmth there now, just a little. "Why isn't she waking? She's breathing, she's warming."

"I don't know, but Terri didn't seem to be worried."

Damien almost said that Terri didn't have as much reason to be concerned as he did, then he stopped himself. Such a thought was unfair. He knew Terri well enough to recognize how caring a doctor and a human being she was.

He was just frantic with concern for Caro, a very strange place for a vampire to be.

He didn't want to think about what that might mean, couldn't afford to now. He had to focus on the threat, focus on enhancing his powers, not on the strange places his heart might wander.

There was no time for distractions now. Now he had to concentrate on saving Caro and perhaps other humans from whoever had summoned that elemental. And there must be others at risk. That shopkeeper had been right: organizations lived on after the men who founded them. Right now, somewhere, there was probably a board making plans to continue what Pritchett had started.

The thought made him turn briefly to Chloe. "Is there a board of directors for Pritchett's company? People who might continue with the development plans? Or did all that die with him?"

"I'll check," Chloe said. "That should be easy enough to find out."

"I don't know the law," Jude remarked, "but it seems to me if there isn't a board for his company, all his death does is make the properties available for sale, and along with them all the demolition permits. There'll be an heir somewhere, I should think, and if he or she doesn't want to take over, the buildings will be sold."

"Yes, but that's in the future," Damien said. "I want to know who else might be at risk now."

"Why?"

"Because someone besides Caro may be being stalked. And while I can keep Caro reasonably safe if she'll just stop haring off on her own, there may be others in trouble right now who don't even know it."

"True. Not that I'm especially fond of people who would tear down the homes of others, but I definitely don't approve of using powers to kill people. Any people. If you're right, that would certainly mean we need to act as fast as possible."

Damien looked down at the unconscious Caro and touched her cheek, testing its warmth. "As fast as possible," he agreed. "But after this, we might have a slight delay. I don't know if Caro will be up to enhancing her powers tonight."

"What about you?" Jude asked.

"I can't do it without her."

Chapter 11

Caro awoke in a state of near panic. She couldn't move her arms, she still felt chilled deep inside and her head felt as if it had been pounded by a mallet. But as her eyes snapped open, she found herself looking into familiar midnight eyes.

"You're okay," Damien said. "You're safe."

She let her eyes close for a few seconds, struggling to make the mental shift from the last thing she remembered to her current state. *Cold. Safe.*

She let go of fright and looked at Damien again. "I need to sit up."

Instantly he pulled away the binding comforter and helped ease her into a sitting position. "How do you feel?"

"Weird. My head is killing me. I feel like I'm cold deep inside. But I'm here, obviously."

"You must never do that again, not until we beat this elemental. My God, Caro, it was that close to killing you!"

"I know," she whispered. She was used to taking risks, but she had to admit this had been a stupid one. "I thought I could push it away. I did before."

"But it got your measure then. The bokor must have strengthened it."

"Maybe." She rubbed her temples.

"Coffee?" Chloe asked cheerily. "Or tea?"

"Coffee, please. Maybe it'll help warm me up." Then she fixed her gaze on Damien. "He strengthened it? How could he make it stronger? Why wouldn't he have made it stronger to begin with?"

He settled back on the couch but took one of her hands in his. His skin felt slightly cool to her, which she supposed was a good sign despite the cold that seemed to fill her very center.

"Summoning these forces is a delicate balancing act, *Schatz*. The mage must ever take care that it doesn't become so powerful he can't control it. Naturally he wouldn't want it to be any stronger than it must be to achieve his purpose."

"But it's stronger now?"

"So it would seem. The question is whether he did it to get at you, or whether it's starting to escape his control. I suspect, though, that the bokor was behind this."

"I still don't get why it's coming after me. Why should the bokor have been afraid that I saw what happened? Why in the world did he attach that thing to me? Surely he should have thought that no one would ever be able to prove anything."

Damien shook his head a little. "I don't read minds. But my suspicion is you may have originally been mistaken for one of its targets. Then you started pursuing the matter and became aware of its existence. The bokor might have become worried that you would find him. Certainly

I'd think that he now has heard we're looking for him. People talk. I think at some point the game changed, probably because of something you or we did."

"So he may have strengthened it for that reason. But he can't get at *you,* Damien."

His expression turned slightly rueful. "I can't guarantee that. I'm fairly sure that I'm not as easy for it to get at as you, but no guarantees."

"The elemental, or the bokor, may not be aware you're a vampire."

"I hope not, although you figured it out readily enough."

"I could see your aura," she reminded him. "And then you moved faster than humanly possible. I'm reasonably good at putting things together."

"Better than most, I think."

She accepted a hot mug of coffee from Chloe gratefully. The first sip took some of the edge off the chill deep in her innards.

"So," Damien said sternly, "will you promise not to go out alone again until we settle this?"

"It goes against my nature to be cooped up all the time. But yes, I promise I won't do it again. I may need to get out and about, but I'm not stupid. I learned my lesson."

"Thank you. You were so close to death, *Schatz.* Too close. I could feel that elemental draining you of life."

"I felt it, too. I won't get cocky again."

"Good." Then he astonished her by reaching out and hugging her to his side. He seldom did that, and after the way he had warned her there was just so much that he could pretend to be ordinary, she hadn't looked for comforting touches from him.

She definitely liked it, however. Definitely liked his arm around her, liked being pressed to his side while she sipped her coffee. If she wasn't careful, she might start to think there was something normal going on there.

But none of it was "normal" start to finish. Although as the department's shrink had mentioned during her interview after that shoot-out recently, "What's normal? There *is* no normal."

Right now those sounded like wise words.

Then she remembered. Her breath caught. Anxiety filled her along with an inescapable heat. Frightened and longing both, she asked, "Aren't we supposed to do something tonight?"

He hesitated. "After what just happened, I'm not sure you have the strength. Let's wait and see."

Wait and see? How long could she stand having this looming over her? Another day of anticipation and nervousness that put her on edge so badly that she'd hardly sleep. That had probably played a large part in her decision to risk that walk.

"I don't know if I can wait another day."

His smile turned wry. "I wish you meant that the way it sounds."

"What are you two talking about?" Chloe demanded.

Damien lifted a brow, eying Caro. "Do you feel well enough to go to your place?"

She felt an unexpected urge to laugh. "Yes, of course."

Chloe grumbled, "Nobody tells me a damn thing. Get out of here, you two, and keep your secrets. I'm just the assistant anyway."

Damien borrowed Jude's car for the trip. First he loaded it with the bags full of his purchases, and then he escorted Caro out.

"So being a vamp has its limitations? Too many bags to carry?"

"I could carry them and you, but I don't want to expose you to the cold just now."

That was thoughtful of him. But as the buildings zipped by on the way to her apartment, her stomach turned to lead with apprehension. She had agreed to this ritual of his, but that didn't mean she was entirely comfortable. Even more, she was on tenterhooks wondering if he would postpone it yet another day. How would she endure that?

But what if he was right that she wasn't up to it now, after what had happened? She didn't exactly feel as if she had regained all her strength yet, and her head still pounded, though not quite as much.

Not tonight, dear, I have a headache. The old joke popped into her head and made her smile. When they arrived at her place, he carried all the bags while she led the way. Her legs felt a bit stronger now, but the butterflies in her stomach hadn't eased one bit.

What now? The question hovered over her like that elemental she sensed was still nearby.

Once in her apartment, however, things turned disappointingly ordinary. She made more coffee. Damien put the bags in her bedroom, then made his protective circle of salt once again, chanting in that strange language.

Then...nothing. They sat side by side on her couch, not touching. Neither of them moved. Oh, this was going to be maddening. Her nerves were already stretched tight.

Finally his voice filled the silence and agonizing anticipation. "Let's see how fast you improve," he said. "We have time."

Time was what was killing her right now. Nervous as she was, she still wanted him to touch her. Wanted him closer. Even wanted him to drink from her again if that was the most he would do tonight.

It had been such an amazing experience and she was

still trying to absorb the fact that giving a vampire her blood could be as pleasurable as any sex she had ever had. More enjoyable, actually.

"Have you fed?" she asked, her voice a little throaty.

"Of course."

"Oh."

A quiet chuckle escaped him and she looked at him. Smiling, he reached out to touch her hair, trace her cheek and bring his fingers to rest in the hollow of her throat. "I warned you would want to repeat the experience."

"So?" His amusement irritated her. "I want to repeat it with *you,* not with just any vampire. There's a difference, you know."

"I know." His face darkened. "Believe me, I know." He turned his head, concealing his expression from her briefly. "I know," he said yet again. "There's danger there, too, Caro. Don't become too attached to me. I might not be able to give you what you want."

"What do you mean?" Her heart sank as she realized that she *did* want more from him than just a good lay. A lot more.

"I'm not exactly sure," he admitted. "There's danger here. I told you of it. But I've been around for nearly three millennia, Caro. In all that time I have never claimed anyone. Perhaps I can't. But I have also never lingered that long with any one person. Perhaps I can't."

"So you've been a playboy all along?"

He considered before answering. "I suppose you could call it that. But I do have an opinion on this much. There is nothing sadder than to give your heart and not receive a heart in return. After all this time, you are the first to make me wonder if I have a heart. Perhaps I do. But what if you're unhappy with what comes from that? Or worse, what if it turns out I don't have a heart to give?"

Her stomach took another plunge to her toes, warning her that she was steadily getting into trouble. But along with that warning came the realization that she might not be able to control this. "That's a risk in any relationship," she finally said.

"It is," he agreed. His fingers caressed her throat, sending shivers of delight to every nerve ending in her body. "I would drink from you, but you've been weakened enough by that attack."

As she watched, his eyes grew golden again, and he smiled. "You are an adventure for me. I like it."

"I'm an adventure how?"

"You surprise me. You engage me in ways few do. You don't give in easily to restrictions, yet you enforce restrictions in your job. An interesting mix."

"There are laws, and then there are other restrictions."

"True," he agreed. "But I sense a free spirit behind the uniform and badge. You don't have to keep it cooped up all the time."

"What do you mean by free spirit?" Although she liked the sound of it, she wasn't sure what he meant.

"There's a person inside who'd like to come out more often. I see glimpses of her. She's a person who can desire a vampire, consider performing a ritual that scares her, that even wanted to be drunk from just to find out what it was like. The same person who took a dangerous walk today."

"Maybe not so smart."

"There's a wealth of experience to be had by those willing to take the risks. I think you know that. Your job isn't without its own set of risks."

That was true. Every day that she put on her uniform, she never knew what she might face. Of one thing she was sure: her job seldom bored her. Maybe that was part of the reason she had chosen it. Not just as a reaction to what her grandmother tried to teach her, not as a reaction to a worldview that hadn't been able to save her parents.

"I never thought of myself as an adrenaline addict." But maybe she was.

"I wouldn't call it that. But I think you like new experiences. You're curious, and you want to taste a variety of fruit. So let yourself."

Then he took her by surprise, sliding down the couch a bit and drawing her over until her head rested on his lap. "Do you mind?" he asked, running his fingers through her hair.

"Just don't act so ordinary I start to expect it from you."

He cracked a laugh and caressed her cheek with his cool fingertips. "I'll never be ordinary."

"Do you wish you were?"

"Before you, never."

"And now?"

"Now, a few times, I've wished I were an ordinary man so I could be what you need."

"How do you know what I need?" she demanded. But even as she made her demand, she felt the touch of his fingers, oh so gentle, like a caress to her soul. It softened her, and weakened her, in ways she liked. It was almost like a kind of relaxation, almost like the way she felt when she climbed into bed after a hard day. Her soul unleashed a sigh of contentment.

"Sometimes," he said, "you need a man who doesn't have to be afraid of comforting you. Or holding you."

"Are you really that afraid?"

His fingers paused in their light strokes of her cheek and neck. "Not anymore," he said finally. "Rest a little. Then we'll see if you're refreshed enough for the ritual. If not, it'll have to wait another day."

"I don't want to wait. This is nerve-racking. And what if someone else dies?"

"But we can't proceed if you're still weak, *Schatz*. It won't help either of us. It could even drain one of us. So we'll wait and see."

He could tell she didn't like the part about waiting, but there was nothing else to be done about it. Self-denial in and of itself could enhance one's strengths. He had frequently practiced it as a priest, often fasting. Then there was the other part—her weakness right now. She might be feeling strong enough, but he could tell she was still not fully recovered. There was a danger in that, the danger that she could take power away from him, albeit unconsciously, to restore her own.

No, this had to be as equal a give-and-take as he could ensure, one that would empower them both, not weaken one of them.

Otherwise he would have gladly started the ritual right this moment. He closed his eyes, his nostrils filled with all her enticing aromas, and imagined how it would be. The ritual cleansing, full of delights itself, to be carried out thoroughly and gently. His hands passing over every inch of her to wash away the detritus of the mundane world, hers washing him the same way.

The mere thought was enough to bring his Hunger to the brink of madness.

Then the candlelit, perfumed room, laying her down in her robe, binding her tenderly to her bed posts so she wouldn't awaken the predator in him. Uncovering her delights little by little, massaging her with scented oils until her skin gleamed and she was breathless with need for him.

Until she glowed like white-hot fire beneath his ministrations. Oh, that was going to test his self-control.

Yes, he'd done this before, both as mortal and vampire, but it had been centuries since the last time, and he knew it would be a hard test to restrain himself for so long.

Because nothing must be hurried, and he had to be sure they had both reached an absolute fever pitch that could get no higher before they united their powers.

Damn, he was nearly there just thinking about it. But when he opened his eyes, he thought her lovely face still looked a bit tired. When he checked the heat emanations of her body, they didn't seem quite warm enough.

She wasn't ready.

And therefore, neither could he be.

He refused to think about how much he wanted her. How easy it would be to fully make love to her right then and there. Take her all the way, finally joining their bodies as they had not yet done. But doing so might affect the ritual badly, and no matter how much he wanted her, he couldn't risk that.

Never had it been so hard to counsel himself to patience.

Though he might refuse to think about it, his body was throbbing with need for her, every cell shrieking to feed, to love, to take her to that place right between life and death. Sitting here with her head in his lap was one of the hardest things he could remember doing, primarily because it was not simply a step along the road of seduction.

No, he meant to comfort her, to help her rest. To relax. He was not using his wiles to get what he wanted, and that made this very different and a whole lot harder.

He wondered how it would be after the ceremony. Would his Hunger lessen or would it grow? And what if it did grow? Would he have the strength to walk away after they dealt with the bokor?

He had better, because if there was one thing he was absolutely certain about, it was that life with him would not be good for Caro over any sort of long term. A few weeks, a few months, a few years—it would not be good for her. As a mortal, she had needs and wants no vampire could ever slake. She needed to walk in the sun, to have mortal friends, to have the life she had built, not to share the nights with him and only with him. He couldn't even give her children.

She would not want to come to Cologne either. He could move himself—he had moved himself before many times—but how difficult would he make her life by being the lover she could never introduce to her friends and co-workers, the person who would always lead a shadowy existence on the edges of her life?

She might endure for a short while, but even with the example of Jude and Terri before him, he didn't believe it could last forever.

Too many sacrifices would be required, and when love required too many of them, things often turned sour. He didn't want to be the sour note in her life.

So as soon as they faced down this bokor and got rid of the elemental, he would have to leave. For both their sakes.

The thought saddened him more than he would have expected, but there was nothing he could do about it.

Realities were realities, after all.

Caro got some of the sleep her nerves had denied her during the day. She dozed off with her head in the lap of a vampire, feeling oddly comforted. How extraordinary that he could comfort her with gentle caresses when he had warned her repeatedly how dangerous he could be to her.

How strange to sink into dreams of him, dreams of flying across rooftops on his back, dreams of him drinking from her, dreams filled with some of the greatest experiences of her life. Places once beyond her imagining, and now a part of her life. In her dreams, no end loomed before them. It went on forever, that racing ride on his back, that blood sharing, his touches and even his rare laughter.

Then something jolted her instantly awake. Her eyes snapped open and she saw Damien looking down at her.

"What's wrong?" she asked immediately.

"It's trying to cross the circle. I guess the bokor no longer cares about witnesses, if he ever did."

"Can it cross?"

"I doubt it."

"But why should anything be able to stop it?"

"Because there must be limits on everything. Rules. Can you imagine the total anarchy if there was no veil between worlds? If powers could act without restriction? No, there are always limits. It seems the bokor has lessened a few of his own, but he can't lessen mine. I've restricted this space."

She didn't want to sit up, to leave the comforting pillow of his lap, but the need to look around for reassurance took charge. She pushed up until she sat and scanned the room. Everything looked the same. So she closed her eyes and reached out with her other senses.

"It passed Jude's wards." The thought scared her.

"Mostly likely because we disturbed them with our comings and goings. If you want, I'll get out the chrism he left here and restore them. We'll have to before the ceremony regardless."

"But you'd have to leave the circle to do that."

"Yes."

Her heart squeezed and her chest tightened as she remembered what that thing had tried to do to her on the street earlier. "No. I don't want you to take that chance. Tell me if I'm wrong, but if you cross that circle, the elemental can get at you."

"I'm not worried about that. I *am* worried if I break the circle the elemental might be able to get at you."

"This is a fine kettle of fish," she said acidly. "We're trapped in a circle of salt."

"Not indefinitely. If the elemental doesn't withdraw as daylight approaches, I'll get Jude over here to do some more warding of his own. He's already outside the circle, so he won't expose you."

She leaned forward, sensing that thing just beyond the circle. "Why the hell is it trying so hard now? It must know I can't do a thing about it."

"You'd have to ask the bokor, and since we still haven't found him—or her—that question will have to wait. For whatever reason, you personally became a target. And now the bokor knows you've been pushing the elemental back. Whatever his goal, he seems determined to deal with you."

"I feel like I keep running around the same maypole, never getting any real answers."

He half smiled. "I agree. It's becoming a very familiar maypole. If Jude doesn't find the bokor tonight, we'll certainly find him once we enhance our powers."

"How can you be sure of that?"

"Because when I'm in that state I've *always* been able to follow the flow of an energy to its source."

"Really? And you didn't bother to mention this sooner? Like days ago?"

He eyed her skeptically. "And what would you have said days ago if I had suggested this ceremony? I think I'd have been lucky to escape with my head still on my shoulders."

She frowned, knowing he was right. "And you can't just have your ceremony with someone else?"

"It does me little good if I meld my power with the powerless. You have power, Caro. You know that now.

We'll build on it for both of us. We'll both become much stronger."

"I admit I don't really get how this works."

"I'm not exactly an expert on the how or why. I just know it works. Just as you know you're alive and you breathe, I know how to enhance my powers. And yours. I've told you before, there are mysteries. Not everything has a specific answer.

"I like answers," she admitted.

"I have none. Mysteries all."

"I guess human life is a mystery, too, when you come right down to it."

"All the chemicals and atoms don't add up to the mind or soul," he agreed.

She cocked a brow at him. "Do you think you still have a soul?"

"My old tradition held that I do. Who knows what others would think these days. I shall assume I do until proven otherwise."

At that she grinned. "I can agree with that." Then on impulse, she swung around until she straddled his lap, facing him. She liked the look of astonishment on his face. "You told me to be a free spirit."

A laugh escaped him, dying as she wiggled until his manhood was nestled against the most sensitive part of her womanhood. She felt him hardening against her and savored the sensation.

"So," she asked, being deliberately provocative, "just how limited are we because of this upcoming rite?"

"Perhaps not as limited as you might think, *Schatz*." His voice almost sounded like a huge cat purring. "You're feeling better."

"Maybe I'm ready for the ceremony." Even as she said it, the butterflies resumed flapping in her stomach. It was amazing how nervous about it she was while still wanting it so much.

"Not yet," he murmured. "Your heat patterns aren't fully recovered."

"You see my aura?"

"Only your body heat. It's not quite the same. I can still detect some coldness in you. But maybe we can do something about that."

She did like the sound of that.

His mouth sought hers hungrily. He knew her mouth now, knew just how to slip his tongue around hers to draw an eager shiver from her. He learned fast, she thought dimly. Very fast.

And he used what he had learned. His tongue mated with hers, finding delicate nerve endings and taunting them in a parody of union, causing her body to rock against him in time with the rhythm he set. The ache he always awakened in her with such ease blossomed to full force almost instantly.

Then he slipped his cool hands up under her sweater, finding the bare skin of her midriff and stroking it lightly, teasingly, hinting at more delights to come, but withholding them. This time when she put her arms around his shoulders, trying to bring him closer, he didn't react like a scalded cat. Instead he deepened his kiss, depriving her of breath, encouraging her to madness.

He must have moved with lightning speed, because she felt her breasts spill free of the confinement of her bra. She dragged her head back to gasp for air, then he claimed her mouth again.

He cupped the weight of her breasts, almost as if testing, then began to brush his thumbs over her nipples. Back and forth, in time with his plundering tongue until she felt as if a fiery arc ran from her mouth to her nipples.

She pressed her hips harder against him, needing stronger touches down there, and a jolt went through her as he arched upward, answering her search for one long, exquisite moment.

His mouth left hers and trailed to the shell of her ear, his cool breath whispering against her cheek and then into her ear until new spasms ripped through her. He ran his tongue around the outside of her ear, teasing, then tucked it inside, setting off new sparks.

Her head fell backward so that her breasts arched into his hands. His thumbs continued to play lightly over her aching nipples, building her needs with every touch.

Then, a jolt so strong that she cried out ran through her as he caught her nipples and pinched them, at first gently, then harder.

She became a slave to desire, right then. Pain and pleasure melded so exquisitely they left her helpless. He was teaching her new things about herself and she was loving it.

The hard clenching throb that gripped her between her legs drove her nearly insane. She became raw need. She dampened until she could feel her own wetness, and it just made her hungrier.

And still he tormented her, driving her ever higher up the steep slope of passion, never giving her all that her body demanded. She felt strung like a bow, drawn and ready to release the arrow, but he kept her there, in a torture so divine she never wanted it to end.

Then cool air whispered over her skin, and the next thing she knew, his mouth had clamped to her breast, sucking strongly. A deep groan escaped her, and she released his shoulders, feeling with her hands for any part of him so that she could return at least some of what he was giving her.

But he caught her wrists and stilled her exploration

while he continued to lick and suck first one breast and then the other. She felt her breasts grow heavy, her labia engorging until the merest touch, the merest whisper of sensation grew acute.

Just at the instant when she felt she could take no more of this exquisite torture, he released her wrists, seized her hips with his hands and drew her hard against his staff.

That was all it took. A cry left her lips, winging toward the moon as she reached the crest in an orgasm so intense it hurt.

Then slowly, her body still throbbing, she collapsed against him and felt his arms wrap around her, holding her close.

A long time later, she found enough voice and breath to murmur, "That was incredible."

"It was," he agreed.

"But you. I didn't do anything for you."

"You did, *Schatz*. I drank from you. Your experience was fully mine."

Lingering weakness wouldn't allow her to raise her head to look at him. "Really?"

"Really. It's one of a vampire's blessings."

"Awesome."

"It is," he agreed, sounding a little amused. But not entirely amused. There was tension in that tone somewhere, and she'd learned him well enough to hear it.

"What's wrong?"

"Nothing's wrong."

"We didn't ruin the ceremony, did we?"

"I wouldn't have done anything that might do that."

She believed him and contentedly let her head remain on his shoulder. Well, she believed him about not ruining the ceremony. But she was also good at reading voices, especially when they were concealing something.

Her brain cells felt as if they had scattered to the four corners of the universe, so she waited a few minutes, collecting them, trying to clear the hazy fog of completion out of her overly contented mind.

"Something's bothering you," she said. "I could hear it in your voice."

"Frankly, *mein Schatz,* I've never experienced anything like that before. Not really. The intensity was…breathtaking."

"It certainly was." Then a thought struck her. "You're worried about claiming me."

"After that, I'd be a fool not to."

"Should I move? Go away?"

"No," he said forcefully. "No."

So she remained, straddling his hips, her head on his shoulder.

"Your warmth feels so good to me," he murmured. "It's such a gift you can't imagine it."

"Then enjoy it. It must be awful not to feel warm."

"It's not awful. I don't really notice it. It's not like I lack something. It's just so pleasurable when I can feel it."

She tried to imagine but failed. Then her thoughts wandered in a different direction. "Why did you have to become a vampire?"

"I didn't *have* to," he corrected gently. "I was asked to."

"But why?"

"Near immortality and some impressive powers. Every religion wants to impress its followers, and having a priest who never aged, outlived all the others and could perform some amazing physical feats was useful."

"But just one?"

"There were several of us at different locations."

"Are the others still around?"

"I'm one of the last, unless there's something I don't know. Sometimes my kind weary of existence. And we do age, albeit slowly. There is, I believe, one older than I, far older, but if she still exists she keeps entirely to herself. Some suspect she may have given rise to the legends of Lilith, but I really don't know."

"It would be fascinating to find out."

"Perhaps. Or perhaps not. With my kind, one must be leery of intruding on territories. We're terribly territorial."

"Then how do you and Jude get along?"

"Some of us manage. For a while. There are presently four vampires in this city. Jude knows us all, but how many have you met? Even when we feel friendship, we don't form tight-knit groups." He paused. "I know the others, of course. But it's not like we hang out together, unless there's a good reason."

She liked how he sometimes sounded so formal when he spoke, while at other times he spoke slang with ease. "Are there other vampires where you live? Cologne?"

"Only me."

"That has to be lonely."

"I've never really noticed. It's just the way it is."

She wondered if she would be able to stand that, then wondered why she was even asking herself. Maybe something changed when you became a vampire, but since that wasn't on her current list of options there was really no point in thinking about it.

This vampire, the one whose lap she straddled, did seem to be enjoying companionship, though. *Enough pondering,* she decided. As he said, there were mysteries, not the least of them the way she responded to him.

She closed her eyes and just decided to savor the moment. Tomorrow night would come soon enough.

Chapter 12

The next night brought some news that shook them all up. There had been another inexplicable death.

Just as Jude was getting ready to join Damien and Caro so that he could ward her apartment once again, Chloe stopped them.

"Another guy associated with Pritchett is dead," she said. "Apparently he was part of the board of directors for the Pritchett business. It's all over the news tonight, but not because of the connection."

"Was killed?" Jude asked.

"Let me call Pat," Caro said. "Maybe she knows something."

"Terri might be on the scene, too," Jude remarked. "You call Pat. If you don't get anything, I'll call Terri."

Pat answered her phone on the first ring. "Matthews, Robbery-Homicide."

"Pat, it's Caro. We just heard one of Pritchett's business associates is dead."

Pat fell silent a moment. "It's true," she said finally. "But there's not a mark on the body. The M.E. is going to have to figure out this one. He was walking into a restaurant with his wife when he collapsed on the street. It could be anything. Absolutely no evidence of foul play, so the case will probably be closed if the M.E. doesn't find something suspicious. Are you doing all right? The captain is starting to make noises about bringing you back."

"I'm doing fine and I'm not ready to come back. You tell me, Pat. Do you think this is all unrelated?"

"Coincidence is always possible, but my hackles are saying otherwise. And you didn't just hear me say that."

"It won't pass my lips."

"Then I'm going to tell you another thing that won't pass your lips. We found a bookstore owner dead yesterday. And guess whose business card was on her desk."

Caro froze. "Jenny Besom is dead?" She saw Damien stiffen.

"Apparent heart attack. But pardon me if I find the presence of Messenger's card there too coincidental. You tell him he may get a visit, although probably not. Cause looks natural. And I'm not going to ask another thing. I need to stay clear of this crazy shit. You know that. Keep your nose clean."

When she disconnected, Caro relayed the information. Jude immediately pulled out his own phone to call Terri. He hung up not two minutes later. "Too early to tell about the guy, but Besom appears to be an ordinary heart attack."

Caro, however, had gone into investigator mode. She looked at Chloe. "Did the board say anything yesterday or today about continuing with the demolitions, with Pritchett's plans?"

"Let me look." Chloe bent to her computer, tapping rapidly.

Caro looked at Damien. "You said Jenny Besom was being prevented from telling you something."

He nodded.

"Well, she must have known something, then. We're running out of time, Damien. I was afraid of this."

"I know you were, but yesterday you were too weak."

"Too weak for what?" Chloe asked without looking up. No one answered her.

"I don't care how awful these men's plans may seem to some," Caro said firmly. "It's wrong to murder. And Jenny Besom didn't have a damn thing to do with Pritchett's plans. So she had to have been killed because she knew something."

"I agree with you," Damien answered. "This bokor is too dangerous. If he means to go after everyone in any way involved with Pritchett's business, as well as anyone who figures out what he's doing, he'll have a lot of blood on his hands. But mostly, *Schatz,* I'm concerned that he's after you. You don't even have anything to do with this."

"He must think I do. I was there when Pritchett was murdered." She turned things around in her head, considering. "He's changed his method, this bokor. His first murders, of Pritchett and his immediate family, were gruesome beyond belief. It was intended to scare everyone associated with the project. But apparently people haven't become scared off, so he's murdering in a more stealthy fashion, trying to make it look natural. And that means he doesn't intend to stop."

She remembered only too clearly what had happened on the street yesterday and was fairly certain the newest death had been caused in just the same way. She could barely repress a shudder when she remembered that feeling of cold crawling into her very bones and her inability to draw a breath no matter how hard she tried.

She looked at Jude. "Tell Terri to look for evidence that his breathing was interrupted somehow. Besom's, too. That's what was happening to me."

Jude nodded and pulled out his phone.

She looked at Damien. "Not that this is going to help us solve this or stop it. We need to get to work."

"I know, *Schatz*. But this is a time for supreme patience. Everything in it's time and proper place. Then we go hunting in earnest."

"We've been hunting all along and where has it gotten us? We're no closer to the bokor."

"I agree traditional methods haven't worked. That's why we're going to use older methods. No power can be used without leaving traces. None. It rends the fabric between the normal and the paranormal. It leaves a trail. It may not be easy to follow, but I should be in a better position to follow it later. I used to be very good at that."

"Really?" She lifted an eyebrow, trying to imagine it. "One of your duties?"

"There are always those who seek to pervert power. They have to be dealt with, just like this bokor."

"What happens when we find him?"

"We'll have to fight him power for power. Unless you just want to shoot him, which I doubt. It wouldn't get rid of the elemental he's loosed, though. It would just leave it directionless."

"That doesn't sound good either."

"Trust me, it's not. These forces have no conscience. Without direction they can inflict a lot of harm simply because they don't care. They simply act."

"Sounds worse than a demon to me," Jude remarked.

"You can at least argue with a demon," Damien replied. "Maybe not successfully, but there's consciousness there. These forces are truly elemental. They exist without any kind of being, despite the writings of Paracelsus. They are the building blocks of this reality, without will of their own unless called on. And once they are called on, unless they are returned to their original state, they function beyond their normal duties often to the detriment of anything they encounter. It's like starting a volcanic eruption. The volcano doesn't care what it destroys—it's a power of nature, doing its work. But what if you were to divert it to wipe out a village? It would keep on in the same direction, heedless of how much it destroys." He paused. "Did that help clarify?"

It certainly did for Caro, and the dimensions of the problem now seemed larger to her than ever. A force of nature without conscience or intelligence, directed to a task, running around without direction, perhaps murdering anyone it encountered.... That was plenty bad.

Damien apparently read her response on her face, or smelled it on her. "Releasing elementals is something a good mage seldom does. There are kinder, gentler powers to call on. But for something like this..." He shrugged.

"For something like this," Caro replied harshly, "you need something without conscience or intelligence. We've got to get going."

It was as if these most recent murders were some kind of last straw for her. She didn't care if Damien wanted to tie her naked to a flagpole in public if it would do something to end this. Too many people had died, including innocent children. Yes, she was scared and nervous, but not just about herself anymore. If this bokor wasn't stopped soon, he might go for more extreme measures, killing other people's families and leaving absolutely no way for the police to find him.

For the first time it occurred to her to be glad that elemental had attached itself to her. Frightened as she had been, much as it had shaken her world, it remained that if it hadn't attached to her in some way, there'd be no one and nothing to stop this bokor because no one would have even suspected something paranormal was at work here.

"Ready?" Damien asked her.

"As ready as I'll ever be."

Jude drove them in his battered car to her place, where he set about restoring the wards. Caro stood watching him, noting that he seemed to be taking extra care this time. He placed a mark over every door and window, then marked every single wall, murmuring something quietly as he did so.

Given her unorthodox upbringing, she didn't have a clue as to what he might be saying. Latin? She wasn't sure.

"Okay," Jude said finally. "You're sealed up as tight as I can make you." He passed a small bottle to Damien. "Seal the door again after I leave, top, bottom and sides. Then do your own protections."

"Thanks," Damien said, accepting the bottle. "I don't feel the elemental in here now. Do you, Caro?"

She reached out with her burgeoning senses and after a moment shook her head. "No, it's not here."

"Seal up quickly after me," Jude suggested. "Don't give it an opening." Then he reached into his pocket and pulled out a small brass crucifix. "I know this isn't your tradition, Damien, but every bit helps. Put it in the room with you."

Then he left. As Damien quickly marked the door according to Jude's instructions, Caro felt her cheeks heat and her stomach flutter. "How much does he know about what we're doing?"

Damien finished the door, sealed the bottle and looked at her with a wry smile. "Only what he suspects. We haven't discussed it. Second thoughts, Caro?"

"I'm just, well, uncomfortable with all of this. It seems so…so…"

"Alien to you?" he suggested.

"I guess."

"Well, it will be my pleasure to ensure you don't feel that way for long. All we are going to do is make love, and our point is to reach the highest levels of delight, where the life force flows freely and without inhibition. Does that sound so bad?"

She hesitated, the butterflies resuming their agitation in her stomach. "I'm just not used to putting things like this on a calendar."

"Only because you've never had the opportunity before. Imagine you are going on a date with someone who attracts you. Don't you spend the entire evening wondering how it will end? Don't you hope and perhaps expect that your date will make a pass?"

He had a point. Sort of. She drew a couple of deep breaths. "Promise you won't tell anyone about this."

"Why would I? This is between us and no one else."

He set the bottle down and crossed the room, moving slowly enough that he didn't startle her. "Think of it as a date," he purred. "And all I am going to do right now is kiss you. Then I'll prepare the room."

The kiss, as always, left her light-headed and hungry for more, much more. Damn, he was good at that. The need filled her, a sweet ache that refused to dissipate even as she followed him around, watching his preparations.

He chose her bedroom, and she knew instantly he intended to tie her to her bedposts. The thought of *that* caused her insides to clench in anticipation now, and the uneasiness seemed to have faded to the background.

He stripped her bed of everything, then spread out a brand-new white sheet, stretching it to fit the corners tightly. A new pillow popped out of another bag and was centered on the bed.

Apparently he was serious about removing detritus.

Thick white candles appeared on every flat surface in large numbers. *A ring of fire around the bed,* she realized.

He added an incense burner with a long stick of incense and ignited it with a pocket lighter. Within moments the room started to fill with the unmistakable scent of frankincense. Her nose twitched a little, then settled down.

He glanced at her, as if gauging her response, then brought out rolls of wide white ribbon. He held out one to her.

She took it, surprised at how soft it felt. "Satin?" she asked.

"Yes. All natural. All of this has to be natural. Even the candles are beeswax. I promise not to bind you too tightly. It won't hurt. It's just that I have to protect you."

She stroked the ribbon, imagining it twined around her wrists and probably her ankles. Her stomach churned nervously, but lower down she felt that sweet ache renew. *Quit fighting it,* she thought. She wanted it, nervous or not. And the fabric was so soft as to feel sensual in itself.

She passed the roll back to him, watched him cut long, long lengths of it and tie it around all four of her bedposts. Apparently he meant what he said about not tying her too tightly. Looking at those lengths, she knew she would have some room to move.

Her mouth was starting to grow dry, and she didn't think it was from a need for water. Conflicting needs buzzed in her, and whether she was longing for this or not, she couldn't entirely get rid of her nerves.

He finished his task in the most surprising way: he sprinkled rose petals across the bed and around the room.

Their fragrance was heady and joined the incense to create a perfume of unearthly beauty.

Beside the bed, he placed a few vials. Then, after surveying everything, he turned to her with a smile and held out his hand.

"Come," he said gently.

Her hand was trembling as she took his. He drew her close and kissed her deeply, causing her to tremble in a very different way. "I know this is all new to you," he murmured as his lips brushed teasingly against hers. "But it is beautiful beyond imagining. Try to trust me, *Schatz.* I'll lead you every step of the way."

She couldn't find her voice but managed a nod. She wanted him more than she had ever wanted anything in her life. Facing that, how could she not face the rest?

He picked up a garment bag from where he had laid it over a chair, then carried it as they went to her small bathroom. It was designed for a couple, with two sinks, but hardly big enough to hold them both at the same time. He hung the garment bag from the hook on the back of the door.

"Adjust the water to your liking," he said. "I have no way to tell if it's the right temperature for you."

Her mouth now felt like the Sahara, parched almost to cracking. Without a word, she went to turn on the faucet in the tub. With only one knob, it was easy to set because she knew exactly where she liked it. Then she turned on the shower and closed the curtain to prevent splashing.

When she turned around, Damien was pulling two long white robes from the garment bag and hanging them. "One for each of us," he said, giving her a smile.

But only after the shower, she thought. First she had to do something she'd never done with him before: get naked.

She gripped her sweater with shaking hands, prepared to strip, but he stopped her.

"Allow me," he said. "You won't be alone long in your nudity."

She licked her lips, dropped her arms and waited.

"You are so beautiful," he murmured. Leaning toward her, he kissed her again, this time deeply and passionately. Her lingering doubts fled before the thrust of his tongue and the feeling of his hands wandering over her back, breasts and belly. She sighed, the breath caught by his mouth, and felt welcome heat flood her, draining her last doubts.

Some part of her felt she had been made for this moment. It seemed so right.

He moved slowly, carrying her step by step up the mountain of passion. His every move seemed strangely languorous as if they had all the time in the world. She remembered what he had said about spending hours to make sure everything was perfect, and apparently he had meant it.

By the time he began to lift her sweater over her head, her entire body was thrumming with need. Nor did he give her a moment to feel shy. As soon as her sweater was gone, her bra vanished and his hands covered her breasts, teasing and squeezing until she threw her head back and began to melt.

"Gently, slowly," he murmured.

"You're not making it easy."

A quiet laugh escaped him. "Good," he said. "But there's absolutely no rush. None at all. In fact, I want to avoid it."

The butterflies had vanished, leaving nothing in their wake but longing and an impatience she tried to tamp down. Not that Damien was going to let her hurry a single moment.

His hands continued their wandering, fueling the ache deep within her, cherishing her as much as they stirred her. It was as if he were memorizing her every curve.

Then, in an instant so fast she didn't see it happen, his shirt vanished, and their naked chests met. She had just a moment to enjoy the view of his smoothly muscled torso, then he tugged her close, pressing her breasts to him as his mouth returned to plundering hers in a deep kiss.

Oh, could he kiss!

She lifted her hands and traced the smooth contours of his back, reveling in the strength she felt there, as well as the slight coolness of his skin. He felt solid everywhere she touched him. And for now, he let her touch.

It occurred to her that he must be exercising great restraint right now, considering that he felt it necessary to bind her later to prevent her from waking his predatory nature.

Drowsy with need, she tilted her head back and looked at him from passion-weighted eyelids. "Am I making this harder for you?"

"You are making this an absolute delight."

Then he knelt, kissing her belly, sending a powerful shudder of longing through her. Never had a touch or kiss there seemed so intimate or exciting.

She felt the snap on her jeans give way, and caught her breath in anticipation as he began to pull the denim down. Its slow scrape against her skin was as sensual as any touch he gave her. She shivered again and resisted the urge to hold his head close, trying to remember why he needed her to be still.

But remaining still was turning into a torture of its own, a very special one.

Lips followed the fabric downward, trailing along her thighs, brushing briefly but so temptingly against the thatch of hair between her legs. The lightest of touches, it ignited her needs to an even higher level. How was she going to stand this for hours? How could she not?

Already she felt as if she had been transformed into a knot of nearly mindless need.

His own clothes disappeared at last, and she managed to open her eyes to take him in. He was a perfect picture of masculinity. His staff was already rigid, assuring her she was not alone at this peak just below heaven, but when she reached out to grasp him, he stayed her hand.

"Soon, *Schatz*," he murmured. "Soon."

Then he swept her up and deposited her in the shower. An instant later he stood there with her and pulled the curtain closed.

"We can do this whichever way you prefer," he said.

"What do you mean?" She didn't want to make decisions anymore. Talking had become a huge effort.

"We can either wash ourselves or wash each other."

For an instant, shyness reared its head, but then she realized just how much she wanted to run her hands over every inch of him, to come to know him intimately before it was too late and he tied her up. Soon she wouldn't have this option.

"I'll wash you," she said thickly.

He smiled and passed her the cloth and bar of soap. She wet the cloth and soaped it and began.

His chest and shoulders first, all the way down to his waist. She luxuriated in the freedom to touch him this way and loved the soapy way the washcloth passed over each of his contours. Then, when she reached his waist, she gave him a little nudge to turn him around.

It tickled her that she might be teasing him as much as

he teased her. Again the cloth passed from shoulders down to waist. Then she hesitated.

"Everywhere, *Schatz,*" he said with unmistakable emphasis.

Taking her courage in her hands, literally, and helped along by the heavy throbbing of hunger in her own loins, she bent to scrub his legs and feet. Then slowly she straightened and began to rub his buttocks, soaping the cloth once more.

"Everywhere," he prompted again and leaned forward a bit.

Oh, man. She didn't know…and then she did. She slipped the cloth into the cleft and rubbed her hand along him, all the way to his testicles, then back again. It thrilled her to feel him shudder with pleasure.

Then he turned, presenting his front. Tenderly, her inhibitions finally gone, she captured his genitals and washed them, drawing her hand and the soapy cloth along his erection. His body jumped in response, and she felt a surge of power at being able to make him respond this way.

Then it was her turn, and she was certain he didn't miss an inch of her either. When he had her bend so he could attend her bottom the way she had washed his, she felt so exquisitely exposed and so perfectly cherished that she thought her knees would give way from the pleasure.

Then at last he scrubbed her womanhood with a surprising roughness, but the roughness turned out to be welcome, pouring more heat through her veins.

No one had ever learned her this intimately. Ever.

Then he washed her hair and his own, and they took turns standing under the spray until all the soap was gone.

"Are you okay?" he asked her, taking her again in his arms.

"I'm wonderful."

He smiled. "You certainly are."

He moved quickly then, turning off the water and stepping with her onto the mat. Then came a new form of delightful torture as he scrubbed her dry with clean towels and squeezed the last of the water from her hair. He wasted a lot less time drying himself.

At this point she'd have walked into the bedroom naked to be bound without a single bit of hesitation. She hadn't guessed she could sustain such a fever pitch of desire for so long, but somehow he kept her there on a high plateau, every inch of her begging for more.

He draped one of the white robes over her. Only when she was wearing it did she realize that it was two pieces of cloth joined at the shoulders and the waist by ties.

So easy to remove. And his appeared to be just the same.

He took her hand. "Are you ready, Caro?"

She wondered how she could be any readier. She would have gladly fallen on the damp bathroom floor to be taken by him right now. The ache between her legs had grown hard and insistent, throbbing in a way that demanded an answer. How could she want this any more?

"Yes," she whispered, all she could manage.

He led her slowly into her bedroom, then guided her to lie down on her bed. One by one, he bound her wrists and her ankles, snugly but not painfully, and a new spear of hunger shot through her.

As she lay there, rendered helpless by his bonds, it occurred to her that there was plenty to be said for bondage. She needed to make no decisions—she needed only to experience. It filled her with an even deeper hunger and a delicious sense of freedom.

Damien lit every candle in the room, creating a ring of fire and ring of warm light, bright yet cozy. The candles also helped warm the room even more and kept Caro's damp hair from feeling chilly around her face.

Then Damien returned to her, his own face looking slumberous with passion, and he reached for the ties at her shoulders.

Her heart quickened, and she drew a breath. Almost instinctively she tried to pull her hands closer to her body and found she could move them only a few inches.

"See?" he murmured. "You are truly helpless to my whims. I promise you will like them, even the unexpected ones."

Before she could wonder what he meant, he pulled the robe down to her waist, exposing her breasts. She wanted to squirm as the lack of control warred with passion in her. He took one of the vials and sprinkled the contents onto his hands. Then he knelt on the bed, straddling her, and began to rub her with oil, starting just behind her ears and working his way slowly down.

She caught her breath again as her skin seemed to heat. The clenching at her core renewed with a vengeance. Every stroke of his hands painted her with fresh fire, filling her with need.

She felt her nipples harden before he even reached them. She felt her labia swell with eagerness, and then grow damp. She was ready, so ready, but he had just begun.

When his hands at last found her breasts, she thought she would come right then. Almost, but not quite, as he traced her over and over, working the oils into her skin, ratcheting her need to heights she had never imagined.

Then he astonished her by pinching her nipples. At first she cried out, shocked by the sharp pain. But pain quickly gave way to a new kind of pleasure, and with each pinch and twist of his fingers, her hips began to rock in helpless rhythm, needing, no, *demanding,* more.

But still he lingered, tormenting her in the most delightful way, refusing to hurry at all. She forgot everything except the touch of his hands and the endlessly building hunger within her.

Damien watched her succumb, his own pleasure mounting. The most exquisite torment of all was making himself wait, and he felt it in every cell. His staff was so swollen now it felt as if it might burst, but satisfaction was a long way away.

He gave himself up to the pleasure of drawing out her responses, teaching her new sensations, particularly of how pain could heighten pleasure. He had seen her initial shock when she'd felt him pinch her nipples, but now he pinched even harder and she writhed and groaned helplessly.

And there was more to come.

It had been millennia since he had devoted himself to a woman this way in this ceremony. He murmured the incantations and prayers under his breath so as not to disturb her, but he still remembered them as if it were yesterday. And what he remembered most from his tradition was that women were truly the source of the life force as no man could ever be. While a man played a role, a woman grew life to fruition in her own body as no man ever could.

This woman was full of the life force, and as a man he needed some of it for himself. He had other powers that he could now share with her, but he needed her strength flowing through him as well, the most important strength of all. As a vampire, he knew himself to have less life force than most.

He needed, first and foremost, to unlock that power in them both, to share it between them, and to do that he had to carry her so far beyond the mundane world that the key would turn in the lock all by itself.

He lost all track of time, but time didn't matter. What mattered was the way she writhed so helplessly under his ministrations, and the way he responded to her arousal. They were headed to a place where time ceased to have meaning, where nothing would exist except themselves, their union and their mutual celebration of life.

She had such beautiful breasts, he thought as he massaged them and pinched them again. Not too large, not too small, firm yet soft to his touch. He paused to place a few drops of oil in her navel and then work them outward and upward.

He liked having her helpless, liked teasing her to an incredible pitch. A vampire in more ways than one, he soaked up her feelings as surely as he would have drunk her blood. They filled him and carried him along with her until her throbbing became his, her need enhancing his own.

Some instinct told him it was time. He pulled away the last of her gown, revealing her beauty in all its glory to his eyes. *Exquisite.* His own body responded with a gripping, hammering need.

Then he bent to oil her legs, starting at her small feet, rubbing between her toes, working the muscles and joints gently until she arched with pleasure. Working his way slowly up and down her legs, he watched the thatch of hair between her legs grow dewy, filled his nose with her scents, so erotic now, and reached for paradise with her.

Finally, ages later, the moment had arrived. He parted her legs gently, turning them outward so that her lovely core was fully exposed to him.

She murmured something, but her eyes were closed, and he saw no resistance in her face.

Kneeling between her legs, so she could not clamp them together, he reached out with oiled hands and ran his fingers along her labia, first on the outermost part, drawing a deep groan from her. Again and again he repeated the caress, watching her swell for him. When at last her clitoris had engorged until it could no longer be concealed, he reached for a bundle of soft leather thongs.

Swinging them gently, he slapped them against her most tender flesh. Her eyes flew open, but her body bucked helplessly. He waited a moment, giving her a chance to object, but she didn't.

He swung the thongs repeatedly, lightly until she was rising to meet them as if she wanted them. Then he swung them a little harder, knowing they would sting.

Again her eyes widened. "Damien…"

"I can stop, but I don't want to," he answered.

She looked at him, drowsy, inflamed, unsure, but then her eyes fluttered closed.

He whipped her again, harder, and a deep groan escaped her. With each flick of leather, he throbbed himself, in time with her pleasure, feeling her need grow. He didn't know how much longer he would be able to hold out himself, but that was the point.

Caro could scarcely believe she was allowing herself to be whipped in this most intimate fashion, but disbelief gave way quickly to the incredible pleasure every stroke of that leather brought her. Stinging, yet good, carrying her to a place beyond thought and time until all that existed was the ache he kept building with every stroke. Her internal clenching grew painful, more painful than the strokes of that whip. At any moment she would…

Then he stopped. Before she registered that the stinging slaps were gone, she felt his fingers on her, stroking her, slipping inside her, feeding her frenzy with contrasting gentleness. Again and again he just barely rubbed her, opened her, then pulled away.

The next thing she realized, his mouth was on her, licking her every fold repeatedly, dancing around the most delicate bundle of nerves, a bundle that was begging for him. She felt his tongue enter her and arched up against him, wanting him deeper, wanting more, needing more, and desperate for any way he chose to give it to her.

She could no longer tell where she was, where she ended and he began. She existed out of time, in some place where there was nothing at all but passion, need, hunger, desire.

"Damien," she heard herself groan as if from a distance. "Please…" Never before in her life had she begged.

She gasped as she felt him nip her clitoris, a pleasure-pain so intense she felt as if she had been launched from a catapult.

He murmured something and then, at last, he slid up over her, sliding into her all too ready and wet depths, filling her body, filling her soul. He pumped into her, slowly at first, giving her a chance to fully enjoy the feelings of union.

But then he speeded up, carrying her away, erasing everything from her mind but the point at which their bodies joined, making her forget everything except that intense concentration of feeling.

Up, up, until she could no longer catch her breath. Then with one deep thrust, he caused her to shatter into a million flaming pieces as if she had fallen right into the sun.

Stars exploded behind her eyelids, her body gave one last huge clench and then she fell into empty space, drifting as light as feather down.

Chapter 13

Caro returned to reality slowly. She discovered she was unbound and wrapped in Damien's naked body as he cradled her close.

When she opened her eyes, the view over his shoulder told her the time. Nearly three in the morning? She felt a little shock, as she had certainly not been aware of how many hours had passed.

Her movement drew his attention. "Are you all right?" he asked.

"I've never been better," she admitted frankly. "That was something else."

A quiet laugh escaped him.

"Did it work?" she asked.

"On which level?"

"Power?"

"Oh, definitely." He moved a little away from her and held up his arm. "See?"

Indeed she could. Those crackles of electricity she had

before seen only around his fingers now danced along his entire arm. They vanished when he lowered it and drew her back into his embrace.

"Now reach out," he suggested. "See if you've been enhanced."

She did. It grew easier every time, and moments after she closed her eyes and sent her senses forth, she gasped. "I can see through Jude's wards now."

"It worked," he said quietly. "We combined to create greater power in us both."

"We combined to have one helluva time."

He laughed, one of those rare laughs it always made her so happy to hear. "That we did," he agreed.

Much as she didn't want to move a muscle yet, much as she wanted to stay wrapped in him and savor the afterglow, she said, "We need to go hunting."

"Indeed we do, but I'm not sure there are enough hours left. So relax a little while longer."

"I thought you said this would take only a couple of hours."

"Usually. But I wanted to share it all with you, and take my time. Are you angry?"

"Angry? How could I be after the most amazing experience of my life?"

"You make me happy, *Schatz*. Very happy. Thank you."

"No, thank *you*." She snuggled in closer, telling herself that if they didn't have time tonight, they didn't have time. He would know. "Will our power weaken by tomorrow?"

"No, it'll last at least a few days. We'll be as strong tomorrow night as right now. Ready to face a bokor."

"So we won't need to repeat this?"

Again he laughed. "We can repeat this anytime you want."

That sounded suspiciously like a promise, but she

warned herself not to take it that way. He'd already said he couldn't give her what she wanted, that he would be returning to Cologne. She refused to think about losing him, though, because the mere thought of it made her heart ache.

Oh, crap, had she gone and given her heart to a vampire who didn't want it? *No,* she assured herself. That wasn't possible. It couldn't have happened so quickly. No way.

No, she was just feeling the afterglow of the best sexual experience of her life. She was so very glad she hadn't allowed fear to hold her back. Who would have thought that she'd respond in such a way to being bound and whipped?

The memory of the gentle whipping between her legs made her cheeks heat a little. No, that thought would never have entered her head. And now that she knew how it could make her feel, she was going to want a lot more of it. A lot.

Too bad Damien and his clever little whip would be leaving. Especially since she didn't know if she'd ever be able to give anyone that much trust again.

She certainly couldn't imagine having done this with anyone in her past.

Damien had opened entire new worlds to her in a short space of time, and as she rested against him, she honestly wondered what had happened to the woman who had wanted nothing more than to become a detective.

That Caro seemed to have vanished. She hoped it was only temporary, because after Damien left she was going to have to pick up the pieces of her real life. She certainly wasn't going to become one of those women who ran shops full of esoterica simply because she had discovered the powers her grandmother had always told her she had.

But maybe she could find ways to use her newfound skills to solve crimes. At least then it might be easier to handle.

Jude seemed to make a business of this kind of thing. Maybe she could help him as she had time.

Then she realized she was planning for Damien's departure. Her throat ached and her chest grew tight. She didn't want to think about that now, didn't want to be planning it. There was time left, and if she were smart, she'd set her sights on enjoying every last bit of it.

"*Schatz?* What saddened you?"

"Nothing."

"I can smell it," he reminded her.

"Damn your nose. It was just a passing thought. Nothing important."

Without even looking at him she could tell he didn't really believe her. She could almost feel him deciding whether to question her further. Maybe her senses *were* growing.

"If you're worried about another death," he said slowly, "we can at least hunt for the bokor tonight, although I'm not at all certain we'll find him in time to confront him. Sadly, I have a limitation at dawn. It'd be very bad to get into the middle of the fight and then have to quit, giving him another day to prepare after he knows what he's up against."

"I get it," she admitted reluctantly. "No, I see the point."

"Then?"

"Nothing. Truly nothing." Because there was no way she was going to admit how much she wanted him to stay for a long, long time. How little she wanted to give him up.

He'd not only shown her new worlds, but he'd filled some emptiness in her that she hadn't even known existed until him.

But what was that emptiness? Not having a lover? Not acknowledging her powers? Or a combination of both? She supposed she would get her answer only when he left.

"You know," he said, distracting her from her morose line of thought, "I'd believed I lost my powers."

"Really?" She tipped her face back to look at him. "Why?"

"Because I hadn't been able to summon them for so long. I thought perhaps centuries of being a vampire had caused them to wane. Then when I'd been near you for a few days, I could feel them start to come back. I think it was being near your powers that reawakened mine."

"Awesome. But I don't have that much power."

"You have a great deal more than you yet know. Since I met you I sensed it. Apart from your beauty, it was one of the first things to engage my attention. It was at a low level, to be sure, but it was there. You have no idea how long it's been since I met someone with innate power."

"There must be others. What about this bokor?"

"I don't know if his power is innate, or something he's built through spells and practice. There's a difference. People like you just have it, whether you ever use it or not. I was like that once. Apparently I am again, thanks to you."

"I'd feel a whole lot happier if I knew how to direct and use these powers. Right now it's hit and miss. I'm never sure of what I'm doing or whether it's right."

"Close your eyes."

She did so, wondering why.

"Now imagine this power of yours as a light at your very center. See it. Feel its heat."

She tried, and gradually she could clearly envision a white flame at her center. And little by little she felt its warmth.

"Some need spells and incantations," he said quietly. "Some use them for focus. Some use them to call upon powers they don't have themselves but can summon. A mage like you needs no spells. In fact, you can make your very own if you concentrate. So now imagine that light flowing down your arm and out of your fingers. Feel it."

It took a while.

"Don't try too hard—you can stymie it. It's part of you like your blood. Let it flow."

As soon as he said "Let it flow," something in her seemed to shift and click into place. She lifted her arm a bit and felt the warm light moving down it to her fingertips.

"You see?" he asked.

She opened her eyes and nearly gasped when she saw faint white light shooting from her fingertips. "Oh…" she breathed.

"Now think of it doing something, preferably innocuous."

She saw one of the candles still burning on her dresser. Pointing her finger at it, she imagined the light snuffing the flame. At once the candle went out.

"I can do it!" Amazement filled her.

"Your grandmother was right. You're a powerful mage, Caro. Try something else."

So she pointed her finger at her dresser again, and thought of the top drawer opening. At first she feared she would fail, but then, jerkily, the drawer pulled out.

"Woohoo!" An excited cry escaped her.

Damien laughed and hugged her close. For a moment she luxuriated in the embrace, but questions remained. "What about the bokor?" she asked. "What do I do when we meet him?"

"It's simple, *Schatz*. I'll fight him because I have the experience. What I need you to do is see the darkness that's gathered around him, and imagine your light extinguishing it."

"That sounds easy enough."

"It's never easy when power meets power." His voice

had grown deadly serious. "Don't go in there tomorrow night thinking any of it will be easy. Whether this bokor has powers of his own or has simply summoned them, there will be a fight and we could lose. He clearly has a lot of experience, too."

The warning sobered her. "Should I be scared?"

"It's never wise to go into this afraid. Fear weakens us. But yes, things could go wrong. Very wrong."

She thought about that. "Well, that's not so very different from being a cop. Every time I make a traffic stop or answer a call, things could go wrong. I'm used to that."

He ran his hand down her back, a cool touch. She liked the cool silkiness of his skin and caresses. Not cold, not icy, just cool. She wiggled closer and he sighed.

"Your warmth is like heaven to me," he said. "Like heaven."

So she wrapped herself even more closely around him, as if she could surround him in her warmth. It seemed to her, really, that she had little enough to offer him. He had powers she could barely imagine, he had abilities beyond the human and he was sexy with every breath he took. The world must be his for the asking.

"So I'm just food," she said finally, because some aching, worried part of her needed to know.

"You insult me."

"I do?" She couldn't hide a spurt of irritation.

"You do. I may be a predator, I may need human blood to survive, but there's more to me than a jungle cat. I give thanks for every gift of blood. As for you…"

He suddenly rolled her over so that he lay on top of her. "As for you," he said, dipping for a quick kiss, "you're far more than food to me. Far more. I like you. I like being with you. I like arguing with you. In fact, I like you too damn much for the good of either of us."

With that she had to be content, she supposed. At least he wasn't just after her blood, as he so amply proved in the next hour as he made love to her all over again, this time without bonds, this time without ceremony or ritual. This time he held her still only by gripping her wrists gently.

He still managed to carry her to the stars as he united them in the mystery of love.

Caro collapsed on the couch at Jude's office, having agreed to do nothing foolish during the day. Chloe greeted that promise with a snort, but Caro ignored her. Tonight they would face the bokor. That was enough to keep her in line until later. Regardless of her promise to Damien, she knew for a fact that she had no intention of taking any unnecessary risk until the right time.

Chloe ordered them some breakfast, and remarked that Caro looked exhausted.

"Just sleepy. I was up all night."

"Why do I find that easy to believe? Vampires." But her tone was teasing. "Actually, I'm going to need some sleep today, too, since I gather tonight is the night. Jude will want everyone on deck."

Caro hesitated. "What's your view of working with a vampire? Or living with one."

"Uh-oh," Chloe said.

"What *uh-oh?*"

"Another one bites the dust. In the past year I've seen three women fall for vampires."

"And?"

"They're all married to them now. Don't ask me how it works. I only see enough of Terri and Jude to figure out how they work it out. Basically, Terri took permanent night duty at the M.E.'s office, so they work the same hours and fit everything else in around the sun. Seems to make them happy enough."

"And the others?"

"So far so good. A few months isn't a great sample, though."

Caro nodded, taking it in. "Were they claimed?"

"Oh, sweetie," Chloe said, "now that's the thing."

"Why?"

"Because they were all claimings. And you have absolutely no idea how hard vampires fight it. One of our friends, Luc? He totally lost his mind when his claimed mate died. He was so far gone he kidnapped me and kidnapped another woman too to try to get his vengeance."

"No."

"Yes. He was willing to do just about anything to end his pain, including asking another vampire to kill him."

"What happened?"

"Well…" Chloe smiled faintly. "However unwillingly, he got involved in a dustup we had here a few months ago. Some rogues—vampires who don't want to obey the rules about not treating humans as cattle and slaves—tried to take over the city and run Jude out. Luc came to give us a warning and the next thing I knew, he was up to his eyeballs in another claiming. Maybe you'll meet her. Dani."

"And they're married, too?"

"Yup."

"How the heck does a vampire get married?" She knew the rules. Birth certificates, residency, filling out forms in offices that were closed by dark.

"I do a little computer magic, make the legal licenses, and then Father Dan marries them."

"*Father* Dan?"

"Hang around with us for a while," Chloe suggested.

"Jude fights demons. He has a few clergy who work with him."

"And they know he's a vampire?"

"Yes." Chloe's eyes danced. "Not everyone thinks they're soulless killers. Father Dan just considers it to be one of the mysteries, and I heard him tell Jude once that God has an odd sense of humor."

"Apparently so." Caro pondered all this new information. "I was thinking that I may not be so happy being an ordinary detective after this. Do you think Jude might want some part-time help? I mean, I'd still have to keep my regular job, but..." She hesitated.

"You've got a taste for the supernatural now. I get it. It's part of what drew me in." Chloe dropped her perkiness and showed an unusual intensity. "What I've seen working with Jude? People have no idea how much danger there is out there, or how lucky they are to have someone like Jude fighting for them."

"And Damien," Caro added.

"Damien for now," Chloe said. "Every so often he talks about going back to Germany. Would you even consider going with him?"

Well, that was the rub, wasn't it? Caro thought. Could she give up everything to follow him back to his life? And hadn't he said something about too many sacrifices killing love? "I don't know."

"Well, he could always stay here." Chloe shrugged. "You never know."

"There's nothing definite," Caro said, more to remind herself than Chloe. "Nothing at all."

"There never is until there is" was Chloe's philosophical comment. Then she added, "You know, they have to move every ten to fifteen years anyway. So maybe it's not as difficult for them."

"How come?"

"People start to notice that they're not aging. Sooner or later, they've got to move to a new place or risk outing themselves. So Damien's roots in Cologne might not be all that deep. I know when Jude decides its time to move on, he plans to follow wherever Terri can get a job. Assuming, of course, the place isn't already overpopulated by vampires."

"How so?"

"Didn't Damien tell you? They're territorial, first of all. And second, gathering in large numbers could make folks aware of them. Admittedly that's not as likely these days between vampire fetishists and the real vamps drinking canned blood. But there are four of them in this town right now, and sometimes I get the sense they might feel a bit crowded."

Which would probably drive Damien back to Cologne, Caro thought. She stifled a sigh, afraid of how Chloe would interpret it.

It was a relief when their breakfast arrived and she could turn the topic to something far safer. Damien had warned her that he couldn't be ordinary for her, and now she had to live with the consequences of that, however it came out.

She didn't think it was going to come out well for her.

With effort, she pushed all such thoughts aside. The important thing was to stop this bokor before someone else died. She was a cop, after all, and while these methods might be unorthodox, they were the only methods available to save lives.

She was dedicated to that, wasn't she? Totally and completely. Saving lives and catching criminals to make the public safer. She'd never counted the cost to herself before, and now would be a lousy time to start.

She knew all too well what could happen if you answered a call with your mind all mixed up or filled with irrational fear for yourself. That was a helluva good way to wind up dead.

The training of years took over and pushed aside the things that could weaken her or distract her. She finished eating, determined to catch enough sleep to make her feel fresh tonight.

She went to the bathroom before stretching out on the couch, and while there she tried what Damien had taught her.

She closed her eyes, imagining the white heat of power at her center, then directing it to flow along her arm. When she opened her eyes, she could see it. It worked.

She smiled, sure she was as ready as she could be for tonight.

Caro slept long and deeply on the couch that proved to be as comfortable as any bed. She awoke to hear Chloe ordering dinner and guessed that it couldn't be long until sunset.

She rose, stretched and headed for the bathroom to shower and change.

As she lathered herself under the spray, she remembered how erotic it had been when Damien had scrubbed her with a soapy washcloth, making her skin tingle, touching her intimately in ways no man had ever touched her before.

Odd to think of the liberties she had never shared with anyone, but then she had to admit most of her relationships had died before they'd gone on very long. She hadn't had a single one that had gotten to the point of sharing a shower.

It wasn't as if she'd never heard of lovers sharing a shower or bath before. She just hadn't wanted to do that with anyone until Damien. In fact, there were a lot of things she'd never even thought of trying until Damien.

Things like being tied up and helpless. Things like that delightful little whip of his. She could feel the sensitive tissues between her legs blossom at the memory, and she lingered a little while washing herself, reminding herself of how good it had felt.

Whole new worlds indeed.

Outside Caro found Chloe setting the table for three. "I didn't mean to wake you," Chloe said, "but it was time to order dinner."

"I needed to wake up. It's been a while since I've slept that long."

"I slept a lot, too. Can you check on the coffee? Terri can't start her day without it."

Caro returned a minute later with her own mug in hand. She could hear Chloe down the hall, paying the delivery-man for dinner—she shortly returned with a stack of foam containers.

"Italian tonight," Chloe announced. "I hope you like chicken marsala."

"I love it."

"These folks make it really well." She allowed Caro to take some of the containers and set them on the tiny table.

Three places for five people, Caro couldn't help but note. She was getting used to Damien not eating human food, but she wondered if it would seem odder over the long run to always be dining alone. Then she reminded herself she would probably never know. Chloe had reminded her, as if she needed reminding, that Damien intended to return home. Even if he were to ask her to join him, she doubted her willingness to give up the life she had built here. She had worked so hard to become a detective. What in the world would she do in another country?

Anticipated sorrow fluttered darkly around the edges

of her mind and heart, but she forced it away. There'd be plenty of time to face that after they dealt with this bokor. Right now she had to maintain her focus. She was about to go out on a dangerous job. After all these years, she'd learned to put aside everything except the task right in front of her. This was a matter of life or death.

The women ate at the table. The two vampires drank their dinners from glasses—better, Caro supposed, than downing it directly from a bag. It at least seemed more polite, she supposed. Certainly it allowed them to join the others even if they stayed on the sofa.

Conversation remained casual until Terri left for work. Then everyone gathered around the table, while Chloe carried leftovers into the kitchen.

"What's the plan?" Jude asked. "What do you need me to do?"

"I'm going to follow the power skeins directly to the bokor."

Jude looked at him. "You can do that? Why didn't you do that to begin with?"

"I didn't have the power. Now I do."

Jude glanced at Caro, a certain understanding in his golden gaze. "Ah. Okay. So you both have enhanced powers now."

"Yes," Damien answered. "And now I can follow the trail of this elemental right back to its source."

"And then?"

"Then I'm going to use every power at my disposal to weaken the bokor and send the elemental back."

Jude's smile was crooked. "You make it sound so easy."

"As I'm sure you know only too well, these things are never easy. Fighting power with power is always a touchy thing."

"And Caro?" Jude looked at her.

"She's going to back me up. She's found her power, Jude. All she has to do is direct it at the bokor or the elemental. It'll bolster what I do."

"The two of you together should be able to match a bokor."

"I hope we do better than match it. Otherwise we're lost."

Jude nodded. "And what do you want me to do?"

"Stay close with your oils and holy water. So far they've worked to keep the elemental back. I may need you to surround us with them when we have the elemental contained with the bokor."

"So it can't escape?"

"Exactly."

"But you'll be locked inside with it."

That was the point at which Caro felt butterflies in her stomach again. All of a sudden the chicken marsala didn't seem to be sitting well, and anxiety ran along her nerve endings.

"Locked inside with it?" she repeated. "That could be a mistake."

Damien turned to her and took both her hands in his. Strong hands, cool hands. She had a flash of memory at what they were capable of doing to her.

"We have to be inside with it. If we're outside, Jude's wards could be as much a wall to us as to it."

"But I can see beyond Jude's wards now," she reminded him.

"Seeing beyond them and casting power beyond them are two very different things."

She supposed she could understand that. So she was about to get locked inside a circle with an elemental and a bokor. Not her everyday sort of experience. Her mouth turned a bit dry as she considered every possible thing that could go wrong, and there were a multitude of them.

Damien's grip on her hands tightened. "I could fight them alone, *Schatz*."

The offer immediately stiffened her spine. "No. I won't have that. I've been tracking this thing for a week, people have been killed and it has to stop. If there's any chance my powers might make the difference, then I'm not staying out of this fight."

Damien searched her face and she tried to look as determined as she could. After a few seconds, he nodded.

"And I'm bringing my gun," she announced. "If necessary, I'm going to use it against this bokor."

Damien shook his head. "Your power is the whitest of lights, Caro. Don't dim it by bringing a weapon of violence with you, or violence in your heart. Please."

Everything in Caro rebelled. Going into a dangerous situation unarmed? It violated every precept of her training as a cop. On the other hand... She closed her eyes and felt for that light within her. It was still there and even seemed a little stronger now that she knew how to call upon it.

Maybe he was right. Her grandmother had always warned her about the way evil backfired. She had never thought of her gun as evil, merely as a tool to be used only in extreme circumstances, but perhaps it would have the wrong vibe for this job.

Finally she sighed, pulled the holster off her belt and laid it on the table.

Damien smiled. "Trust. It's important. Trust me, trust your own power."

She looked at her holstered piece and thought that was a whole lot of trust she had just put on the table.

At Damien's direction, she bundled up warmly against

the winter night. The two vampires, impervious to the cold, simply wore their usual leathers.

Outside they darted into a dark alley, then Damien lifted her on his back. She clung tightly as they climbed straight up a building. Rock climbers had nothing on a vampire, she thought. Not only did he seem to be able to cling where there was hardly a finger or toe hold, but he moved so swiftly that they reached the top of the building in an eyeblink. Even though she was getting used to the speed at which he could move, she was still astonished at how quickly he set her on her feet.

"Now?" asked Jude.

Damien didn't answer. He closed his eyes, murmuring something, and then held out his arm. Caro could see the blue sparks dancing along it, and from the expression on Jude's face he could, as well.

Still murmuring under his breath, Damien turned slowly, extending his arm as if it were a pointer. A minute ticked by, then he dropped his arm.

"To the west," he said. "The bokor hasn't moved since last I sensed his general direction. But I'll have to keep checking so I can home in on him."

Then they were off again, on a wild ride from Caro's perspective, but one she was beginning to love even though the cold wind of their movement threatened frostbite to her nose. She loved being wrapped around Damien this way, loved the way she could feel his muscles bunch and unbunch, so fast it was hard to believe any muscle could twitch that fast.

It felt like a speeded-up roller-coaster ride, leaps followed by gentle landings but enough that her stomach couldn't decide whether it was rising or falling. *Like being on a crazy elevator,* she thought, and she had a wild urge to laugh because she liked it. No amusement park would ever again seem exciting.

They paused again, and she took the time to get grounded, feet firmly planted, stomach settling, as she looked out over the rooftops. This wasn't a vantage she was used to, and it proved a bit difficult to get her bearings.

Damien was holding out his arm again, but this time he wiggled his fingers a bit, as if trying to get more detailed information.

She closed her eyes and reached out with her own senses, feeling for the elemental. It was nearby.

"Damien. It's here."

"I feel it," he agreed. "Jude? Sprinkle some of that holy water on us, will you?"

Jude obliged, pulling a spray bottle out of his pocket. He must have read the astonishment Caro felt on her face, or smelled it, because he smiled faintly. She still had to get used to that smelling part.

"It's efficient," he said as he walked around her, spraying. After he sprayed Damien, he handed the bottle to Caro. "Do me, too, if you don't mind."

A moment of absurdity, she thought as she used an ordinary spray bottle to cover Jude in holy water.

Then she closed her eyes and reached out. "It pulled back a bit."

"Let's go," Damien announced. "Not much farther." He swung Caro up onto his back as if she weighed nothing at all and the roller-coaster ride began again.

Fear fluttered in her stomach as she wondered if she would survive this night.

Chapter 14

When at last they stopped, some deep instinct told her they were in the right place.

They walked cautiously to the parapet and looked down on the street below. Caro gasped as she recognized the shop. "Alika! Not Alika!"

At once she thought of the talisman in her pocket and pulled it out. As she started to hurl it away, Damien snapped his arm out and stopped her.

"You said you felt nothing ill about the gris-gris."

"I didn't. But if she's behind this…"

"We don't know she's behind this. Not at all. I just know it started here. It could be someone else. Regardless, if she's part of this, she gave you the talisman for protection. Maybe she wanted to protect you from the force she unleashed. Or maybe she just wanted to protect you from something else she was aware of."

Caro tightened her grip on the talisman, hesitating. It

was true they couldn't be sure Alika was the bokor. It was equally true that she had sensed nothing evil about the pouch in her hand. More confident in her special senses, she checked it once again. It still glowed with a lavender light and seemed to offer no threat. Slowly, she returned it to her pocket. "It didn't protect me that day on the street," she remarked.

"But that elemental may have been strengthened. Or perhaps you survived only because it couldn't do its worst work."

She looked at Damien. "You don't feel anything bad from it?"

He shook his head. "We don't discard anything that might be helpful until we're sure it's not."

"Okay, then."

Jude crouched beside Damien. "You're sure it's in that building?"

"Most definitely. I can't tell exactly where it's coming from, though. But it's definitely emanating from there."

"Then let's go. Carefully. I'll surround the building just as soon as you're close enough."

Just before they descended the building, Damien drew Caro close. "Know this. I'll keep you safe at any price. Trust your instincts about what to do. And don't use any more power until we know who we're facing. Just as I can sense the use of it, the bokor may, as well."

She nodded and swallowed hard. This was it. An experience beyond her imaginings. She had at least been able to imagine the ritual he had suggested, but for this she had no known paradigm. This would be so totally and completely outside her realm of experience that it staggered her.

What had he meant by protecting her at any cost? Her heart squeezed and she grabbed his arm. "Damien? Don't do anything foolish on my behalf. Please."

He smiled and brushed a chilly kiss against her cold lips. "It's certainly not my intention."

That had to satisfy her, because he quite clearly wasn't about to make promises of any kind except that he would keep her safe.

She didn't like that mentality. Partners were supposed to look out for each other. A joint effort. She should have made that clear from the outset.

Well, she promised *herself* that she'd have his back no matter what. And clearly he felt he needed some backup or he would have insisted on doing this alone. Vampire or not, he still had plenty of male arrogance about him at times.

Then she noticed something. "Wait," she whispered.

"What?"

"Don't you feel it? Listen."

"To what?" Damien asked, then said, "Oh."

There were no sounds at all, as if they'd been caught in a soundproof bubble. A glance down at the street, despite the early hour, showed that no one was about.

"We've been cut off," she murmured.

"Yes." Damien closed his eyes. "The bokor knows we're here."

"Damn it," Jude said.

"He's drawing power." Damien's eyes snapped open, and now they were as dark as the depths of space. "It's going to be a helluva fight. Caro…"

"Don't even think it. I'm going with you. Only an idiot goes into a dangerous situation without backup, and you're not an idiot."

He gave her a crooked smile. "I would die for you."

But would he live for her? she wondered. The question was painful. No time for that. "You're not an idiot," she repeated.

"No," he said after a beat. "No, I'm not. But are you being unwisely stubborn?"

"I've never let my partner go into a situation without backup. I'm not going to start now."

He offered no more argument. Instead, he stood quietly, as if feeling the world around them, but he did nothing to display his powers. Maybe he was using his vampire senses.

"There's no one nearby," he said eventually. "Except in that building."

"That's not one of the ones set for demolition, is it?" Caro asked.

"No," Jude said. "But that doesn't mean the bokor is simply acting to protect this one building. Friends or family could be involved. Or he or she could live in one of those buildings."

Caro nodded. "I was just wondering if we knew of a direct link."

"As of now, no."

"All right," Damien said. "I think it would be wise for us to get down from here out of sight of the bookshop. While we won't exactly be a surprise, we can at least avoid providing additional information."

"How about heading away a bit?" Jude suggested.

"Good idea," Damien agreed. Turning, he held out his hand to Caro. She could have sworn she felt an almost electric zap as they touched. Then she was on his back again and had no idea where they were going.

When next they alighted, she looked around and realized they were no longer on the same street.

The sense of being in a bubble had vanished.

"It might look like we missed him. Her. It," Damien said. He gave a quiet chuckle. "Maybe we bought a few minutes."

Perhaps out of deference to Caro, they made their way down a fire escape. Though it creaked and clanged, no one even looked out a window. Maybe, Caro thought, this was a neighborhood where seeing things could be dangerous. It wouldn't surprise her. As a cop she was intimately acquainted with how many people never saw or heard a thing, even when the ruckus should have wakened the dead.

Once they reached street level, they began walking at a human pace. Not that anyone would have seen if Damien had lifted Caro on his back and flown. The streets were amazingly empty, although that might be in part because of the bitter cold, and in part because this wasn't a safe part of town. Still, her instincts rose into high gear.

"There's something wrong," she said. "Cold, night, whatever, there's no part of this city where you don't see groups of young men out until the wee hours."

"Gangs?" Damien asked.

"Often, but not always. Something's going on. Maybe somebody put out the word to keep inside."

"Who would have the power to do that?"

"A bokor," Jude and Caro answered simultaneously. But Caro continued. "Someone everyone is terrified of."

"Then it seems we may have come to the right place."

"I thought you already knew we had."

He flashed a grin. "I do, but I'm just talking for the sake of talking."

"Are you nervous?"

"A bit. Aren't you?"

"I'd rather not think about it." It was true. Nerves were to be ignored, not fed. They were useful only insofar as they kept you alert. Beyond that, they could become a hindrance.

They covered two blocks before she again saw the storefront. She kept waiting to feel the bubble again but didn't. "We fooled them," she said.

"For a little while," Damien agreed. "Not much longer, though."

Only a few steps later, she felt it like ice on her neck. "The elemental is here."

"I feel it."

"Get to the door," Jude said. "Let me know when you're sure it's there with you and then I'll get to work warding the area."

"The bokor is already warding it," Caro said uneasily. "Do you feel it, Damien? The bubble is coming back."

He turned to Jude. "Can you sense it?"

"Only vaguely."

"Surround the entire block, then, as soon as I tell you. Caro, where's the elemental?"

"All around me," she answered as ice began to seep into her. "It's after me again."

"Let's hurry."

Without further ado, Damien gripped her arm, lifted her and began heading for the shop door. "Stay close. Stay very close. My power will cloak you, as well."

"What about mine?" she croaked.

"I feel the light of it. What it will do I don't know. Use it carefully. Only you can direct it. But not yet, not unless you feel that thing getting too far into you."

She had begun to shiver and wondered if it was already time. Then she remembered she needed to carry the thing into the store with her, so that Jude could create a circle around the entire area. She let the cold seep in even more, until her teeth chattered.

At last they reached the door of the shop.

"It's in me," she said.

Damien spoke. "Go now, Jude. Caro has the elemental."

Jude disappeared as if he had never been.

"Can you manage, *Schatz?*"

"A little longer. I'm so cold inside."

He took her gently by the shoulders. "Imagine yourself as a vessel. A container for this thing. It cannot hurt the vessel that holds it. Like water in a jug."

"It can't?"

"Think of it that way. Believe it."

Even as she shook from head to foot, and felt her lips stiffen from the cold, she got it. See herself as an inert vessel, holding it but not affected by it. She formed a mental image of a clear jug holding ice water, and as the image grew clearer, she felt the strangest thing. The cold didn't leave her, but it felt a whole lot less threatening. It also didn't get any worse.

"Ready?" Damien asked.

"As I'll ever be," she said, and she realized she had regained use of her lips, even though she was still shivering.

Damien reached out and pushed the door open. A bell rang, announcing their entrance but no one was in sight.

"Alika?" he called out. Then again when no one responded.

Finally the curtain at the back moved and a tall man stepped out. He looked to be in his thirties and resembled Alika, but only a little. His hair was almost white despite his youth, and his eyes, dark, held a burning intensity.

"My mother is unwell," he said. "You need to come back another time if you wish to see her."

"I just needed a book," Damien said, apparently playing along. "Maybe you can help me."

The young man shrugged. "I don't know the store the way she does."

Caro narrowed her eyes, wondering if she saw a bright red halo around him. It came and went so fast that she couldn't be sure. "I'm so sorry Alika is sick," she said. "How bad is it?"

"I'm sure she'll be on her feet in a few days. But right now the store is closed."

"Then you should have locked the door," Damien said. He stepped closer to the man. "I'm Damien. You are?" He offered his hand.

"Who I am doesn't matter," the other said, refusing to shake hands. "I think I asked you to leave."

"Well, unfortunately, we seem to have something that belongs to you. Or maybe it belongs to Alika."

The man's brows lifted. "What?"

"An elemental."

"A what?"

But Caro could see something in the way he shifted that told her he was lying. Thank goodness for the street smarts she'd gained over the years. "Oh, come on. You know all about it," she said. "I'm carrying it right now."

"That's impossible. You're crazy."

Caro closed her eyes and envisioned putting a stopper in the jug of ice water. As soon as she did it, she felt a little warmer. "It's not impossible," she said. "I contain it and it's not going anywhere unless you're willing to send it back to where it belongs."

"What makes you think I can do that?"

"Because," said Damien, "you're the one who called it."

"I don't know what you're talking about."

But Caro could see his aura deepening. He was summoning power. She hoped Damien could see it, too. She had a feeling this was about to get very ugly, but she could hardly imagine in what way.

Moved by an impulse she couldn't explain, she pulled the gris-gris Alika had given her from her pocket and showed it to the man. "We need to talk," she said in her best cop voice.

"About what?" he demanded truculently.

"About how these murders are going to stop."

"I don't know what you're talking about. Did Alika give you that?"

"Yes, to protect me. Apparently she knew something was coming after me. You miscalculated on that. Your elemental is following me because I saw what it did at the Pritchett house. That was your mistake."

He shook his head. "Are you crazy? What are you talking about?"

"We're talking about you," Damien said silkily. "And your very big mistake. You're apparently not a very good bokor."

The man took a step toward them. "I'm no bokor. No way. Crazy or not, you're talking to the wrong person."

"Someone here," Damien said flatly, "called upon an elemental to kill people. That's a very big mistake. Especially when it then turns its attention to a cop who had no part in Pritchett's activities. Otherwise you might have left a trail of unsolved murders. As it is, you're going to recall this elemental and stop murdering people now."

"No one in his right mind becomes a bokor!"

"So I would have thought. But the power was called from here, so that leaves you, doesn't it?"

Suddenly the curtain moved again, and Alika stepped out. She looked drained and unsteady, and at once the young man took her arm to help her. "Mother..."

"No, Jerome, I'm not going to let you fight for me." She looked at Damien and Caro. "Yes, I called on the power. And I'm not going to stop, not while there's a single person who might become homeless because a wealthy man doesn't give a damn about the lives of the poor. You can't stop me."

"Mother…"

She patted the young man's hand and settled onto a chair. "I tried to protect you," she said to Caro. "I knew you weren't part of it. And now my son tries to protect me. He cast a spell to keep you away. You should have stayed away."

"Not while people continue to die," Caro said. "I'm grateful for the gris-gris, Alika, but I nearly died anyway. How long do you want this to go on? How many have to die?"

"As many as it takes. In less than a month my son and his family will lose their home. Where will they go? What will they do? The rich never think of these things. Pah!"

Caro had to admit some sympathy with the woman's view. "But there has to be a better way to fight."

"We went to the meetings. We argued for our homes. They didn't listen."

"How does this justify murder? You took the law into your own hands. No one has that right."

"Easy for you to say," Alika spat furiously. "You won't be sleeping on the street."

Caro gave up the argument. The problem here wasn't that Alika was wrong about what was happening to all those families. No, she was simply wrong in how she was dealing with the problem. Finally she said, "Leaving people homeless is wrong. But murder is even worse, and it won't stop what's happening. There has to be another way. I'm sure there are agencies—"

"Pah," Alika interrupted. "Agencies. As if they care. Believe me, they don't care the way I do, the way my son does. How many homes will be destroyed? You tell *me* where there are homes these people can afford to move into."

Caro didn't have an answer for that. Worse, she wondered if anyone did.

"No," Damien said quietly. "Don't weaken yourself."

She looked at him and realized she had lost the image of the corked bottle. The cold was creeping through her again. At once she mentally reconstructed the container and slapped the stopper on it. The elemental remained contained.

"Please," she said to Alika. "Innocent children died because of your anger at their father. I might have died and may still. You need to recall this thing. What if it slips your control?"

Alika smiled faintly. "It's in *your* control now, woman. What will you do with it?"

Caro didn't have an answer for that. She had the thing bottled up inside her, but with no idea of how to get rid of it. If she even could.

Damien's voice changed, taking on that eerie note again. He was trying to command Alika. "We both know the rules. You summoned it so you are the only one who can send it back. Send it back now."

Alika shrugged. "You won't kill me, because then it will never go back. And if you won't kill me, you cannot stop me."

"Woman, I am Magi. You don't know what you're bargaining for here."

"Your powers are gone, vampire."

"Actually," Damien said softly, "they are not. Believe me, I can make you wish you'd never been born. Or perhaps you would prefer I make your son wish he'd never been born."

Caro smothered a gasp.

"You can't," Alika said calmly. "It would violate your oath as one of the Magi."

"Not when it will protect the lives of others. You threaten my lady. You've killed many already. You plan to kill more. Which way do you think my oath flows? To life or to death?"

Finally, something that gave Alika pause. She said nothing, her face frozen, for at least a full minute. "Leave Jerome out of this. I left your lady out of it."

"Not entirely," Damien countered. "It almost killed her despite your gris-gris. Are you strengthening it? Is it already slipping your control?"

Again Alika remained silent.

Then Damien moved faster than sight, and the next thing Caro could see, he held Jerome in his grip, with his hands behind him. "I have no desire to hurt your son. I have no desire to hurt you. But this must stop and it must stop *now.*"

"Leave Jerome out of this," Alika demanded, shoving herself to her feet.

Jerome was beginning to look a little wild-eyed and his gaze kept darting to his mother.

"Then call off your elemental," Damien insisted. "Send it back. I don't even need my magic to deal with your son. He's a mere human. Before you could do a thing I could snap his neck. Or rend him to pieces the way you did with the Pritchett children."

Caro was appalled by the threats. She hated threats of violence. Yet this time she understood them. Others would die if Alika didn't back down.

"Release my son or I'll call on powers you can't even imagine."

Damien smiled, showing teeth. "You think I haven't learned every one of those powers? You're talking to a mage who has walked this earth for three thousand years. Your knowledge is that of a child's compared to mine."

"Let him go or I will kill her!"

Damien said nothing for a moment. He looked at Caro.

"Let her try," Caro said, feeling a steely resolve grow in her. "Let her son go, and let her try. *I have had enough.*"

Whatever Damien saw or sensed about her, his smile widened. "Indeed you have, *Schatz.*" With that he let Jerome go, but stopped him with a word. "If you love your mother, talk sense to her before I have to act."

Jerome approached his mother, taking her hand. "Mother, you always told me that using power for dark purposes would rebound. I don't want anything to happen to you. Please, send it back."

"And let dozens be homeless, including my own son?"

"We'll find another way."

"There is no other way. We tried and tried again. They don't listen, those rich men who own the world."

Caro felt the elemental in her struggling to escape. She guessed Alika must be calling it to take care of her and Damien. While it was contained so that it couldn't hurt her, she could feel her strength draining as she fought to keep it in check. Was there no way out of this?

"In what way," Damien asked, "are you any better than they?"

For an instant Alika's eyes widened. Then they narrowed again. "If you're so powerful, mage, send it back yourself."

Damien looked at Caro. "Melt it."

"What?"

"Melt what is inside you with everything you've got. Then release it."

She stared at him, uncertain, then noticed that somehow he seemed to be growing larger. That wasn't possible, was it?

"Caro!"

She nodded and tried to do what he said, although it was all guesswork at this point. She found the white flame inside her and imagined it growing hotter and hotter. Little by little she felt her insides warm. Little by little the container she had created to hold the elemental seemed to shrink. It was working! She focused more of her energy on it, until she felt it grow small and almost lukewarm.

"Now," said Damien.

Mentally she pulled the stopper from the bottle. At once she felt the elemental recoil, pulling away from her and back toward Alika.

Alika gasped and took a quick step back. But then she seemed to gather herself. "So we fight," she said.

"Not if you send it back."

"I can call another."

"Not while I breathe," Damien said. "I don't have to kill you, you know. I have other methods."

Alika's response was surprisingly fast. With a fingernail, she clawed her own wrist and let blood spill on the floor while she began to chant.

Caro looked at Damien, saw the inevitable flare of his nostrils at the scent of blood. Was Alika hoping the blood would distract him? If she was, it didn't work.

Damien lifted his arms and blue lightning began to dance along both of them. "I am mage," he said. "I am also vampire. You have no idea, woman."

She laughed and continued her chant, pulling things from deep pockets in her dress and scattering them around.

Jerome, looking horrified, backed up. "Mother..." But she ignored him.

Damien began to chant, too, his voice growing thunderous. And before Caro's eyes, he grew, becoming larger and suddenly appearing to her to be wrapped in some kind of white cloak. What was going on?

But then Alika grew, too, though not as big as Damien.

It was as if power was changing their aspects. Maybe only Caro could see it and she wondered. But she didn't have time to wonder very long. She felt the elemental strengthening again, and with every ounce of will she had in her, she sent hot white light toward it.

Damien's voice had begun to sound like the roll of thunder from a nearby storm. It drowned Alika's chant, but as an eerie red light began to glow around her, Caro knew that she was still building power.

Jerome appeared to be wishing he could fade into the wall.

Caro watched with fascination, wondering what if anything she could do. When her skin started to prickle as if there was lightning in the air, she wondered if it came from Damien or Alika. Or whether it even mattered.

As the elemental stirred again, she sent more white light toward it and felt it recoil. Good. If that was all she could do, then she would do it.

Blue lightning spread all over Damien's body. She could hear it snap and hum like a thing alive. Alika's red glow increased until it looked like flames leaping outward. Should she direct white light that way, too? But almost as soon as the thought distracted her, she felt the elemental surge again, its power growing. Holding out her own arms, she imagined white heat flowing toward it, holding it in check.

Blue lightning met red flame. The bokor and the mage seemed to fill the room and reach beyond it, impossible or not. To Caro they seemed to become towering giants wrapped in their power, mythical beings no longer human.

As soon as their powers connected, a deafening crack

sounded and the entire shop seemed to shake. Startled, she almost lost track of the elemental but quickly cornered it again. She watched as her own white light shot forth toward that force, but then her power did something odd. It seemed to twine around Damien's blue light, adding just a bit.

Was she helping? She wished she knew. The only thing she knew for certain at that moment was that nothing must happen to Damien. Nothing.

Although given how large and powerful he looked right now, she doubted anything at all could harm him. He seemed to hurl blue bolts at Alika from his hands. *Zeus on a rampage,* she thought inanely.

To her it seemed almost as if time had stopped. Seconds and minutes became meaningless in a point of eternity. Blue bolts met red flames again and again until she wondered if the powers were evenly matched. Nothing seemed to change except for those bolts.

"Send it back now," Damien thundered, "or I swear I'll leave you with nothing!"

Then to Caro's amazement, the blue lightning seemed to be sucking the red flames toward it. Oh, God, she hoped Alika wasn't winning. Frantically she tried to think of what she could do to help.

But Damien, she realized, didn't look as if this change bothered him at all.

"I told you, woman. I am mage and I am vampire. You have not met the likes of me before. Send the elemental back!"

Alika said nothing. She tightened her face, as if fighting with every ounce of her strength. For an instant the red flowed back to her. But only for an instant. Then it started flowing toward Damien again, and as it reached his blue lightning, it faded toward lavender.

"You're running out of time," Damien warned.

"I can leave it and you won't be able to stop it," Alika gasped.

"If you leave it, can you prevent it from harming your son? Or his family?"

More red flames disappeared into Damien's blue aura. Caro blinked, as it seemed to her that Alika was shrinking a bit, that her fiery aura was fading.

"Do it!" Damien demanded.

Caro felt it happen. One moment she was holding the elemental back, and the next it was gone. Completely gone. While the air still sizzled with electricity, it had also grown lighter, clearer.

"Caro?" Damien asked.

"I can't feel it anymore."

"Wait a minute, and be sure."

Alika continued to shrink, her aura growing dimmer. "Stop," she begged.

"I'll stop when I'm sure the elemental is gone."

"It's gone," Alika groaned. "It's gone."

"Caro?"

"I really can't sense it anymore."

Another clap sounded, this one quieter. All of a sudden there was just an old woman sagging into a chair, and Damien, the Damien she had known all along, standing there.

Damien surprised her by squatting before Alika. He waited until he had her attention.

"I took power from you."

"I know."

"You still have enough. You can build it again but it will take time. But do not do this again, Alika. I don't want to have to come back."

"But the people," she whispered. "My son, his family."

Caro stepped forward. "If I may?"

Damien nodded and moved to the side a bit so Caro could squat beside him. "Alika, you tried to protect me. I know that. And while I don't approve of what you did, I understand why you did it."

The woman's eyes, looking ancient now, stared glumly back at her.

"I'll work with my friends on the force to find places for your son and all the other people to live. I can't promise they'll succeed, but I think everyone will want to help."

Alika barely nodded.

Damien stood. "You'll be all right, Alika. I just hope you didn't pick up a lot of bad—what do you call it?"

"Juju," Caro supplied. She, too, straightened and turned to Jerome, who looked as if he had aged a dozen years. "I'll find a way to help you."

He just nodded, but there was no hope in his face.

Outside on the street, Caro breathed the cold air, enjoying the freedom of no longer being stalked and watched. The city looked so damn normal that it was almost impossible to believe what she had just seen.

"Damien?"

"Yes, *Schatz?*"

"I have questions."

"Of course you do. But let's get somewhere warm first. You're merely human, after all."

She laughed, feeling so good all of a sudden. It felt even better when he lifted her onto his back, and along with Jude they headed back, leaping from rooftop to rooftop. Someday she hoped to be able to actually see it, not just feel like she was riding a crazy elevator.

Then, in the midst of her relief and happiness, she realized something. Tomorrow, or the next day, she would have to return to her mundane life.

She loved being a cop, wanted to be a detective, but nothing in her life was ever going to be the same again. She wondered how she would mesh this new world into her old world. Surely there had to be a way to use her new-found skills and power in her job?

But as she clung to Damien, even that didn't seem all that important. Not as important as how much longer she might have with Damien. Not as important as how soon she was going to lose him.

Her face pressed to his back, she fought down a sudden urge to weep.

So much had changed so fast, and one of the things that had changed was her heart.

Somehow she had to deal with that.

Back at Jude's office, Chloe started pumping coffee into Caro to warm her up. Jude and Damien disappeared, probably to feed, then returned to join the women.

Chloe demanded immediate explanations, and Caro added her voice.

"What did I see? What happened in there? What did you mean when you warned her that you were both a vampire and a mage?"

"I was warning her that she had never seen my like."

"I got that part," Caro said a little sarcastically as she cradled the hot mug of coffee to warm her hands.

Damien sat beside her on the sofa and wound his arm around her shoulders. Liking the embrace, she leaned into him and let her head rest on his shoulder. She wished she didn't fear this might be the last time she would be so close to him.

"A long time ago," Damien said, "the Magi realized something. There were those who would do evil, and while they could be thwarted, they couldn't always be prevented from trying again. Power is power, after all, and how it's wielded is a personal decision."

"Okay. I get that part."

"It was told to me that one of our most powerful priests was changed, long before my time. It wasn't by choice, but it proved to have an unexpected benefit."

"And that was?"

"That a vampire priest, one who held true power himself, could drink the power from others. Take it away as surely as if it were blood."

"Really?" At that Caro sat bolt upright.

"Really," he said, still keeping his arm loosely around her. "The secret was closely guarded by the temple. Only a very few of us were selected after proving our trustworthiness for years, and then we became the guardians of the secret. It was important that no one else know."

"I can see why. But you didn't drain Alika completely."

"I hope I never have to. I suspect that until this event she's always tried to use her power for good. And she *did* give you that gris-gris to protect you. For that I am grateful to her."

"She didn't seem like a bad person," Caro agreed. "Mostly she just seemed desperate." She listened to herself, and realized that henceforth she was apt to be a very different sort of cop. Not that she would excuse murder, but she was probably going to be a lot more sympathetic to some of the reasons why people broke the law.

"You said you were going to help those people find homes," Damien said. "How will you do that?"

"The force works with several charitable organizations. I'm sure I can get them working on it. It would be good for the community."

"I agree."

"What would have happened if you had continued to drain Alika?"

He gave a slight shrug. "I could have left her with no power at all. I could have burned it out of her. Or I could have killed her. I really had no desire to do the latter."

"A predator who prefers not to kill," she remarked.

At that, both Damien and Jude laughed.

Then, without warning, Damien swept her up in his arms. "Time to go home, *Schatz.*"

Home. Where he'd probably say good-night and maybe goodbye now that the problem was solved.

With a very heavy heart, she let him take her.

Chapter 15

Her apartment still smelled of incense and burned beeswax, and even the faint aroma of rose petals lingered in the air. After what she had been through tonight, she suddenly noticed how small the place was, how little she had really done to make it homey. Why that suddenly seemed important, she didn't know.

Unless she was trying to avoid thinking about the things that might tear her heart apart.

"Well," she said brightly, a brightness she definitely did not feel, "I'm home, I'm safe and you no longer need to be my watchdog."

She thought his eyes narrowed a bit, and he didn't answer immediately.

"I should vacuum up all the salt," she prattled on. "Change the sheets, air out the incense…"

She jumped as she realized he was standing right in front of her. "Will you stop doing that?"

"What?"

"Moving so fast I can't see you. I jump every time."

"Not every time, *Schatz*," he said, reaching out to capture a lock of her hair between his fingers. "Are you giving me my walking papers?"

Was she? The thought made her chest tighten and her throat ache. "Well, I don't need to be guarded anymore, and you have a life and were talking about going back to Cologne. I just assumed…"

"Are you assuming what I want?" he asked silkily. "Or assuming what you think must be?"

Her mouth turned dry as she saw his eyes grow as dark as night. "What are you asking?"

He hesitated. "I'm asking you if you're telling me to leave."

"No!" The word popped out of her instantly, without thought. Truth often did that.

"Then perhaps we should talk," he said quietly. "Can you just talk with me and not buzz around cleaning?"

She bridled. "Of course I can."

He motioned to the couch and they sat side by side but not touching.

"You've seen how I live," he said after a moment. "Haunting the night, never seeing the sunlight. My friends are limited to a very few I trust. There is nothing *normal* about my life, as you would think of normal."

"*Normal* is a relative term."

A smile lifted the corners of his mouth, just barely. "Relative indeed. I live a normal life for a vampire. I have a great many things to amuse me and keep me occupied. By contrast, you have an important job, one I am quite convinced you want to keep. You have friends, and I'm sure you couldn't introduce me to most of them. I'd make them uneasy, even if they never guessed what I am."

"So?"

"So?" he repeated.

"Look, if you're trying to find a graceful way to let me down, don't bother. I know you plan to leave. I know you plan to go back to Cologne. I get it."

"I don't think you get it at all." He lifted her swiftly until she straddled his lap and had to balance herself with her hands on his shoulders. All of a sudden her growing sorrow gave way to the inevitable passion that was never far away when he was close. She wanted him beyond all reason, even now as she believed he was trying to say goodbye.

She saw him smile as he caught scent of her rising desire. It didn't bother her anymore that he could read her that way. In fact, it heightened her desire for him. There was something to be said for being emotionally exposed. In its own way it was as frighteningly erotic as being bound to her bed.

"Schatz," he said.

"Yes?"

"I told you about claiming."

"Yes, and how much you want to avoid it."

"I'm not sure you fully understand. Claiming is a matter of life and death for me, not just love. I cannot lose what I claim without losing my sanity or my life. It's an obsession beyond all obsessions. Were I to claim you, I would need you as much as I need food and air to breathe. You see?"

She nodded. "I can see why you don't want to do that."

"Ah, Caro, I think I have already done so. The question is whether you want it."

"You've claimed me?" The words rocketed through her like an explosion, bringing a mixture of joy and fear at once. "How did that happen?"

He shrugged one shoulder. "I don't know. I'm not in

control of it. I thought it might be happening, but last night I was certain. I would have died for you."

"You said so," she agreed, still trying to absorb this. Her heart thudded so fast now.

"I meant it. That's when I knew. But it is not yet final. Much as it would be like walking out into the sun, I could still leave you. The pain would be execrable but most likely survivable. So I ask you, do you want my claiming? Think hard, think carefully. Think of what being with me will do to your life, what it may cost you."

She tried, but it was getting really hard to think. Every bit of her wanted to lean into him and cry, "Take me forever."

"I can't go to Cologne," she said finally, the only shred of reality she seemed able to cling to.

"I'm not asking you to. I can stay here."

"It's my job," she said almost apologetically. "It means a lot to me."

"I know, my darling Caro. I know. Of the two of us, it is far easier for me to move here. But think carefully, because once I take the final step, I will not willingly let you go ever again."

It should have sounded like a threat. Instead, it sounded like the promise of paradise. "Really?"

"Really. Think, Caro, please, for both our sakes. This is one time you won't be able to change your mind later. Well, you will, but if you do, I'll have no choice but to end my existence. I don't want that on your conscience."

Nor did she. So she closed her eyes and tried to think about all of it. She could still be a detective. She could live with his odd hours as she had discovered. And while she was certain she would have to change her life in some ways, none of them seemed all that important.

She opened her eyes and found him waiting, as still as if he were carved from rock.

"It's not final yet?"

"No. There's one more step to take. At this moment, painful though it would be, I could still leave."

She thought about that. "Is this what you want, Damien?"

"It has happened."

She didn't like that answer. "What about love? Do you love me or are you just obsessed?"

"Of course I love you!" He seemed startled. "I have claimed you. No claiming occurs without love."

"It would have been nice if you'd explained that. How was I supposed to know?" But the fears seemed to be fading, and deep inside she felt almost as if she were purring. "I thought I was going to lose you. I've been dreading it for days."

"*Schatz,* you will never lose me unless you wish it."

"I love you," she admitted.

A smile began to widen on his face. "Truly?"

"Truly. I didn't know how I was going to be able to stand it if you left. Every time I thought about it, I hurt so much."

He leaned forward and kissed her. "I will never leave unless you tell me to," he whispered. "I vow it."

She knew he was one to keep his vows. Sighing, she let go of everything and leaned into him, wrapping her arms around his neck.

Just one last fear halted her answer. "What happens when I grow old and die? What will you do? I can't bear to think of you ending your life because of me."

"Without you I would have no life. But if it worries you so, perhaps one day I can make you like me. It will be up to you."

She couldn't deny herself any longer. Selfish or not, the need drove the words out of her. "Claim me, Damien. Claim me, please."

"No doubts?"

"Not a one." She was tired of talking. Now she wanted action. He seemed to sense it because the world whirled wildly, then she felt herself lying on her bed. He towered over her, looking like a powerful Teutonic knight, and stripped his clothes so fast she didn't see it happen except for a quick blur.

He was so beautiful. Head to foot, he was perfect. And he was so ready for her. She started to reach out to touch his staff, to encircle it and claim it for herself, but he stopped her.

Then her own clothes vanished, leaving her utterly naked before him.

"Can I move this time?" she asked, her voice thick with passion.

"Absolutely. *Meine Liebe,* move all you wish."

The words set her free. She reached for him, and he lowered himself beside her, for the first time, other than the shower, giving her free rein to discover every inch of him, to stroke him until he groaned and moved restlessly.

It filled her with both joy and power, that the predator lay so tamely beside her, reveling in her touches. That with the gentlest of touches she could make him move so she could explore more, or with equally small touches make him writhe.

But when she at last stopped teasing him and reached for his staff, he suddenly flipped and was on top of her. She gasped, loving the feel of his weight, his hardness along her length, his penis pressing the sensitive tissue between her legs.

"Last chance," he said, his own voice thick.

"For what?"

"To avoid a final claim." His eyes were as black as a starless night. "If I drink with you at the same time I am inside you, it will be done. Are you sure?"

She had never been surer of anything in her life. She reached up, drawing his head to her throat. At the same instant she felt him enter her, making her feel so full and so possessed.

She never felt his teeth plunge into her throat, but she knew when it happened anyway.

They became one in that unimaginable way. She felt his heart pounding as if it were her own, felt her blood running in her veins and his. Felt every thrust he made as if she were making it as well as receiving it.

Pleasure doubled, grew, lifting her higher than she'd ever gone, even on the night of the ritual. No longer did she feel as if she were separate in any way. Never had she imagined such a union was possible.

Yet it was. Entirely one body, one heart, one mind, they rose to dizzying heights, and when culmination came, they exploded at the same time.

Together they hovered at the pinnacle of completion, awash in a tide of feelings and sensations that didn't end.

Love for eternity.

A week later they had a condo in a building across town. A vampire named Creed Preston and his wife, Yvonne, helped them find it, and Creed helped them make a room that was safe for Damien during the daylight.

Caro was surprised, but apparently money was no object for Damien, so they bought the penthouse, and the work to fix it for him was completed rapidly. They held a small housewarming party, though they hadn't finished decorating yet, and even Detective Pat Matthews came.

It was night—the city lights glowed beyond walls of windows. Pat drew her aside.

"You look damn happy," she said.

"I am," Caro admitted. "Happier than I ever imagined I'd be."

"Good. Got yourself a bit of a weirdo there, but I like him."

Caro smothered a smile. "He's good to me."

"Only thing that counts," Pat agreed. "Malloy sent a message, by the way."

"And?"

"Get your butt back tomorrow or the next day. All is forgiven. Apparently those additional murders made him reconsider your sanity."

Caro laughed. "Really."

"Really. A lot that's weird is going on. He just asked you to please not mention it."

"I won't. I promise." There was no need now.

"And that request you made to help those folks find homes?"

"Yes?"

"We've started working on it but it would be nice if *I* didn't have to run your program. So come back soon, will you? And make sure I get a wedding invite."

"I promise." She watched Pat drift away to talk with Jude and Terri, then felt familiar arms close around her from behind.

"Are you pleased, *Schatz?*"

She turned within the circle of his arms and looked up at the vampire she loved more than life. "I'm very pleased. And one of these days…"

He laid his finger over her lips. "Don't ask yet, *meine Liebe*. Not yet. The day will come when we'll have to consider changing you, but not yet. Please. Let me enjoy you just as you are."

"Okay," she agreed.

But deep inside she knew the question wouldn't be shelved for long. There'd come a day when she would want to share his nights completely, to see them the way he did.

And when that day came, she had no doubt she would get her way.

"I love you," she murmured and watched his eyes grow golden with pleasure.

She was forever claimed, and forever his.

* * * * *

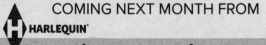
#167 THE LOST WOLF'S DESTINY
The Pack
by Karen Whiddon

Shape-shifter Blythe Daphne is desperate to save her child's life. So desperate that she turns to a prominent—but controversial—Faith Healer. But Lucas Kenyon, the healer's son, is the only man who knows the truth: his father is evil personified. Determined to prevent Blythe and her daughter from becoming the healer's next target, Lucas forms an uneasy alliance with the beautiful shifter. But when sparks begin to fly between Blythe and her protector, she forces herself to pull away. Because falling for the man she wants most may put her daughter's life on the line....

#168 RELEASING THE HUNTER
by Vivi Anna

Ronan Ames knows all about infamous demon hunter Ivy Strom. So it doesn't surprise him when she attacks him. But when nothing happens to him—no burning, no melting flesh—Ivy can't figure it out, especially since her protection amulet still glows in warning. He informs her that he's a cambion—half human, half demon—and that he, too, has been hired to track a demon who may know Ivy's brother's whereabouts. Forced together, the two battle the common enemy...and each other. Until the attraction between them can no longer be denied.

HNCNM0813

REQUEST YOUR FREE BOOKS!

2 FREE NOVELS FROM THE PARANORMAL ROMANCE COLLECTION PLUS 2 FREE GIFTS!

YES! Please send me 2 FREE novels from the Paranormal Romance Collection and my 2 FREE gifts (gifts are worth about $10). After receiving them, if I don't wish to receive any more books, I can return the shipping statement marked "cancel." If I don't cancel, I will receive 4 brand-new novels every month and be billed just $22.76 in the U.S. or $23.96 in Canada. That's a savings of at least 17% off the cover price of all 4 books. It's quite a bargain! Shipping and handling is just 50¢ per book in the U.S. and 75¢ per book in Canada.* I understand that accepting the 2 free books and gifts places me under no obligation to buy anything. I can always return a shipment and cancel at any time. Even if I never buy another book, the two free books and gifts are mine to keep forever.

237/337 HDN F4YC

Name	(PLEASE PRINT)	
Address		Apt. #
City	State/Prov.	Zip/Postal Code

Signature (if under 18, a parent or guardian must sign)

Mail to the Harlequin® Reader Service:
IN U.S.A.: P.O. Box 1867, Buffalo, NY 14240-1867
IN CANADA: P.O. Box 609, Fort Erie, Ontario L2A 5X3

Want to try two free books from another line?
Call 1-800-873-8635 or visit www.ReaderService.com.

* Terms and prices subject to change without notice. Prices do not include applicable taxes. Sales tax applicable in N.Y. Canadian residents will be charged applicable taxes. Offer not valid in Quebec. This offer is limited to one order per household. Not valid for current subscribers to Paranormal Romance Collection or Harlequin® Nocturne™ books. All orders subject to credit approval. Credit or debit balances in a customer's account(s) may be offset by any other outstanding balance owed by or to the customer. Please allow 4 to 6 weeks for delivery. Offer available while quantities last.

Your Privacy—The Harlequin® Reader Service is committed to protecting your privacy. Our Privacy Policy is available online at www.ReaderService.com or upon request from the Harlequin Reader Service.

We make a portion of our mailing list available to reputable third parties that offer products we believe may interest you. If you prefer that we not exchange your name with third parties, or if you wish to clarify or modify your communication preferences, please visit us at www.ReaderService.com/consumerchoice or write to us at Harlequin Reader Service Preference Service, P.O. Box 9062, Buffalo, NY 14269. Include your complete name and address.

THE LOST WOLF'S DESTINY

by Karen Whiddon

In this wild journey filled with danger and
sizzling sexual tension, a shape-shifter trying to
make amends for his past finds family and love
beyond his deepest longings.

As he slanted his mouth over hers and breathed in her scent,
Lucas dimly realized he didn't know how she'd react. If she
was truly intent on spiraling out of control, she could fight
him. In which case, he'd immediately withdraw.

Or she could freeze. Shut down. Turn all that wild fury and
panic inward, into self-regret and loathing.

In fact, Blythe did none of those things.

Instead, she focused all of that passion toward him, singeing
him so bad he thought they might both go up in flames in a
blaze of heat.

Damn. Aroused, on fire, aching, he desired her, this woman
he barely knew but with whom he had shared the most intimate
of acts—the change from his human form into his wolf.

And now he wanted more. More than wanted, *craved*.

So of course Lucas pushed away from her and crossed to
the other side of the room, struggling to get his breathing
under control.

"What now?" Color high, eyes wild and hair tangled, Blythe

taunted him. "I need this. I need you. Hard and fast and deep. Now."

Even as her words inflamed him, he knew he had to stay strong. Instinctively, he knew having sex with her would change things for him forever. He'd been content living his life alone. Safe. Furious with himself and with her, he reined in his temper and his need.

"No." He lifted his head, letting her see in his face how much letting her go had cost him. "This isn't the time or the place. You're hurting. You're fighting feeling powerless. I refuse to take advantage of that."

For a moment, the thudding of his heart in his chest was the only sound he could hear. He thought she might argue—she looked spitting-mad as she cocked her head and eyed him, almost as if she wasn't sure if he was serious or completely insane.

**Don't miss THE LOST WOLF'S DESTINY
by Karen Whiddon, coming September 2013 from
Harlequin® Nocturne™.**

NOCTURNE™

They must battle demons…
and their desire.

All that's left of infamous demon hunter Ivy Strom's family is the brother who vanished three years ago. Now that she's finally close to finding him, the last distraction she needs is sexy half human, half demon Ronan Ames. She can't resist his help in the search for the vicious enemy. Nor can she deny the searing desire that draws them together…even though a passionate alliance might destroy them both.

RELEASING THE HUNTER

by

VIVI ANNA

**The hunt begins September 2
only with Harlequin® Nocturne™.**

www.Harlequin.com

HN88578

SADDLE UP AND READ 'EM!

This summer, get your fix of Western reads and pick up a cowboy from some of your favorite authors!

In September look for:

STERN by Brenda Jackson
The Westmorelands
Harlequin Desire

COWBOY REDEMPTION by Elle James
Covert Cowboys Inc.
Harlequin Intrigue

CALLAHAN COWBOY TRIPLETS by Tina Leonard
Callahan Cowboys
Harlequin American Romance

THE BALLAD OF EMMA O'TOOL by Elizabeth Lane
Harlequin Historical

*Look for these great Western reads and more
available wherever books are sold or visit*
www.Harlequin.com/Westerns